THE SISTERS GRIMM

9

D0089806

THE S.
GRI.

10th Anniversary Edition

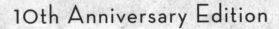

9

THE COUNCIL OF MIRRORS

MICHAEL BUCKLEY

Pictures by PETER FERGUSON

AMULET BOOKS   NEW YORK

Cataloging-in-Publication Data has been applied for and can be obtained from the Library of Congress.

ISBN 978-1-4197-2009-3

Originally published in hardcover by Amulet Books in 2012
Text copyright © 2012, 2018 Michael Buckley
Illustrations copyright © 2012 Peter Ferguson
Book design by Siobhán Gallagher

Printed and bound in U.S.A.
10 9 8 7 6 5 4 3 2 1

Amulet Books are available at special discounts when purchased in quantity for premiums and promotions as well as fundraising or educational use. Special editions can also be created to specification. For details, contact specialsales@abramsbooks.com or the address below.

ABRAMS The Art of Books
195 Broadway, New York, NY 10007
abramsbooks.com

For Sylvie and Phoebe Sanders.
Thanks for riding this flying carpet.

O nce upon a time there was a sleepy little town called Ferryport Landing. It was nestled on the banks of the Hudson River in upstate New York. Quaint little shops lined Main Street, and people spent days strolling along the town's cobblestoned lanes and through its community gardens. Apple pies cooled on windowsills, and few people locked their doors at night. Some visitors thought Ferryport Landing had been plucked right out of a storybook.

But that was a long time ago.

Now, the town was in ruins. Its death wasn't slow, like that of so many tiny communities that decay and, eventually, disappear after the mill closes or the steel plant shuts its doors.

No, Ferryport Landing was murdered—by its own citizens. They looted shops and smashed in windows. They overturned cars, leaving them scattered in the streets. They lit fires and watched hungry flames burn homes to the ground.

Sabrina and Daphne, the sisters Grimm, stood over its remains to pay their respects to a fallen friend.

"Is that it?" Daphne asked. "Is that the end?"

Sabrina nodded. "Yes. And it's about time."

1

Two Weeks Earlier

OCTOBER 14

My name is Sabrina Grimm, and this is my journal. My family has been bugging me to write in it for a while. I tried a few times before, but I never really wanted to get all that involved with the family business. I wanted to be a normal girl, living in New York City. I wanted to go to school and have friends and buy bagel sandwiches at the deli on York and 88th Street every morning.

If you're reading this, it means you know that didn't happen. It also means you're either Puck (stop snooping, stinkface!) or you're a future Grimm. Maybe you're like me, and you didn't choose this life. Instead, you got dumped into it, and nothing makes sense. Well, I suppose the least I can do is try to help you. There's a lot of stuff you need to know, so you might want to sit down for this.

You know those bedtime stories your parents read to you at night? The ones filled with fairies, giants, witches, monsters, mad tea parties, sleeping princesses, and cowardly lions? They're not stories. They're history. They're based on actual events and actual people. These real-life fairy-tale characters call themselves Everafters, and a lot of them are still alive today.

That's where our family comes in. We're Grimms, descendants of one half of the Brothers Grimm, and for hundreds of years we've kept an eye on the Everafter community. Believe me, it's no picnic.

OK, I know you're probably thinking I've been sitting too close to the microwave, but I'm telling the truth. I didn't believe any of this at first, either, so let me start at the beginning. Two years ago, my parents, Henry and Veronica Grimm, mysteriously disappeared. My sister, Daphne, and I thought they had abandoned us, but it turned out Mom and Dad had been kidnapped (long story). Enter Granny Relda, our long-lost grandmother who we thought was dead (an even longer story). She brought us to live with her in a little town called Ferryport Landing, where most of the Everafters live.

You've probably never heard of Ferryport Landing. As I write this, there's an angry mob of ogres, trolls, talking animals, and other assorted monsters running loose on its streets, terrorizing everyone. Anyone with any sense at all has left or gone into hiding—but not us! Oh no, not the Grimms! Our family has no interest in running for safety, so we're knee-deep in trouble, and things don't look like they're going to get any better.

But you still need to know about Ferryport Landing and everything that happened here. Of course, there might not be any more Grimms after

THE COUNCIL OF MIRRORS

me. I might be dead, and then there won't be anyone to read this journal. Like I said, things are looking pretty bleak. But that's enough backstory for today. I'll write more when I can. For now, I have to go save the world.

Sabrina snapped her journal shut and tucked it into the folds of her sleeping bag for safekeeping. She rubbed her eyes and stretched, sore from sleeping on the cold marble floor of her new bedroom.

Not that the place where she and Daphne were sleeping could actually be called a bedroom. A bedroom contained—at the very least—a bed and a window and a place to put your clothes. The girls were sleeping in an empty room with stone walls and more than a few cobwebs draped in the corners. Every night, Sabrina told herself that this was temporary, that someday they would have a real room again. But to make that happen, she knew she had to get to work.

Sabrina dug into the foot of her sleeping bag for the drumstick and rusty cowbell she kept there, then padded over to her still-sleeping sister. She called out to Daphne, even gave her a few shakes, but the little girl could sleep through a tornado. Waking her often required drastic measures.

DONK! Sabrina felt the sound of the cowbell deep in the pit of her stomach, but Daphne did not stir.

"Time to wake up!" *DONK! DONK! DONK!*

Nothing.

"Wake up! We're under attack. Monsters and lunatics and weird dudes with pitchforks! They'll be here any second!" *DONK! DONK! DONK! DONK! DONK! DONK!*

"You are a terrible human being," Daphne croaked, pulling her sleeping bag over her head. As she sank inside, a big snout popped out. It belonged to Elvis, the family's Great Dane. He eyed Sabrina sourly.

"C'mon. Get up, both of you. We've got stuff to do," Sabrina said.

Daphne grumbled but did as she was told. She and the dog crawled out of the sleeping bag, got to their feet, and yawned at the same time. Daphne scratched her armpit, and Elvis went to work on his rump.

Sabrina noticed a book hiding in the folds of her sister's bedding, and she frowned. The Book of Everafter was a collection of fairy tales, but it was also a magical object. Its readers could step into its stories, alter them, and in turn change things back in the real world. It should have been under lock and key, but Daphne was determined to keep a close eye on it.

"You shouldn't leave that lying around," Sabrina said. "Hasn't it caused enough trouble? What if it falls into the wrong hands?"

Daphne snatched it up. "Elvis is protecting it."

"At least tell me you've found something in there that will help us free Granny from Mirror."

The little girl shook her head. "There are a lot of stories—like, thousands! I'm still reading."

"We're running out of time, Daphne," Sabrina scolded.

"I know!" her sister shouted.

The girls were silent for a moment, and the tension melted away.

"I'm sorry," Sabrina said. "I know you're doing your best. Let's see if anyone else is having any luck."

She led Daphne and Elvis out of their room and into a vast hallway with a barrel ceiling as high as the sky. Hundreds—maybe even thousands—of doors lined both walls. The rooms they hid had once housed monsters and magical items but had recently been looted. Now most of the rooms sat empty, but others still held a few surprises.

The sisters walked along the hall until they reached the door they were looking for. They pushed it open and stepped inside. Mirrors—twenty-five of them—were mounted on the walls.

Sabrina and her family had moved the magic mirrors to one of the Hall of Wonders' newly empty rooms that was closer to the portal, so that they could more easily access the Room of Reflections, as they called it. But only five of the mirrors remained intact. The others were busted and broken. Sabrina and Daphne were collecting the shards one by one and carefully gluing them onto the walls. When light hit the fragments just right, they created a dazzling effect.

Two people guarded the room. The first was an elderly man wearing a suit several sizes too large for his thin frame. His arthritic hands trembled in his lap. He went by the name Mr. Canis. The second figure was almost his opposite. No older than Daphne, she had amber curls that spilled down her shoulders, and she wore a red hooded sweatshirt and hand-me-down jeans. Her face was full of possibility and hope. Everyone called her Red. Both of them looked exhausted.

"When was the last time either of you got some sleep?" Sabrina asked.

Red smiled. "He won't sleep. He's been up for days."

"I'll sleep when your grandmother is safe and sound," Canis growled, then turned to Daphne. "You should lock that book up where no one can get it."

"I won't let anything happen to it," Daphne promised. "See anything new?"

"As a matter of fact . . ." Canis said, gesturing to the five intact mirrors. Instead of reflecting back Sabrina's image, they each showed a bird's-eye view of Ferryport Landing. Ugly purple and ebony clouds hovered in the sky. The clouds had appeared two days prior, blasting the town with lightning and ear-smashing claps of thunder. "Show them, mirrors."

The reflections suddenly glowed with an otherworldly light. The surfaces of the glass shimmered and rippled, and when they finally stilled, four odd faces materialized. In the first mirror, a brutal barbarian named Titan appeared; the second showed a seventies-era nightclub owner who went by the name Donovan; the third was a laid-back beach lover with long dreadlocks named Reggie; and the fourth was Fanny, a roller-skating waitress with fire-engine-red hair. The fifth mirror remained empty.

"Well, hello, darlings," Fanny said in her thick southern accent. She chewed gum while she talked and blew bubbles between phrases. "I was telling Mr. Canis that one of the reasons we couldn't find your granny is because we were lookin' in the wrong places."

"Well, the world is pretty big," Sabrina said.

"That's just it, honey. She's not out in the world. She's still here in Ferryport Landing!" the waitress cried, then did a happy dance on her roller skates. She lived in the Diner of Wonders, an old-fashioned ice-cream shop, complete with red counters and matching stools. Behind her, a milkshake machine hummed, and a jukebox waited patiently for nickels.

"What?" Sabrina asked.

"But stealing a human body was Mirror's plan for getting out of the town. Why hasn't he gone?" Daphne asked.

"Well, I don't rightly know," Fanny admitted. "But I do have a theory."

"And that is?" Sabrina urged.

"He's stuck, Ms. Sabrina," Reggie said from his Island of Wonders. "The bad weather outside isn't a storm. It's his temper tantrum."

Daphne slipped her hand into Sabrina's and gave her a hopeful smile. Mirror had hijacked their grandmother's body two days ago in the hope of skipping town and taking over the world. With his powers, there would be little any human being could do to stop him. But now . . .

"Serves him right!" Titan roared from the Dungeon of Wonders. He was a rugged man with long, rust-colored hair and a scraggly beard. He often worked himself up into a blustery rage, turning his face the shade of his mane. Titan made Sabrina nervous. The medieval torture chamber he lived inside was filled with spikes, sharp weapons, and boiling oils. But he seemed to be on the Grimms' side. "If only I were a living, breathing man, I would put a painful end to our brother's atrocities!"

"He's no brother of mine," Reggie grumbled. "The firstborn is a scoundrel of the worst kind."

"Firstborn?" Sabrina asked.

"That's what we've been calling him, sister. He was the first magic mirror the Wicked Queen ever made—you know, the proto-type," Donovan explained as he fixed his Afro with a comb. He lived inside the Disco of Wonders, a nightclub that never closed with a dance floor that lit up like a rainbow.

"Anything is better than his other name," Red said. "*The Master is—*"

"Creep-tastic?" Daphne asked, pretending to shudder.

Sabrina didn't have to pretend. Every time Mirror's name was mentioned, it felt like her blood flash froze in her veins. How could she have ever called him a friend? She had confessed all her hopes and fears to him. She had trusted him, but he was using her, all the while making his horrible plans. The second he got the chance, he betrayed her and her entire family.

"Whatever his name, our brother will pay! He has stained the honor of magic mirrors everywhere!" Titan roared, pounding on his chest.

"You mean, the four of us?" Donovan said. "We're all that's left, big daddy."

Titan snarled. "All the more reason to protect our legacy."

"Calm down, sugar. You'll get your blood pressure up again," Fanny said as she applied a coat of ruby-red lipstick. "Now that we know where the firstborn is, it's time to focus our energies on catching him and freeing Relda Grimm from his control."

"Please tell me you have some ideas," Sabrina said. Her plea was met with heartbreaking silence.

"What about this one?" Daphne asked, pointing to the fifth undamaged mirror. She approached its surface, touching the glass and watching it ripple. "What do you think?"

Canis sighed and shook his head. "I haven't heard so much as a peep from that one."

Daphne turned back to the group with a sigh. "Well, at least we know where Granny is now. How about Uncle Jake?"

Donovan shook his head. "He's been harder to find than your granny, dancing queen. He disappeared right off the map."

"We can sense his presence, but we can't pinpoint it," Reggie added. "Wherever he is, he doesn't want to be found, and I think he's using some serious mojo to make sure it stays that way."

"What about these broken pieces of mirror? Have you caught any glimpses of him in them?" Sabrina asked, peering at the shards on the wall. In one, a man was putting on a necktie in a department store; in another, a woman washed the makeup off her face. In yet another, a high school student practiced a speech in a cramped bathroom.

"Nothing," Canis said.

"Well, I'm worried about him, but Uncle Jake has always been able to take care of himself," Sabrina said. "Right now, we should focus on finding Granny. Now that we know she's still in town, we can rescue—"

"Forget it! You and Daphne are sitting this one out," said a voice from behind her.

Sabrina spun around to find her parents approaching. Her mother, Veronica, was carrying Basil, her two-year-old brother. Henry, her father, was dressed in a heavy jacket and hiking boots. Like Mr. Canis, he looked exhausted. "Mirror is way too dangerous," he argued.

"But danger is my middle name," Daphne said.

"Your middle name is Delilah, young lady," Veronica said. "Some jobs are for grown-ups. Besides, I could use your help with Basil."

"Babysitting?" Sabrina cried.

"Your mother was up all night with him," Henry said. "He's . . . he . . . well, he won't sleep, and he isn't eating."

As if to illustrate Henry's point, Basil cried and squirmed in his mother's arms, pounding on her chest with his little fists.

"Just tell them the truth, Henry," Veronica said. "Basil misses Mirror."

Sabrina scowled. Basil had been kidnapped as a newborn by Mirror, who planned to put his own mind inside the boy's human body. Basil barely knew his real family—he only knew his captor.

"I'll take him, Mrs. Grimm. He knows me," Red offered, reminding them all that Mirror had manipulated Red to act as Basil's nanny for some time.

Veronica looked pained. She didn't want to let the boy go, but Basil needed sleep, and Red would be able to calm him. Veronica reluctantly placed Basil into Red's outstretched arms, and his tears quickly transformed into giggles.

"I'll get him something to eat," Red promised, and then took the boy from the room.

The moment they had gone, Veronica broke into sobs. Henry swept her into his arms and held her tight.

"It's going to take time, 'Roni. He just doesn't know us yet. But he will soon," he assured her.

Veronica clung to Henry as he tried to absorb her grief, but Sabrina could see he had plenty of his own. If people could break in two from pain, it seemed that Henry and Veronica were very close to snapping. It frightened Sabrina to see her strong, confident parents so fragile.

"So, what is your plan of action, Henry?" Canis asked. "I hope you aren't going to chase Mirror down and confront him."

"No." Henry shook his head. "For now, I think it's best if we keep our distance. But I do want to get a good look at him. Maybe I can spot a weakness. That thunderstorm he's conjuring has been hovering over the southern end of town for a day. I assume he's at the train station off of Route 9. I'll start there."

"I'm coming with you," Canis said, snatching up the cane that leaned against his chair. He used every ounce of his strength to struggle to his feet.

"Mr. Canis, I would feel better if you were here, keeping an eye on things. We don't know if any of the monsters the Scarlet Hand set free from the Hall of Wonders are still lurking around."

Canis frowned. "Your mother and I worked as partners. I was not her assistant, and I certainly wasn't anyone's babysitter."

"That's not what I'm saying at all! There are plenty of things that need to be done here, and you're the only one I can trust to get them done," Henry said quickly, almost sheepishly. "What if I go down there and find a way to rescue Mom? She's going to be exhausted, maybe even hurt. We'll need to get a room ready for her. Or I might stumble upon some more Everafter refugees. Veronica's got her hands full, and—"

Canis threw his cane against the wall. His face was red with rage, and his hands were shaking. Sabrina braced for an argument. Feeding babies and preparing bedrooms was not how the old man was accustomed to helping. He had, until recently, been the family's fiercest and most intimidating ally. He'd struck fear into the wickedest of villains, wielding the strength and savagery of the Big Bad Wolf. Henry's request that he stay behind hit the old man like a sucker punch. Canis turned and stomped out of the room.

"He wants to feel useful," Daphne said to her father.

"I know, but he'll slow me down. If something happens, I can't worry about getting him back here," Henry said, though Sabrina could see he immediately regretted his choice of words. "Not that anything will happen, of course."

"I'd feel better if someone was going with you," Veronica said.

"Someone is," Henry replied as he buttoned his jacket.

Sabrina heard a fluttering of wings and a voice above their heads. "Incoming!" Something wet and sticky landed on her head with a splat and trickled down her face. It smelled like the live-stock tent at a state fair. Sabrina looked up and saw Puck floating above her, laughing and aiming another balloon filled with funky, sloshing green ooze right at her.

"What's in those balloons?" Sabrina growled as she wiped the muck off her face.

"I don't have a clue. I found it collecting in a pool near the sewage treatment plant. It was just sitting there—free for the taking! Can you imagine?" He flung the second balloon, and it hit her in the shoulder, splattering all over her neck. "This is grade-A filth! It's top of the line."

Sabrina clenched her fists and scowled.

Puck looked genuinely shocked by her anger. "You're mad? You should be honored. There's a list of people a mile long I could throw this slop at, and you're at the top!"

"C'mon!" Henry shouted to the boy fairy, and Puck darted to join him, narrowly escaping the knuckle sandwich Sabrina was preparing to serve him.

"You're really leaving us here?" Daphne cried. "Again?"

"We are," Henry confirmed.

"You can't keep us locked up in this mirror forever! We could help you," Sabrina shouted, but Henry waved her off. He and Puck stormed out of the Room of Reflections, through the portal that led to the real world, and then they were gone.

"Mom! This is ridiculous. Granny Relda trained us for things like this. We've got crazy skills," Daphne grumbled.

Veronica patted them each on the shoulder. "Your dad's right, girls. It's too dangerous. And believe it or not, there really is plenty to do around here. Go find Pinocchio and ask him to help Canis with that room. He could start lending a hand. We are feeding him, after all."

When the girls were out of earshot of their mother, the complaining began again.

"They treat us like we're babies!" Sabrina said.

"Yeah, why not put us in diapers?" Daphne replied.

"We've been in dangerous situations before."

"Very dangerous!"

"We've fought dragons and Jabberwockies and creepy guidance counselors!"

"You're right. We're tough!"

"I killed a giant once!"

"I ate 'fish surprise' in the orphanage cafeteria!" Daphne shouted.

The two continued complaining until they found Pinocchio's room. The odd little boy had chosen one far from the others. Sabrina didn't blame him. He was largely responsible for many of the family's problems. He was the one who had opened the doors in the Hall of Wonders and let all the magical creatures into the real world. Those monsters had destroyed the Grimms' home. On top of that, he was condescending and arrogant. Sabrina was flabbergasted when her father invited him to stay with them. In her opinion, Pinocchio should have been sent out into the wilderness to fend for himself. But Henry believed the boy deserved a second chance to prove himself. So far, he had only proven himself to be rude and lazy.

Sabrina pounded on his door harder than was necessary.

"Whoever it is, go away! I'm having some me time," the boy whined from behind the door.

"I have keys to this room, you know," Sabrina shouted back. "Open the door, or I will open it myself!"

"You wouldn't dare!" Pinocchio cried.

Sabrina scowled and dug into her pocket for her keys. She made quick work of unlocking the door, and then she and Daphne burst into the room. There, they found Pinocchio lying on a brass bed, flipping through an architecture magazine.

"Hey! This is private! You're invading my . . . what on earth is that smell? You're putrid!"

"What does *putrid* mean?" Daphne asked.

Before Sabrina could answer, Pinocchio spoke. "It refers to something that is in a state of foul decay. You children have always lacked a sense of personal pride when it came to cleanliness, but you seem to have reached a new low."

"He's saying I stink," Sabrina clarified.

"Actually, I'm saying you both stink," Pinocchio said.

Sabrina might have gotten angry at the insult if she wasn't so distracted by what she saw in the boy's room. While she and her family were sleeping on floors, Pinocchio was living in the lap of luxury. He had a king-size bed, an armoire, an ornate rug, an overstuffed chair for reading, and a box of chocolate bonbons. "Where did you get all this stuff?"

"I discovered these items in some of the other rooms," Pinocchio huffed. "Hey, you're getting that slop all over my things. Some of these pieces are antiques!"

Sabrina grabbed the boy by the collar and dragged him from the bed. He flailed and kicked until he freed himself from her grip.

"Did your tiny little brain ever think there might be other people who need this furniture more than you do? Mr. Canis? My mom and dad? My baby brother?!"

"Not to mention me, hello!" Daphne whined as she stretched a cramp out of her back.

"It's every man for himself now, Grimms," Pinocchio said, shooing them away.

Sabrina fought the urge to strangle him and nearly lost. Instead, she grabbed him by the shoulders, spun him around, and kicked him in the behind so hard, he went flying through the doorway. "Get out!"

"You're evicting me? You wouldn't!" Pinocchio cried, straightening his clothes.

"I can and I will," Sabrina snapped, stalking out after him. "We have a million major emergencies going on right now: We're practically homeless, a maniac has stolen our grandmother's body, our uncle's girlfriend was just killed, there are monsters running wild all over town, there's a psychopath escapee from a magic book on the loose, and there's a lazy, worthless freeloader hogging beds and taking up space. Which of those problems is the easiest to solve?"

Pinocchio shoved his sharp little nose into her face. "Fine! What do you require of me?"

"Go back to wherever you found all that furniture and bring back whatever you can—if you spot a crib, take it to my parents' room pronto!"

"I will not be ordered to do manual labor!" the boy shrieked. "That kind of work is done by the uneducated classes."

"Get moving, or my foot is about to be filled with splinters!"

"I haven't been made out of wood for centuries," Pinocchio grumbled as he walked away.

"You better change that attitude, pal!" Daphne called after him. "Next time we say jump, the correct response is 'How high?'"

Sabrina watched the boy disappear down the hall.

"Did that sound tough?" Daphne asked. "I felt tough."

"Get your jacket," Sabrina said.

"Uh-oh! I know that look," Daphne said, grinning. "You're thinking about shenanigans!"

"Shenanigans?"

"It's my new word. It means 'fun troublemaking,'" Daphne explained. "You've got a plan to get into some shenanigans."

Sabrina nodded. "We're going to help rescue Granny Relda, whether Dad likes it or not."

"Right after you take a shower," Daphne said.

Sabrina sniffed her glop-covered shirt and gagged. "Right after I take a shower."

2

INOCCHIO PROVIDED AN EXCELLENT DIS-
traction. His endless grumbling and whining kept
Veronica so occupied, she didn't even notice the girls
leaving. Daphne stashed the Book of Everafter somewhere safe,
and then she, Sabrina, and Elvis slipped out of the portal unseen.
As they passed through, they were met with a rush of air and
a dramatic drop in temperature. They stepped out into a heavy
thicket, deep in the Hudson Valley forest. The bushes were the
perfect place to hide the huge mirror, but not a very convenient
exit from the Hall of Wonders.

They pushed free of the thorny vines and stepped into the open
and a chilly spatter of autumn rain. Drops trickled down Sabrina's
face and neck, sending shivers all the way down to her feet. She
quickly zipped up her sister's jacket, then did the same to her own.

"It was raining like this the day we came to Ferryport Landing," Daphne said, catching some of the drops on her tongue.

Sabrina recalled the freezing drizzle, gray skies, and brisk chill that had greeted them when their caseworker, Ms. Smirt, had marched them down the train platform to meet their grandmother for the first time. Sabrina had sworn to Daphne that they would run away from the crazy old woman the second they got a chance, but destiny had other plans for them. Now, she couldn't imagine her life without Granny Relda. She and Daphne needed to rescue her from Mirror. No one could get in their way, not even their father.

"We have to be patient with Dad," Daphne said, seemingly reading her sister's mind.

"Now you're on his side?" Sabrina said. "Five seconds ago you were shouting about how unfair he was being."

"I'm trying to give him some credit. When Mom and Dad went to sleep, I was five and you were nine. I was obsessed with princesses—"

"You still are."

"Don't interrupt. What I'm saying is, they're still trying to catch up to us. I think we need to wait a little longer for Dad to recognize we've grown up."

"I'll try, but Granny never treated us like little girls. She would want us leading her rescue," Sabrina said.

"Actually, she would have told us to stay home. We just never would have listened."

Daphne was right, but it was still frustrating. "So you think we should go back?"

"No way!" The little girl leaned down and kissed Elvis on the snout. "Find Granny, buddy."

The dog shook himself off, sending water in every direction. He sniffed the air and trotted up a steep incline. Sabrina and Daphne followed, trudging through spongy mounds of brown leaves and over slick black rocks. Soon, they were both soaked to the bone, but Sabrina didn't mind. It felt good to be outside the Hall of Wonders, in the real world. It made her feel useful.

After an hour of following Elvis, they realized his keen nose wasn't really necessary. All the girls had to do was walk in the direction of the tremendous storm. Lightning slashed the horizon, followed by thunder so loud, it rattled Sabrina's teeth. Anyone else might have rushed for cover, fearing an approaching tornado or hurricane, but Sabrina knew better. The storm was no act of Mother Nature. It would lead them to Mirror and Granny Relda.

The girls stumbled out of the forest and onto a deserted road. They walked along its edge, despite the fact that neither of them had seen a car in weeks—not since the Scarlet Hand took over the town. It felt to Sabrina as if she and her sister were the only two people left in the world. She took Daphne's hand, not only to reassure her sister that they would be OK, but to calm her own anxiety. Eventually, Elvis slowed near a bend in the road. He looked frightened, pacing in circles and panting heavily. Daphne rubbed his neck, but it did little to soothe him.

"Granny's nearby," Sabrina said.

Daphne nodded and turned back to the dog. "You stay here, OK?" Elvis pulled at Daphne's sweatshirt with his teeth, but she stepped away. "We'll be careful, Elvis. You stay."

Remarkably, Elvis did as he was told, and the girls continued down the road. They followed the sharp bend, and there they saw their grandmother for the first time in three days.

It was not a pretty sight. The old woman was engulfed in a light so intense, it hurt to look directly at her. She held her wrinkled hands held high above her head, and they glowed like two giant torches. Energy rocketed from her fingertips and streaked into the sky, leaving plumes of smoke and magic in their wake. The target was Jacob and Wilhelm's invisible barrier, built long ago to keep Everafters from leaving Ferryport Landing.

The magical force bounced off the barrier without any effect. Each blast slammed into it hard, bursting into a million vivid colors that spread out over the dome's surface. Aftershocks shook the earth and air. One attack followed another and another and another. Granny Relda wouldn't stop, and it was clear that she was not in command of her actions. Mirror's spirit was inside her, controlling her as if she were a puppet. Sabrina felt the urge to confront him, demand that he set the old woman free, but the explosions were too strong. After just a few short moments, the heat was already almost more than Sabrina could bear.

"I'm soooooo telling." The taunting voice behind them made

Sabrina jump out of her skin. She spun around to find Puck, waving a disapproving finger in her face. "You two disobeyed your parents! I'm both really shocked and really impressed."

"We're tired of being under house arrest," Sabrina said.

"Yeah! We're not babies. We've fought monsters," Daphne added.

"Actually, you've done a lot more running away from monsters than actual fighting of said monsters," Puck said. "And it is always hee-larious. Still, I love this big, brave turnaround. Sabrina's whole 'I don't want to be a Grimm' thing was getting a little tired."

Daphne nodded. "He's right. You were getting lame."

Suddenly, their father, Henry, raced into the clearing, snatched each of his daughters by an arm, and dragged them back into the trees. Sabrina had never seen someone's head explode, but her father looked like a volcano just waiting to erupt.

"Get back to the Hall of Wonders right now!" he demanded.

"We want to help! Granny trained us to be brave and take action," Sabrina argued.

"And look where that got her!" Henry roared, then launched into a long rant about respect, trust, and sneakiness. When he eventually came up for air, he said, "You're grounded."

"You can't ground us. We're homeless," Daphne said.

Henry was momentarily derailed. "Fine! But once we get a home, you are going to be locked inside it until you are very old and very gray! Come on, I'll take you back myself. We've learned all we can anyway."

"Which is?" Sabrina asked.

"An all-powerful monster has control over my mother, and if we confront him, he'll incinerate us with his magic."

"So we're just going to give up on the old lady?" Puck asked.

"Of course not," Henry said. "But we can't just go running headfirst into a fight we can't win. We need help."

Elvis approached, looking even more frantic than when the girls had left him. He was whining and growling and racing around in circles.

"I've never seen him act like this before. It must be the storm," Henry said as he tried to calm the dog.

"We have." Sabrina cringed.

"Yeah, around monsters," Daphne added.

A loud crashing noise from deep in the woods drowned out the girl's words. It sounded like a tree falling over—a very big tree. Sabrina peered into the forest, trying to find the source, when she spotted a monster so terrifying, she nearly fainted. Its mammoth body was covered in thick, matted hair. Its arms were long and spindly, but it stood up on two thick, muscled legs. A ridge of sharp spikes lined its spine all the way up to its head, which was enormous. Its most grotesque feature was its fang-lined mouth. It unhinged at the jaw when the creature roared, opening so wide that Sabrina was sure she could step inside with no trouble.

"Grendel!" Henry cried, snatching the girls once more and racing in the opposite direction.

"What's a Grendel?" Sabrina asked.

"There's a poem about him. He killed hundreds of Vikings—and ate most of them. If we don't get moving, he'll kill us, too," Henry cried.

Puck flew leisurely overhead. "Yawn! I've never been afraid of anything that appeared in some silly poem. Next you guys will be trembling over the Cat in the Hat."

"He's no joke, Puck," Henry said. "The warrior Beowulf chopped off his head once, and even that didn't stop him."

"Big deal! Who here hasn't had their head chopped off?"

"This is exactly why I wanted you girls to wait in the Hall of Wonders. Your grandmother isn't our only problem. This town is overrun, both with the Scarlet Hand and with all the monsters that should be locked away."

"He's gaining on us," Daphne warned.

"Just keep running until I can come up with a plan," Henry said.

"Plan?" Sabrina said. "The only plan we need is to keep running!"

"We can't outrun him," Henry said. "Puck, do you still have those stink balloons?"

"I never leave home without something disgusting!" Puck reached into his hoodie pocket and pulled out four more of the disgusting sludge bombs he had tested on Sabrina earlier that morning.

"Good!" Henry cried. "Hit him high. I'll take him low."

Sabrina could feel panic squeezing her neck. "Wait! You're going to attack him? With some water balloons and your bare hands?"

"And my feet, too," Henry said. "Your grandfather always said not to underestimate the power of your own body as a weapon. If you know what you're doing, you can be very dangerous."

"What should we do?" Sabrina asked.

"Hide!" he commanded, shoving the girls behind the thick trunk of an ancient maple. "If something bad happens, run for the mirror. All right, fairy, let's do this!"

"Wait! You just said it was stupid to run headfirst into a fight," Sabrina grumbled.

"Hush up, and you might learn something," their father said, and then took off at a sprint toward Grendel, roaring like a barbarian.

"Your dad rules," Puck said, darting into the air and mimicking Henry's wail.

Puck tossed his disgusting bombs at the monster, nailing Grendel in the face. Enraged, the brute snatched at the boy's leg, but Puck darted away from the deadly claws. While Grendel was busy with Puck, Henry snuck up behind him.

"Lesson number one!" Henry called out to the girls. "When you are about to fight someone—or something, for that matter— you need to take them by surprise. Screaming like a maniac startles your opponent. The distraction will allow you to observe his weaknesses. Look at Grendel's left knee. It's bigger than the right one. It's bulging and red. He's injured it, and now it's infected, which means that if I kick it . . ."

Henry delivered a vicious kick with his boot heel. Grendel shrieked and bent over, cupping his knee in his massive hands.

Henry circled around the creature until they were nearly face-to-face. "Now, while Grendel is bent over, we can get an even closer look. Notice his left eye. The pupil is milkier than the right, which means he's going blind on that side, so he can't see me as well when I'm standing on the left side of his body. So he won't see this coming!"

Their father punched Grendel hard on his left temple. The monster fell to the ground and lay silent.

"Whoa," said Sabrina, Daphne, and Puck at once.

Sabrina was stunned. Back in New York City, Henry had been a man who refused to step off the curb to hail a cab. He wouldn't eat hot dogs from the carts in Times Square because he was afraid of food poisoning. He never left the house without hand sanitizer. What had happened to her super-careful father? Who was this . . . daring, heroic man?

"You knocked him out? Awww, man! Who am I supposed to throw the rest of these balloons at?" Puck complained when he landed next to the fallen monster. "It's no fun to pelt someone when they're unconscious."

He threw one of his balloons at Grendel, and it exploded on his cheek.

"OK, it's still fun, but not as much fun!"

"Geez, he's big," Henry said, kneeling to get a closer look at Grendel. "He's gotta be nine feet tall and mostly muscle. Your uncle and I used to spy on him through the window of his door in the Hall of Wonders, but this is the closest I've ever gotten to him. The stories says his father was a dragon, and his mother . . ."

"What about his mother?" Sabrina asked, unsure if she really wanted an answer.

"Forget it. That will give you nightmares," Henry said, standing upright again. "We need to get him back to the Hall of Wonders. He's too dangerous to be running—" But Henry didn't get to finish his sentence. Grendel sprang back to life and was up in a flash.

"DAD!" Sabrina screamed.

Henry somersaulted out of the way just as the brute's hulking fist smashed into the ground where he'd been standing. A wicked backhand followed, but Henry dodged once again. The tree directly behind him was not so lucky. It cracked in half, and the forest floor was showered in splinters.

Puck blasted the creature with more of his gag bombs and buzzed around his head. Grendel swatted and roared, nearly blind from the glop.

"Girls, get back!" Henry shouted just before the monster connected a brutal punch to his chest. Sabrina watched as her father fell to the ground. She raced to his side and cradled his head in her lap. He was unconscious and bleeding from his left ear.

"Is he OK?" Puck cried as he continued his assault.

"He's breathing, but we have to get him back to the Hall of Wonders, now!" Sabrina shouted.

"I think I can help," Daphne said. She fumbled through the front pocket of her sweatshirt. A second later, she was laying out objects on the ground: bejeweled rings, a pair of golden slippers, a few wands, and some other odds and ends.

"You brought magic weapons!" Sabrina exclaimed, overjoyed.

"It's not much. The bad guys took all the good stuff, and I don't know what some of these things do."

Sabrina pointed out a ring with a rose engraved in its clear crystal. "What's that? Does that kill monsters?"

"That's the Kingmoor Ring," Daphne said. "It stops nose-bleeds."

"Are you serious, Daphne?"

"You won't need any of those trinkets," Puck said as he continued taunting the monster. "I think he's getting tired!"

With a sudden burst of speed, Grendel landed an uppercut so powerful, it sent Puck sailing straight up into the sky and out of sight, leaving just the girls and Elvis to fight off the creature. The big dog stood before Grendel, barking and baring his fangs, which only made the hideous monster do the same.

All the while, Daphne sorted frantically through her magical items. Sabrina prayed she would find a magic sword, but the little girl was busy waving a silver wand with a glittering star on its tip. It looked like part of a cheap Halloween costume, but Sabrina knew what it really was: a fairy godmother's wand. When Grendel charged them, Daphne unleashed its magic. Grendel disappeared behind a puff of purple smoke and light. Sabrina heard a loud thump, followed by a groan.

She lost sight of her sister in the haze. "Daphne!"

"I took care of it," Daphne said. When the smoke faded away, the little girl was standing over the fallen monster, her wand in hand and Elvis by her side. Grendel squirmed and struggled to escape a formfitting silver taffeta dress. He roared, and the gown tore down his back, freeing him. "Maybe not. I guess he didn't like that dress. I'll try another."

Daphne flicked her wand once more. The gown vanished in another puff of smoke and was replaced by a clown outfit, complete with floppy yellow shoes, a rainbow wig, and a bright red nose. Grendel looked down at himself, befuddled.

"Can't you put him in a straitjacket or something?" Sabrina cried.

"I'm trying. This isn't easy," Daphne complained, twirling the wand in a big loop, then zapping the creature over and over again, changing his outfits: a tuxedo with tails, a conquistador suit, a ballerina tutu, Raggedy Andy overalls, and a banana costume. Each abrupt change only made Grendel more and more enraged, and eventually he snatched the little girl off the ground, forcing her to drop her magic wand.

In desperation, Sabrina jumped to her feet and scooped up the enchanted weapon. A wave of nausea rolled through her, an experience she felt every time she touched something magical. The feeling was too intense, and she had to drop the wand. She was going to have to fight Grendel without magic. But how? What had her father said about the monster's knee? It was swollen and infected. Thankfully, being an orphan had taught her a lot about kicking and punching.

Grendel gripped Daphne in his claws and stared at her with hungry curiosity. Sabrina knew she had to act fast, before her sister became the monster's breakfast. She raced toward him, leaping into the air and landing a swift kick to his kneecap. Grendel cried out in agony. She looked down at her foot, stunned by her own strength, but spotted a quick flash of fur and claws. Something else was attacking the monster—its movements were too fast to follow.

Grendel dropped Daphne, and the little girl fell into a wet mound of leaves. She crawled toward Sabrina, and the two raced to their unconscious father. Sabrina looked around to find that they had not one savior, but four. Three massive brown bears were attacking from all sides. These were no ordinary bears, though. The biggest wore overalls, the middle one a polka-dotted dress, and the littlest a beanie cap with a propeller on the top. Watching the action from the relative safety of the trees was a beautiful woman with curly blond locks and big eyes.

"Goldilocks," Sabrina gasped.

"Let's get your father to safety," Goldie said, and Sabrina saw that she wasn't alone. Another woman helped Goldie heave Henry to his feet. She had long auburn hair, creamy skin, and green eyes.

"Beauty?" Daphne cried.

"I don't think your bears can take him, Goldie," Beauty said. "Mind if I give it a try?"

"Be my guest," Goldilocks said.

Beauty turned to face Grendel, seemingly fearless in the face of the massive beast. She sang a sweet lullaby, loud and clear. Grendel stopped fighting and stared at her, perplexed. Each beautiful note she sang seemed to further soothe the brute. Soon, all the fight had drained out of him, and he stood weaving back and forth on his feet in a happy daze.

"That's right," Beauty said as she reached up to caress Grendel's horrible face. "You know I like a man with a big smile. Can you smile for me?"

Grendel did as he was asked, baring his disgusting fangs. Then he cooed like a newborn baby, which was equally nauseating.

"Oh, we've got a real charmer on our hands, Goldie." Beauty giggled.

"Can you get him into the Hall of Wonders?" Henry, now conscious, begged weakly. The girls helped keep him upright.

"Right now, I could get him to do the cha-cha!" Beauty said with a wink.

"Thank you. You saved our lives," he said to her, and then gave Goldie a quick, awkward hug.

Goldie stepped back, blushing. "Don't be silly, Hank. It's only, like, the fifty millionth time."

Sabrina watched as a lifetime of memories passed between them. Sadly, Goldie's eyes hinted at heartache. It upset Sabrina that this woman still loved her father, but at the same time, she had to be grateful to Goldie for those feelings. If Goldie had truly moved on, her kiss would never have woken her father from Mirror's sleeping spell.

"What were you two doing out here?" Henry asked Beauty and Goldie.

"Looking for you," Beauty explained.

"Us?" Sabrina cried.

"Yes, and we have to hurry," Goldie said. "We need your help. It's Jake."

"You've found him?" Henry asked. "Our magic mirrors couldn't locate him. It was like he vanished."

"He's been with us," Goldie said. "There's a diversion spell on our camp. He's safe, but—Hank, he's not himself."

"He just lost Briar," Henry said. "It's still hard for him. When our father died, he was so overcome with grief that he left town."

"It's more than grief," Beauty said. "I think he's losing his mind."

"What do you mean?" Daphne asked.

"He's talking to himself, muttering at all hours of the night. And what he's saying—it's troubling stuff."

Suddenly, Puck drifted down from above, seemingly recovered from Grendel's attack. He blasted the brute with three of his glop balloons, smiled at his successful revenge, and landed next to Sabrina. Grendel, still under Beauty's spell, was unfazed. The vile concoction dripped down his dreamy face.

"I heard someone's going crazy. Who is it? Can I watch?" Puck asked. "Crazy people are fascinating."

"Puck, this is serious," Henry said. "What kind of things is my brother saying?"

Goldie looked pained but spoke anyway. "I'm afraid he's talking about murder."

3

OCTOBER 14 (PART 2)

Thought I better update the journal now that I'm back in the Hall of Wonders. Grendel is safely back in his room, where he belongs. Unfortunately, he's just one of hundreds of monsters that Pinocchio set free. The rest are still running around town doing who knows what. Dad tried to focus on the positive by reminding us that we now have one less freak to worry about. I reminded him that we are now sleeping next door to said freak. He told me to zip it.

He's pretty upset with us. Note to self: Don't get Mom and Dad mad . . . ever. I forgot how they are when they're angry, and I think I'd rather face Grendel again. The last time I saw them this furious was when Daphne invited a homeless man to come live with us. She hid him in our closet for six hours before someone found him.

Neither of us are allowed out of their sight, and they swore that if we ever pull a stunt like that again—well, I probably shouldn't write it down.

I'm so embarrassed. In all the family journals I read, I never came across a single entry where a Grimm got grounded for trying to rescue someone. It seems like everyone treats me like a child. Even Daphne's doing it now. Am I really that worthless?

I suspect my sister and I are not completely to blame for all of our parents' stress. Goldie's sudden reappearance has put them both on edge. Anytime she's around, Dad looks like he wants to crawl under a rock, and Mom looks like she wants to toss that rock at Goldie's head. I can't blame her. Who would want their husband's ex around, mooning over him? Goldie doesn't make it any easier. She's so nervous all the time, rushing around moving things. Not to mention the endless chattering. Daphne thinks she's trying to fill the awkward moments (of which there are plenty).

Still, it's good that she and Beauty have come to warn us abut Uncle Jake. We really need to stay focused on Granny Relda right now, especially since we've found her, but Uncle Jake needs us, too. I pray he isn't as broken as they say he is, especially all the talk about murder. Still, I have to wonder: If someone I loved was killed, wouldn't I want revenge?

Well, on that bright and cheery note, I have to go. Dad is calling me. He probably wants to yell at me again. I'll write more when I can. I have a feeling that I'm going to be spending a lot of time with this journal now that I'm grounded.

With the magic mirror strapped securely to Poppa Bear's back, the Grimms, Puck, Mr. Canis, Pinocchio, and the rest of the bears marched through the forest, led by Goldilocks and Beauty. Red and Basil stayed behind in the Hall of Wonders. She'd promised to make sure he took a nap. There was a cold drizzle in the air, and the low-lying clouds made everything seem extra dreary.

"Grendel was as ugly as I remember," Beauty said as she kicked a clump of leaves off her high-heeled shoe. Her outfit was completely wrong for a hike in the woods. Her sweater dress was awfully thin for the chilly air, and she didn't have a jacket, but she didn't complain. She only said that it was "more important to look good than to feel good."

"You have no idea what it was like coming over here on the boat with him," Goldie said, shuddering from either the cold or her memory of Grendel. "All that grunting and groaning. I was sure that at any moment the chains binding him would snap and he'd eat us all whole."

"Plus, with all those monsters running around—ugh. The only way you'll get me on a ship now is if it's a cruise to the Bahamas," Beauty said.

"Why did Jacob and Wilhelm bring all these dangerous weirdos to America?" Sabrina asked.

"The brothers believed everybody had some goodness in them—even dangerous weirdos," Mr. Canis said, as he carefully navigated a rocky passage with his cane. "They took a chance on me, and I will always be grateful."

Henry agreed. "Look at some of the people that we now call friends—Morgan le Fay, Baba Yaga—"

"Baba Yaga is hardly a friend," Sabrina interrupted.

"The fact that she's not trying to eat us makes her as close to a friend as we may ever get." Henry laughed. "In my book, that's personal growth."

Goldie giggled. "Henry, do you remember the time we snuck out into the woods and ran into her? We were up on the cliffs near Mount Taurus, and she came along in that creepy house, and we . . ." Her voice tapered off when Veronica glared at her.

"Hmm, so you say my father used to sneak out into the woods without permission?" Daphne asked, narrowing her eyes at him.

"Funny, it seems like we just got grounded for doing the same thing," Sabrina said.

Henry frowned at them and deftly changed the subject. "Like I was saying, Jacob and Wilhelm didn't believe in writing anyone, or anything, off, and their decision to keep an open mind helped our family immensely. Who knows? You kids might someday think of Grendel as an ally. You might even decide he's ready to be free from the Hall of Wonders."

"Let's not hand out any empathy awards just yet," Pinocchio said. "Your ancestors built a wall around this town, locking everyone inside whether they were dangerous or not."

A big, awkward pause fell on the group, and all eyes turned to Henry.

Mr. Canis broke the silence. "I was there when it went up. It was necessary. A large group of citizens was planning to invade the next town. Innocent people would have been killed, and no one would listen to reason. The brothers did the right thing."

"Still," Pinocchio said. "The barrier punished everyone for the crimes of a few, and even more have innocently stumbled into this town, not realizing they would be trapped here for eternity. Take me, for instance. I wasn't even here when the troubles started, but I'm paying the price nonetheless."

Henry opened his mouth to say something, but Pinocchio cut him off.

"These so-called friends and allies, who have all reformed, are still just as imprisoned as the Scarlet Hand lunatics. Mr. Canis has proven himself a hero. The Wicked Queen has shown herself to be trustworthy. And we're walking beside Beauty, who, from what I understand, sold her child to a monster."

"I did not sell her!" Beauty said, turning on the little boy and leveling an angry stare at him. "I was manipulated by magic."

"My point," Pinocchio said as he stepped back from her, "is simple. Jacob and Wilhelm's prison disguised as a town doesn't reward changes of heart, reformed villains, or magical manipulation of any kind. It treats all Everafters like criminals. To the barrier you, Beauty, are no better than Sheriff Nottingham, or even Grendel. They will never leave this town . . . and neither will you."

Sabrina eyed her mother, then her father, and finally her sister.

They all shared the same troubled expression. She couldn't stand Pinocchio, but he made a powerful argument, one that had kept her up on many a sleepless night. On one hand, the barrier kept evil people safely away from the unsuspecting world. On the other, it imprisoned genuinely innocent, kind people. Was the barrier fair? Was the magic wall solving any problems, or was it causing them in the first place?

"Blah, blah, blah," Puck taunted as he flew above them. "All you people do is talk. Where are we going, anyway? I've scouted ahead, and there is no sign of any camp."

"We're going to the castle," Beauty explained, taking a few deep breaths to calm herself.

"What castle?" Sabrina said.

"The one we built," Goldie replied. "Boarman and Swineheart designed it, and the rest of us have worked night and day getting it ready."

"Ready for what?" Mr. Canis asked.

"War," Beauty said. "Charming's army is going to attack the Scarlet Hand."

"Charming's army?" Henry asked.

Not long ago, Prince Charming and a band of Everafter refugees had parted ways with Sabrina's family. She had no idea where they'd gone or what they were doing. Leave it to Charming to prepare for yet another battle with the Scarlet Hand.

"Didn't you already try and fail?" Pinocchio chuckled dismissively. "You built a fort, trained everyone, and the Hand overran the place and burned it to the ground. Don't you people ever learn?"

"Actually, we learned a lot," Goldie said, gesturing into the woods. "Oh, here we are."

"Huh?" Daphne said, spinning around and looking in all directions. "I don't see anything but trees."

"That's because it's invisible. Hold on a sec." Beauty reached into her purse and pulled out a glass vial filled with what looked like purple glitter. She poured some of the substance into her hand and blew it into the air. The powder collided with the raindrops, and each particle exploded like a tiny firework. Suddenly, a grand castle appeared. It was built from thick white stones, stood nearly four stories tall, and was framed by two towers that spiraled even higher. Each tower was festooned with purple flags and ominous black cannons. It was an impressive structure, especially considering it had been built in only two days.

"OK, I've got to get some of that purple stuff!" Daphne cried.

Goldie winked at her, then stuck two fingers into her mouth. She blasted a loud, shrill whistle, and Sabrina heard a heavy wheel turning and chains rattling. A huge drawbridge tilted forward to span a deep trench filled with spikes.

"We haven't had time to fill the moat with water yet," Goldie explained as if she were deeply embarrassed. "And we're still trying to find alligators to live in it."

"I can help with that," Puck said, landing beside Sabrina. "I know a guy."

Goldie led the group over the drawbridge to the castle's iron gate. It rose, and they stepped into an interior courtyard. There, Sabrina found several crude log cabins. The nutty smell of fresh bread wafted from one of them, and horses neighed from a barn. Old friends were bustling about, pounding hammers and sawing timber. She spotted Puss in Boots, Morgan le Fay, the Scarecrow, and even the Pied Piper and his son, Wendell.

"It's incredible," Veronica said.

"Indeed," Mr. Canis agreed, straining his neck to look up at the fluttering flags.

"So how many people do you have in this army?" Pinocchio asked.

"Twenty-two," Goldie said.

"Twenty-two! That's preposterous," Pinocchio said, chuckling.

"What does *preposterous* mean?" Daphne asked.

"He's calling it silly," Sabrina said.

Goldie shrugged. "Well, as Geppetto says, 'We're small, but we're spunky.'"

Pinocchio's sneer fell off his face. "Papa's here? Is he well? Is he injured?"

"Your father is fine. As you know, he's a very talented carpenter, and he's helped the pigs make the place into something formidable. If you'd like, I can take you to him."

"Yes, yes. I would like that very much," the boy said eagerly.

Across the courtyard, Morgan le Fay's son, Mordred, was busy working his magic. The last time Sabrina had seen the warlock, he was living with his mom and playing video games all day. Now, he was doing something more productive. A stream of white light emanated from his fingers and enveloped a newly constructed water tower lying on its side in the courtyard. Slowly, the tower struggled to right itself, hobbling back and forth.

"Now I see how you got this castle built so quickly," Henry said to Goldie. "How did you get Mordred off his mother's couch?"

"Mordred might be a pill sometimes. But like most kids, he's afraid of his mother's temper," Goldie explained. "He's really made himself indispensable. Unfortunately, there are a few side effects to his magic."

"Side effects?" Sabrina asked.

Goldie didn't need to answer. The water tower suddenly lunged away from Mordred, stomping up and down in an attempt to squash Boarman and Swineheart. Mordred shot a couple of fireballs at the ground beneath it, which seemed to ward off its attack.

Beauty shrugged. "Everything he brings to life turns evil and murderous for a few minutes."

Puck grinned. "That dude is the coolest."

While Mordred attempted to subdue his evil water tower, Prince Charming and Mr. Seven approached. Both needed a shave and a bath, and Charming was wearing his trademark scowl.

Mr. Seven, however, was as friendly as ever—perhaps even more than usual.

Charming growled at Goldie and Beauty. "I thought we had an agreement. No one leaves the castle without my approval."

Beauty flashed him her best smile and batted her eyelashes. "We were only gone for a little while."

"Don't try the 'calming the savage beast' nonsense on me, lady," Charming said. "The rules are in place to keep everyone safe."

Sabrina rolled her eyes. It seemed she wasn't the only one in town being treated like a child.

"We had to find Henry and his family. They're the only ones who can reach Jake," Goldilocks explained.

"Jake is hardly the biggest of our problems!" Charming cried, then threw up his arms in surrender. "Fine! It's not like I can control the two of you anyway."

Beauty nodded. "We were wondering when you were going to catch on."

"Interesting. Sometimes, people break the rules, and it makes things better," Sabrina muttered within earshot of her father.

Veronica shot her a warning look that said it was much too soon for sarcasm.

"It's so good to see you, Billy," Daphne said, wrapping the prince in a big hug. Charming squirmed while the little girl clung to him like a monkey. Daphne adored the stuffy, overbearing man, even if the feeling was not mutual.

"Um, yes, let's get you to your uncle," Charming said, pushing her gently aside. He turned and led the group along the castle wall, where they found even more log cabins.

"So you're going to try to fight the Hand again?" Henry asked the prince.

"I don't see that we have much of a choice," Charming said. "We're all criminals according to Heart and her goons. They're determined to kill us. We either fight or we die. The way I see it, you're in the same boat, and we could really use some help."

Henry looked to Veronica, then back to the prince. "Our energies are focused on rescuing my mother. Once that's done, I'm taking my family far away from this place, barrier or no barrier."

"So you're leaving us to clean up the mess, Henry?" Charming asked sharply. Henry ignored him.

"It's good to see the two of you," Mr. Seven said to Sabrina and Daphne with a big, toothy grin. "Lovely day, huh?"

"Someone's in a good mood," Sabrina marveled, looking around at the dirty castle and the drizzling rain.

"Of course he's in a good mood," Charming said. "The fool is lovesick."

"And it's contagious," a voice sang from behind them. Sabrina turned and saw Morgan le Fay approaching with a basket of herbs and berries. Morgan was gorgeous and glamorous. Even in a hard hat and overalls, she was a stunner. Seven rushed to her side, and when Morgan knelt down to his height, he planted a kiss on her that made everyone blush.

"Mom, please! Can you give it a rest?" Mordred groaned from across the courtyard.

"Sorry, honey," Morgan said. "But my darling boyfriend has simply swept me off my feet. In fact, he popped the question last night. We're getting married!"

"As soon as everything calms down," Seven added, beaming.

Charming grumbled. "All this affection is quite tiresome. There is serious work to do here. The west wall needs fortifying. The armory is still not ready. The stables need cleaning. We can't move into the castle until it's complete. Yet these two are running off every five minutes to stare into each other's eyes!"

"I seem to recall a certain handsome prince staring into mine last night," Snow White said from the doorway of one of the cabins. She wrapped her arms around Charming and planted a kiss on his cheek. Her touch seemed to make him dizzy.

"Snow, I—"

Snow giggled. "I'm just teasing, Mr. Grouchy Pants. Let the happy couple have their fun. Things are getting done around here so fast, my head is spinning."

"Harrumph!" Charming said, though he did flash a hint of a smile. The prince and Snow White had a long, complicated relationship. Hundreds of years ago, she'd left him at the altar.

Since then, he'd married Sleeping Beauty, Cinderella, and Rapunzel. None of those marriages had worked out, and Sabrina knew Snow was the reason. Even after countless centuries, William Charming could not let her go.

"I assume you're here to help us with Jake?" Snow asked the Grimms. "Henry, you might want to leave the girls here with me. He . . . he's not feeling well."

"Unfortunately, we're not allowed out of his sight," Sabrina said. "Apparently, we can't be trusted."

"We get into shenanigans," Daphne said, winking at her sister.

Henry huffed. "Come along, girls."

The group continued along the perimeter of the fortress, stumbling across Geppetto, who, despite his advanced age, was splitting firewood with an ax.

Pinocchio watched him for a moment, and then he sputtered out, "Papa?"

"Pinocchio!" Geppetto dropped his ax and rushed to his son, scooping him up into his arms. "My boy! My boy!"

Pinocchio hugged the old man and shed a few tears. "Oh, Papa! I thought . . . Oh, it's too terrible to say."

"Oh, brother," Puck groaned.

"And the Oscar goes to . . ." Sabrina said.

Pinocchio shot them a hostile look, then turned back to his father. "Papa, you have no idea how bad things have been for me. These horrible people expected me to sleep on the floor. They literally stole my bed. Can you imagine? I've never been treated so rudely in my—"

"I know what you did, son," Geppetto interrupted.

Pinocchio's crocodile tears suddenly dried up. "You have only heard one side of the story, Papa. I can explain!" he said frantically.

"The side I have heard is that you betrayed a family I count among the kindest friends I have had in my very long life. You lied to them, took advantage of their generosity, looted their home, and left them with nothing. You conspired with their mortal enemy, with my mortal enemy. You helped a—a monster try to steal the body of a helpless little boy. When that failed, he took Relda Grimm for his puppet. Don't you remember what it was like to be controlled by a master? To have your strings pulled against your will? And yet you allowed it to happen to someone else!"

"But Mirror promised to turn me into a man!"

"A man! What makes you think you are ready to be a man? Do you think playing chess and reading big books makes you a man? It takes more than the interests of an adult to be one. Why, I wouldn't be surprised if the Blue Fairy's spell keeps you as a child until you are ready to grow up. Is that something you've ever considered? Perhaps you are still a boy because, deep down, you aren't mature enough to be anything else!"

"Papa, please," Pinocchio cried. "You don't understand!"

"I understand perfectly. I've failed you as a father, but I'm considering this my second chance. You are going to become a good person, or I'll have the Blue Fairy turn you back into a puppet!"

"I was a marion—"

"Your first lesson is to shut your mouth when your father is speaking to you!" Geppetto roared.

"Why, you act like you don't love me anymore, Papa," Pinocchio whimpered.

"Oh, I love you more than I can ever say. But right now, I don't like you very much." He picked up the ax and placed it in his son's hands.

"What's this for?" Pinocchio asked.

"Chopping wood, of course," Geppetto replied. "You're the one who wants to be a grown-up. Grown-ups have jobs. Get to work."

Pinocchio looked to the Grimms in desperation.

"Don't look at us," Sabrina said with a laugh; then, along with the others, she turned her back and walked away.

Charming led them onward, around another corner. Sabrina felt something whiz past her head, followed by a loud *thunk!* She spotted a knife impaled in a straw dummy propped on a stake. The dummy bore a remarkable resemblance to Sheriff Nottingham, complete with a leather cape. Another dummy was propped next to it, this one dressed as the Queen of Hearts. A knife was buried in its forehead, too.

"Sabrina!" Uncle Jake cried, racing to her side. "I'm sorry. I didn't see you. Henry, Veronica, Canis—what are you doing here? Oh, I get it. I suppose they told you I've lost my mind."

Uncle Jake scowled and slumped into a chair placed next to a freshly dug grave. A wooden cross marked the mound, which was completely covered by a gorgeous white rosebush in full bloom. This was the final resting place of Briar Rose. A small shrine of candles, beads, dried flowers, and photographs of Briar decorated the cross. Sabrina fought back tears, not only for the loss of such an amazing woman, but for her uncle's heartbreak.

The tragedy had taken a toll on Jake's appearance. He looked exhausted and filthy. He'd lost quite a bit of weight, and his eyes burned with anger. Sabrina knew at once that Goldie and Beauty were right to bring the family to him.

Suddenly, a large black crow landed on the back of Jake's chair. She wore a red ribbon around her neck, and Sabrina recognized her immediately as the Widow, queen of the crows, and a friend of her grandmother. "No one thinks you're crazy, big guy," the Widow said.

"Good, because I'm not!" Jake said. "I'm perfectly fine, so you can all just go away. I have no plans to kill myself, if that's what you're worried about."

Henry gestured to Jake's targets. "It's not you hurting yourself that's got us concerned."

"That's none of your business." Jake stood abruptly, sending the crow flapping awkwardly to stay aloft, and then yanked the

knives out of his targets. He shoved the weapons into his coat pockets.

Henry shook his head. "I understand you're hurt—"

"Hurt? I'm a little more than hurt, Hank," Jake cried, spinning around to face his brother. "I am destroyed. I promised Briar's fairy godmothers I would look after her, and now she's gone. Heart and Nottingham are responsible. They had her killed right before my eyes, and there was nothing I could do to save her."

"Revenge won't bring her back," Canis said. "It will just hurt you more. It will break your soul."

Jake gave the old man a look of utter disbelief. "You've got to be kidding me, Canis."

"We're your family, Uncle Jake," Daphne said. "We want to help you."

"Focus on your grandmother," Jake said; then he hefted a quiver of arrows onto his back and scooped up a bow leaning against the wall. Without another word, he marched in the direction of the drawbridge.

"Where are you going?" Henry called after him.

"It's better that you don't know," Jake shouted back. He disappeared into the woods moments later, before anyone could stop him. Panic squeezed Sabrina's heart as she worried what he might do. Her uncle was obsessed with two incredibly dangerous people. Who knew what might happen if he found them?

"We should stop him," Veronica said. "He's not thinking clearly, and he's in no shape to confront Heart and Nottingham. They'll kill him."

"These woods are crawling with members of the Hand," Charming warned. "It's a miracle you weren't attacked coming here. I can't have all of you stumbling around in the forest. You'll give away the location of this castle and put us all in danger."

"He's my brother!" Henry shouted.

"I can keep an eye on him from the air," the crow squawked. "I'll do my best to keep him out of trouble."

Once the Widow was gone, Charming raised the drawbridge, but it came to a jerking halt barely halfway up.

"Boarman! Swineheart! What is wrong with this infernal machine?" he shouted.

The pigs rushed to investigate, inspecting the chains and pulleys, but they stepped back, scratching their heads.

"Nothing's broken, boss," Swineheart said. "Push the button again."

Charming did, but nothing happened.

"Fix this!" Charming growled. "Keeping this door open makes this castle vulnerable."

"Right away, boss." Boarman nodded.

"Your little door is not broken," a voice called out from across the moat. "I've come for the Grimms!"

"Who is that?" Seven asked as he and Morgan raced to join the group.

"Get to your battle stations!" Charming shouted as the castle's inhabitants rushed to arm themselves. "Someone has found us!"

There was the terrible sound of metal straining, and then the heavy chains on the drawbridge snapped as if they were rubber bands. The bridge slammed down onto the trench. Henry stepped in front of his family, prepared to fight. Puck landed next to him and drew his wooden sword. Even Mr. Canis wielded his cane.

A woman stormed through the gate: She wore a pretty black dress, pearls, and heels. Snow White might have been the fairest of them all, but this woman was a close second.

"The Wicked Queen," Goldilocks gasped. Even her bears roared in fright.

"Mother?" Snow said, pushing her way to the front of the crowd. "How did you find us?"

"Do you think your amateur attempt at a concealment spell would fool someone with my power?" the woman asked.

"Bunny, you broke my drawbridge!" Charming cried.

The witch dismissed him with a wave. "Everyone, follow me. It's time we got to work saving the world."

The witch stepped over to Poppa Bear and, with a flick of her wrist, severed the ropes that held the magic mirror on his back.

She leaned the mirror against a cabin wall, then plunged through its reflection. Sabrina looked at her father, who led her, Daphne, and Veronica into the mirror, as well.

"Hurry, now!" the witch demanded as soon as they entered the Hall of Wonders. Everyone followed, eager to hear what Bunny was planning. "Time is wasting. Don't you want to save Relda?"

Red approached with Basil in her arms. "What's going on?"

Veronica took the child and shrugged. "We don't have a clue."

Everyone followed the witch until she stopped at the Room of Reflections.

She charged into the room, looked around at the five remaining mirrors, as well as all the shards glued to the wall, and frowned. "Someone has not been taking care of these mirrors," Bunny snapped.

"They were like this when we found them," Daphne said.

Bunny took a closer look at the broken pieces, marveling at the different places they revealed. "Fascinating. Somehow your mirror guardian managed to link these pieces to every mirror in the world—not just magic ones. He's been spying on everyone. Quite clever, really."

While she studied the shards, four of the five intact mirrors illuminated, their guardians appearing in the reflections. Reggie, Titan, Donovan, and Fanny watched Bunny with a mixture of respect and fear.

"Good to see you, Ms. Lancaster," Titan said without any of his usual ferocity.

The witch ignored them and turned her attention to the fifth, empty mirror.

"That one might be broken," Canis said. "The guardian has never appeared to us."

"That's because it doesn't have a guardian. This mirror has only a single purpose: to reset the others to their default settings. *Ongegn!*" she cried, and a scarlet-red handprint appeared in the glass. A loud humming shook the air, and then suddenly all the broken shards peeled themselves from the walls and darted around the room like honeybees. They flew into the empty frames, reassembling themselves like jigsaw puzzle pieces, until they were whole once again. Soon, all twenty-five mirrors were as good as new.

"Give them a moment," Bunny said, her hand raised over her head. It was burning bright red, like a hot coal in a fire. "They need to reboot."

A red handprint appeared in each silver reflection and then faded just as quickly. Bunny lowered her hand and smoothed the wrinkles in her dress.

"Mirrors, I require your presence," she said sternly. In the blink of an eye, twenty-four guardians appeared, each floating in their own frame. Only the reset mirror remained empty.

Many of the faces looking out at the group were human, like Fanny and Reggie, but others were bizarre creatures. One had a pointy nose as long as a yardstick, while another had eyes and lips as big as a trout's. One was a huge iguana-like thing with a forked tongue. Another was a beautiful woman with the antlers of a deer. Sabrina was happy to see a familiar face among the strangers—Harry, the manager of the Hotel of Wonders. When his mirror shattered, she had been sure Harry was lost forever.

"Hello, Mother," the guardians called with great respect.

"Please stop calling me that," the witch demanded. "Oh, well, I'll fix that another time. For now, I come seeking a prophecy. Arden, will you please begin?"

The woman with antlers nodded. "Ask what you will, and we will enlighten." Her reflection rippled and shimmied so much that her face was barely visible. The same thing happened with the other mirrors. After a long, unsettling moment, the reflections calmed, and each guardian's eyes glowed a bright silver.

"Mirrors, mirrors, our future is cursed. Tell me how to defeat the First," the queen said.

"THE COUNCIL OF MIRRORS SEES ALL, EVERY DAY THAT PASSES, EVERY DAY TO COME. MANY POSSIBLE FUTURES LIE AHEAD, MANY PATHS CAN BE TAKEN, BUT IN NONE OF THEM ARE YOU SUCCESSFUL AT DE-FEATING THE FIRST."

"Who's the First?" Daphne whispered to her sister.

"I think they're talking about Mirror," Sabrina replied. "He was the first magic mirror."

"You must be mistaken," the witch said to the guardians.

"WE ARE NOT. THE FUTURE IS LIKE A SPIDER'S WEB, WITH A BILLION STRANDS LEADING TOWARD AND AWAY FROM THE CONFLICT YOU SEEK. NONE OF THEM ENDS IN A SATISFACTORY DEFEAT. IF YOU CHOOSE THIS QUEST FOR YOURSELF, YOU WILL FAIL. THE FIRST WILL DESTROY WILHELM'S BARRIER. HE WILL ESCAPE INTO THE WORLD OF HUMANS AND UNLEASH HIS POWER ON THEM. NATIONS WILL KNEEL. BILLIONS WILL DIE. YOU CANNOT STOP OUR BROTHER."

"Nonsense!" the Wicked Queen cried. "I created him! I should be able to destroy him."

"THE FUTURE DOES NOT AGREE."

The witch shook her head. "Then you're saying there is no hope."

"NONE ALONG THIS PATH."

Bunny turned to the crowd. "I'm sorry. I was mistaken. We cannot win. My only suggestion is to run and hide. Get as far away from here as you can. I wish you luck."

Sabrina was stunned. She stepped forward to block the exit. "So that's it? You're just going to give up?"

The Wicked Queen's lip curled in hostility. "The Council of Mirrors doesn't lie, child. It sees the future, every future. If there were a chance, we would take it."

"Then your mirrors are stupid and wrong," Daphne said.

"Girls," Henry warned. "Don't anger her."

"No, this is all her fault," Sabrina cried. "She made Mirror, then abandoned him. She sold him like he was an old chair. It's no wonder he's gone crazy and taken Granny Relda. She can't just walk out. She's got to fix this!"

The Wicked Queen's eyes burned bright with anger, and the room around her seemed to get smaller and darker. Everyone was afraid of this woman, even her own daughter, and it appeared Sabrina was about to find out why.

"Mirrors, it seems the child did not hear what you said," the witch growled through clenched teeth.

"THE QUEEN CAN DO NOTHING TO STOP THE FIRST."

"What about someone else? What about me?" Puck asked, stepping forward and striking his best heroic pose.

"ONE THREAD LEADS TO THE DEFEAT OF THE FIRST, BUT IT MUST BE FOLLOWED CAREFULLY. THE FATE OF THIS WORLD LIES IN THE HANDS OF THE SISTERS."

"The sisters?" Daphne asked.

"MANY STAND BEFORE THE FIRST: HEROES, WITCHES, FAIRY FOLK. BUT IN ALL THE FUTURES ONLY TWO SUCCEED, AND ONLY IF THEY TRUST IN THEIR STRENGTHS AND IN EACH OTHER. ONLY THE SISTERS CAN STOP OUR BROTHER: SABRINA AND DAPHNE GRIMM."

"Um, I'm sorry, I didn't hear you say my name," Puck said.

"Wait! What strengths?" Sabrina cried.

"DAPHNE GRIMM FORMS THE COVEN," the mirrors said. "A CRONE, A TEMPTRESS, AND AN INNOCENT."

"What's a coven?" Daphne asked.

"Shhh!" Bunny snapped.

"SABRINA GRIMM LEADS THE BATTLE," the mirrors continued.

Henry and Veronica pushed to the front of the group. "This has to be a mistake," Henry said.

"They're just little girls," Veronica added.

"THEY ARE THE WORLD'S ONLY CHANCE. ACT WITH HASTE. THE FIRST IS COMING. BLOOD WILL SPILL. HEARTBREAK IS UNAVOIDABLE. THE SISTERS ARE OUR ONLY HOPE."

The mirrors shimmered once again, and the guardians' faces returned to normal. They all looked tired and disoriented.

"But how do we do it?" Sabrina asked. "We need details!"

"They are done with the prophecy," the Wicked Queen said. "There is nothing else they can tell you."

"We're going to save the world," Daphne said, raising her hand to her sister for a high five. But Sabrina just stood there, bewildered, unable to speak or move.

Puck laughed. "We are so screwed."

4

ACOMMOTION ROSE UP AROUND SABRINA that made it impossible for her to think. People shouted and argued. They pressed in around her, stealing the air and space. She felt woozy and short of breath.

Suddenly, her father was there, pulling her out of the room, out of the chaos. Her mother followed with Daphne and Basil, and soon they were all stepping through the portal and marching across the castle courtyard.

"We'll head for the Metro-North station and get on the next train to Grand Central," Henry said.

"Dad—" Daphne started.

"This isn't up for discussion," Henry said. "I should have sent you away as soon as I had the chance. I won't make the same mistake again."

"But you heard the mirrors, Dad. If we don't stop Mirror, he'll take over the world. That's, like, really bad," Daphne said.

"The world will have to worry about itself."

"Henry, I think Daphne has a point," Veronica said.

Sabrina only caught snippets of the conversation. Her mind was back in the Room of Reflections, watching the Wicked Queen's face as the mirrors predicted the future. The witch had been as shocked as the others, but there was also something in her eyes that looked like acceptance, maybe even hope.

They were almost to the drawbridge when the Wicked Queen caught up with them. "The girls are the key to everything. You can't leave."

Henry turned on her. "Watch us."

"I know all about wanting to protect a child from danger, Henry, but this is their destiny. I don't like it any more than you do, but if they don't carry this out, everyone will suffer. Mirror will find a way to break through the barrier. He will unleash his power on a world that believes magic only exists in children's books. Their guns and bombs will be useless against him. There will be nowhere you can hide—he will hunt his enemies down one by one. The girls must fight. It's the only chance they have. It's the only chance any of us has."

"No one can know that, Ms. Lancaster," Henry said. "Your mirrors are busted."

The witch grabbed his arm. "I wouldn't be talking to you if that were true."

Henry pulled away and continued leading his family toward the gate.

"What about our stuff?" Daphne asked as they stormed past log cabins and half-built ramparts.

"We'll buy new things in New York City," Henry said.

Suddenly, Puck dropped down from the sky and blocked their way. "I never thought I'd see the day."

"Get out of my way, boy," Henry muttered.

"You're all a bunch of chickens," Puck said, spinning on his heels and morphing into a red rooster. He squawked obnoxiously and pecked at Henry's shoes. "Are you really going to just give up on the old lady? After all she's done for you? The cooking, the cleaning, the bedtime stories, how she hosed you down at night?"

"She didn't hose us down at night," Sabrina said.

Puck spun around and returned to normal. "The old lady would never run. Are you sure you're actually related to her? I'd like to see some paperwork."

"I'm not giving up," Henry argued. "I'm getting my family to safety, but I'm staying behind to save my mother."

"Wait, we're splitting up?" Veronica asked, stopping in her tracks.

"Just for a little while. I'll come find you as soon as my mom is safe," he explained.

"Henry, let's just stop and talk about this," Veronica said.

"Now you want to argue with me, too?" he said, turning to face his wife.

Mr. Canis hobbled forward with Red helping him along. "Hank, the girls will not be alone in this fight. They'll have all of us by their side."

"I'm sorry if I can't put my faith in an army of old people and talking animals," Henry snapped. "C'mon, girls."

He led his family across the fallen drawbridge and out into the woods, leaving their friends and the castle behind. When Sabrina glanced back, she watched the castle magically disappear from view. Henry marched ahead with determination. The girls and their mother, carrying Basil, did their best to keep up with him. Puck followed in the air.

"Once you get into Grand Central, head for Brooklyn," Henry said. "Dana will take you in for a while."

"Henry, she probably thinks we're dead after all this time," Veronica said. "And what are we supposed to do for money? Do you even have enough for train tickets?"

Henry sighed deeply, but his pace didn't slow. "Right, money. I've got ten dollars in my wallet. Plus credit cards that I'm sure have been canceled. Just get on the train. They may kick you off, but not before you're out of the town. Once you're on the other side of the barrier, you'll be safe. Then, call your sister in Australia."

"Henry, I haven't spoken to her in a decade," Veronica argued.

"Tell her we'll pay her back whatever she can lend. We still have money in the bank . . . somewhere."

Sabrina heard Puck's wings fluttering overhead and craned her neck to see his face. He looked defeated and hurt. Then it hit her: She would never see him again. He was trapped in Ferryport Landing, like the rest of the Everafters. He couldn't follow her back to New York City. This was good-bye, for good.

"The train station is a disaster," Puck called down to them.

Henry stopped midstep. "Then we'll go back to Mom's house and get her car, and—" He threw up his hands and sat down on a fallen log.

"Honey?" Veronica asked.

"I just need to think," he said, waving her off. Then he shook his head and glared up at Puck. "I'm disappointed in you."

"Then things are getting back to normal," Puck said as he landed.

"I thought your puppy-dog crush on my daughter would have made you more protective."

Puck's mouth fell open, and his ears turned bright red. Puck, the boy who proudly collected his farts in mason jars, was embarrassed! He stammered, as if unsure what to say. Then a mischievous grin stretched across his face.

"Well, it's a little more than a crush, old dude," Puck said. "I'm going to marry your daughter someday, so it's sort of important to my plans that she save the world."

"OMG," Daphne cried as she bit the palm of her hand.

Henry fell off his log. Veronica's eyes grew wide with shock. Sabrina couldn't remember a time when she'd been this mortified.

Puck chuckled. "You think you can embarrass me, but you're wrong. I'm the Trickster King—crown prince of the overconfident, leader of the self-deluded, spiritual hero of all who think too highly of themselves. Sabrina has seen the future. And I guess she didn't tell you that I'm going to be your son-in-law. So, are you going to start listening to reason, or do I have to kidnap your daughters so we can get to work?"

"Do I get a vote in this?" Veronica asked.

Everyone turned to her.

"Yes, Mom has an opinion!" Veronica snapped. "We're staying."

"Veronica!" Henry cried, clambering to his feet.

"The safety of Basil and the girls is my priority," Veronica said. "But what if the mirrors are right? What if Sabrina and Daphne are the only ones who can rescue Relda and make things OK again?"

"The mirrors didn't say the girls would save the world. They only said they had a chance," Henry argued.

"Yes, but they were certain no one else had one. If the girls don't try, then it can't be done at all. They're the world's only hope," Veronica replied. "We raised them to do the right thing. Staying and fighting is the right thing."

"Mom's right! Grimms don't run! Especially when we're in a prophecy," Daphne said.

"We've never been in a prophecy before now," Sabrina growled.

"Right, and do you think we'll be in another one if we screw this one up?" Daphne asked, turning to march back to the castle. "We need to go back. It's time for shenanigans."

"And you?" Henry asked Sabrina.

Sabrina nodded, though she was still numb from hearing the prophecy in the first place.

Henry sighed, then followed Daphne.

"You're making the right decision, Dad," Puck said, patting Henry on the back.

"Don't push your luck, fairy boy," he growled. Red, Mr. Canis, and the Wicked Queen were waiting for them outside the invisible castle. The witch said nothing but nodded respectfully to Henry.

"Let's get to work," she said.

October 15

Today is a new day, and I'm hoping it will be a little more relaxing. I mean, all I have to do is train and lead an army. I should have that finished before breakfast (insert sarcastic facial expression).

It seems that everywhere I go, people are staring at me. Now I know what it's like to be a goldfish. Some of them watch me with curiosity, like they might uncover some secret strength they never noticed before. Others watch as if they're about to witness a terrible car accident. Some look out of the corners of their eyes, and others stare at me directly until I notice, and then try to act like they were looking at something else.

Daphne is oblivious. She ate breakfast this morning like it was any other day. I envy her ability to tune out the overwhelming disappointment of Charming's army. On the other hand, hearing her singing her little songs and making a face out of her breakfast (two fried eggs, a slice of bacon, and a pancake) makes me feel as nervous as the others. We are so young.

Charming did not look happy. Then again, neither did anyone else. Most ate listlessly, eavesdropping on Charming's conversation with the girls.

"How long are you going to lollygag around here this morning?" he snarled.

"What does *lollygag* mean?" Daphne asked.

"He's saying we're being lazy," Sabrina explained. "But I'm not exactly sure what we're supposed to be doing."

"Let me be a little more clear," Charming said. "When do you plan on doing something about the prophecy?"

"Cut the kids a break, William," Goldie said from a nearby table. "It just happened last night."

"The people of this camp are not interested in giving these two a break. They are worried that two little girls are responsible for the fate of the world. Morale has sunk to an all-time low.

People are packing and leaving—but you're right, let's make sure the girls have some time to enjoy their pancakes!"

The prince stood in a huff and stormed away.

Canis appeared and took Charming's seat at the table. He bowed his head respectfully toward the Wicked Queen. "May I have a word, Your Majesty?"

"Of course."

"I understand that we have a book in our possession that could fix our problems," he said quietly, peering around to make sure no one was eavesdropping.

Bunny raised her eyebrows but said nothing.

"Relda shared a number of things with me," Canis continued. "I also understand you've had experience with its unusual form of magic. I'd like to propose that you alter its contents so that the whole world can reap the benefits."

Sabrina cocked an eyebrow. Mr. Canis's idea was brilliant. The witch could enter the Book, just like she had before, and rebuild the story of Snow White. She could erase Atticus and stop Mirror.

Ms. Lancaster shook her head. "It's not as simple as it sounds. The story is unruly and brittle. With the slightest alteration, it would fall apart entirely. It took nearly twenty-five years for me to make the changes I've already made, and as you can see, a lot of them did not stick."

"But—" Canis started.

"Relda Grimm doesn't have twenty-five years," the witch interrupted.

"What, exactly, are we supposed to do, then?" Sabrina whispered.

"We need to listen closely to the Council's prophecy," she said. "Daphne must build a coven."

"And I will, as soon as I find out what a coven is," Daphne said, shoving an entire link of sausage into her already full mouth. Elvis sat with his head in the little girl's lap, watching her with envy.

"A coven is a group of witches," Sabrina said.

"Three, to be exact," Morgan added, as she and Mr. Seven approached the table. "Glinda from Oz, Frau Pfefferkuchenhaus, and I were once a coven. When we worked together, our powers were much stronger. I'd be happy to volunteer for yours."

Daphne grinned. "You and Ms. Lancaster are my first choices."

"Very well, but we still need a third," Morgan said.

Sabrina spotted a gleam in her sister's eye. "I have a great idea for number three, but—" Daphne started.

"Why do I think I'm going to hate your choice?" Sabrina asked. She knew that look on Daphne's face. It was practically a glowing neon sign that read TROUBLE.

Daphne folded a pancake in half, shoved it into her pocket, and then grinned at her sister. "Shenanigans!"

☙

"Of all the witches in this town, you had to pick the one that wants to eat me," Sabrina complained as she, Ms. Lancaster, Daphne, Morgan le Fay, Puck, Elvis, and Henry stomped through the woods toward Baba Yaga's shack. None of them were thrilled with Daphne's choice, and they each took turns trying to talk her out of it. But Daphne insisted that if they wanted to build a coven of super-powerful witches, they had to ask the most powerful one in town.

"We can't save the world if we're in Baba Yaga's belly," Sabrina argued. "Why can't we just ask Mordred instead?"

"No boys are allowed in a coven. Plus, it has to be a crone, a temptress, and an innocent, just like the mirrors said," Morgan said.

"Fine, then what about Mallobarb or Buzzflower?" Henry asked. "Briar's fairy godmothers use a lot of magic, and they're already living in the castle."

"They're fairy godmothers—not witches," Daphne said. "Duh!"

"Why not Ozma of Oz?" Sabrina suggested, reminding Daphne that the princess of Oz was part of Charming's army. "She could be the innocent, Morgan can be the temptress, and Ms. Lancaster can—"

An angry glare from the Wicked Queen cut off the end of Sabrina's sentence. Clearly, the woman was offended by being considered a crone.

"So how do you plan on getting her to agree?" Sabrina asked, quickly changing the subject. "She's not exactly a team player."

"We're still working on that part of the plan," Daphne said as she scratched behind Elvis's ear. "Aren't we, buddy?"

"Please! Keep your voices down!" Ms. Lancaster shouted, then lowered her own voice. "We don't have to announce to half of Duchess County that we're coming."

"Is the Wicked Queen afraid of Baba Yaga?" Henry asked, raising an eyebrow.

The witch sneered. "Hardly. My power nearly rivals hers."

"Nearly?" Sabrina asked. "*Nearly* is not the same as *is better than* or *laughs in the face of*."

The queen huffed and marched ahead. The group followed, trudging deeper into the darkest and loneliest part of the Hudson Valley forest. Soon, Sabrina noticed the trees were black and bare and looked more like shadows than living things. The path was knotted with ugly vines that were as thick as chains and covered with thorns. The grass grew in thin gray clumps. She started to feel the throbbing, woozy sensation of magic and told herself to be brave.

Soon, the old witch's home came into view. It was little more than a shack. Its two small windows and single black door looked suspiciously like a face. It seemed to watch the visitors as they approached. The house had a white fence, but instead of pickets, it was constructed from bones. A walkway of bleached skulls led to the front door.

With a grimace, Daphne unhooked the fence latch and swung the bone gate aside. The group followed her into Baba Yaga's yard.

"Who's going to knock?" she asked.

"It's your coven. You knock," Sabrina said.

Daphne cringed. "But I'm scared."

Puck rolled his eyes. "Oh, brother."

"I'll do it," Henry said, stepping forward. "I've dealt with her a few times. You just need to be respectful."

"Yes, remember to say please and thank you when she's chewing on your face," Sabrina muttered.

Henry knocked on the door, then quickly pulled his hand away.

"It burned me," he said, looking down at his blistered knuckles. Sabrina could see painful welts forming on his hand. He blew on the skin as the door swung open. There was no one in the doorway.

"I hope everyone brought a change of undies," Puck sang. "I think this is going to get spooky."

The group huddled together and entered the house. It was as unsettling as the last time Sabrina had visited. Big, rusty cages were stacked in a corner. Filthy tables were covered in pots of strange, bubbling potions and jars filled with animals—some still living. On the far wall, a fireplace raged with a roaring fire. In its flames, Sabrina thought she could see faces.

"Old Mother!" the Wicked Queen shouted. "We respectfully request an audience."

The fire raged as if fed by kerosene, and Daphne leaped into her father's arms.

"Old Mother, this is Bunny Lancaster. I wish to speak with you."

"Maybe she's gone. We should come back later," Sabrina offered, backing toward the door.

"No, she's here," the Wicked Queen said, peering into the shadows. "I can feel her."

"Maybe she's being shy," Puck said as he swaggered around the room. "Some people find me to be very intimidating."

Henry cringed. "Don't taunt her, Puck."

"You guys have got yourselves worked up over nothing. I mean, really—"

And then, quite suddenly, Baba Yaga stepped out of a shadow behind Puck. She had long gray hair that hung from her head like a rotting mop. Her one good eye spun in its socket, and her nose was as pointy as a steak knife.

Puck shrieked. Sabrina would have spent months ridiculing him if she hadn't done the exact same thing.

Baba Yaga examined each member of the group. When she got to Sabrina, she leaned in close. The temperature in the room dropped at an alarming rate. Sabrina's teeth chattered.

"Either you are insane, or you have the courage of a lion. The last time I saw you, I promised to make a coat of your skin," the old crone sneered.

"Hello, Old Mother. I'm sorry if my girls have caused trouble for you," Henry said.

"They are very disrespectful, Henry Grimm!" Baba Yaga replied as she crossed the room to one of her tables. She slipped an apron over her filthy frock. It had the words VERMONT IS FOR LOVERS printed on it. She snatched up a knife and fished a frog out of a jar with her free hand. Sabrina was grateful that the woman's back blocked her view of what came next, but she could still hear the frog's bones crunching between Baba Yaga's teeth.

"Old Mother, do you know why we are here?" the Wicked Queen asked, seemingly unfazed by the crone's disgusting lunch.

"I do," Baba Yaga said. She opened a small tin filled with centipedes, fished out a fat one, and then ate it, as well.

"The fate of the world is at stake," Morgan said.

"Oh, sweet girl, the world isn't in any danger. It's the people who live on it that are going bye-bye."

"Not if you help us," Daphne said.

Baba Yaga cackled, and spittle covered her hairy chin. In her amusement, she kicked a can of something into the fireplace, and it exploded.

"Old Mother, you must listen!" the Wicked Queen demanded.

Baba Yaga raced across the room in a flash and stood within an inch of the Wicked Queen's nose. "You should respect your elders, poison maker. What do I care of this world? The Old Mother will live on. Probably with far fewer uninvited guests."

The queen swallowed hard but stood her ground. "This isn't a request."

Baba Yaga chuckled.

"You dare laugh at me?" the queen cried, her voice like thunder. She stretched out her hand. Resting on her palm was a spinning ball of light and energy.

Baba Yaga had only a moment to register the light before it blasted her across the room. She collided with a table and sent pots of potions splattering in all directions. There was a loud crash, and hundreds of creepy-crawlies covered the floor. The old crone fell to the ground.

"This is not going well," Morgan remarked.

"We can't build a coven if you kill her," Daphne complained.

"The queen doesn't have what it would take to kill me," Baba Yaga muttered before breaking into an unintelligible chant. When she fell silent again, hundreds of pointy legs erupted from her body. They flipped her over, and she scurried along the floor like a centipede, eventually scuttling up the wall and onto the ceiling, where she swung from a dirty chandelier. She leaped onto the queen's back, and the two fell to the floor, rolling and fighting in the filth.

"This is not going well at all," Sabrina groaned.

"You cannot turn your back on the rest of us," the Wicked Queen shouted at Baba Yaga. "Billions will die!"

"A dog feels no sorrow when his fleas are extinguished!" Baba Yaga shrieked.

Ms. Lancaster shouted an incantation, and Baba Yaga once again went flying across the room. She crashed into a wall but quickly recovered, springing to her feet and waving her hands in the air. Her body transformed into twenty flying daggers that shot toward the Wicked Queen with deadly accuracy. The witch cast a spell, and a glowing red shield appeared, blocking the daggers. They hit the ground and melted into a thick black pool, from which Baba Yaga rose. When she fully regained her form, she reached into the folds of her raggedy dress, brought something out, and blew on it. Hundreds of hairy spiders leaped from her hand and onto the Wicked Queen, burrowing under her skin as she screamed in agony.

Before Sabrina knew what was happening, Daphne pushed between the dueling witches. "Cut it out!"

Baba Yaga sneered at the girl but ceased her attack. "I have no appetite for this fight. Gather yourselves and go."

"No!" Daphne cried. "We came to you for help because we need to stop Mirror, and you're the most powerful witch in town. But maybe the rumors aren't true. Maybe you don't have what it takes. Maybe you're afraid he'll beat you."

Baba Yaga's head turned toward the little girl so quickly, Sabrina heard the bones inside her neck crack. "What did you say?"

"You heard me," Daphne said, standing her ground. "I think

you're scared to fight Mirror, and you're hiding it under your usual grouchiness. But I'm not fooled."

"Daphne, please be quiet," Henry begged.

"I will kill you and suck on your bones, little one," the witch raged. "I've made soup from children who were far less disrespectful than you."

Daphne cringed. "Fine. You can go ahead and eat me, but that still won't prove you're not a lousy witch. I see you, Old Mother. You hide out here in this creepy house because you're afraid."

"Daphne, shut up!" Morgan cried.

"I made a mistake coming to you," Daphne continued. "I guess I'll have to go find someone who isn't such a coward. Does anyone know where Ozma of Oz lives?"

Baba Yaga's anger was so intense, her ratty hair stood on end. "Ozma of Oz? That child doesn't have a fraction of my power!"

"Maybe not, but she's got way more courage!" Daphne shouted back.

There was a long, awkward pause, and then Baba Yaga started a new chant. The floor beneath her feet shook, and the walls drew inward as if the group were trapped inside a deflating balloon. Sabrina clenched her fists, preparing for a fight, when her father grabbed her and Daphne by the arm.

"Everyone outside!" Henry cried. Unfortunately, the door was locked tight.

"Step aside," Morgan said, her eyes glowing red with magic. An invisible force knocked the door off its hinges.

The group spilled out of the shack, and they were stopped in their tracks by two unexpected figures. The first was Granny Relda—or, rather, Mirror wearing her body. The second was less familiar. He wore chain mail, armor, and heavy boots covered in spikes. He wielded an immense sword. It had a golden hilt with a ruby inset that looked like a bloodshot eye.

"Granny!" Sabrina cried.

"Atticus!" the Wicked Queen gasped.

Granny was the first to speak. The voice was neither hers nor Mirror's but an unsettling combination of the two. "Hello, Grimms. It's such a lovely day, don't you think?"

"What do you want?" Henry demanded.

"I've come to make you an offer."

"Let go of Granny first!" Sabrina shouted.

Mirror frowned. "I wish I could, but I'm sort of stuck at the moment. It's an unfortunate side effect of the monkey wrench you threw into my plans. If you had given me your little brother, I wouldn't be trapped in this elderly body with all its aches and pains. But, alas, here we are."

"Are we going to talk all day?" Atticus growled. "I have so many people to kill."

"Calm down, prince," Mirror said, then turned his attention back to the group. "Please excuse my business associate. He's quite passionate. Oh, but I'm being rude. Not everyone here has met him. Please allow me to introduce His Highness Prince Atticus Charming."

"Charming?" Morgan gasped. "Like William Charming?"

"Exactly," Mirror replied. "Of course, a few of you are already familiar with him. Isn't that correct, Bunny? You are his mother-in-law, after all."

The Wicked Queen stepped forward, her hands twisted into angry claws. She looked as if she wanted to rip Atticus's heart right out of his chest.

"It's been a long time, Mom," Atticus said with an evil laugh.

"Not long enough." The witch seethed.

"Where is my wife? With my brother, no doubt," he said as he eyed the sharp edge of his sword. "No matter. He will not stop me; nothing will stop me. Not even locking me away stopped me."

The witch and the warrior looked ready to attack each other, but they were interrupted by Baba Yaga. The old crone charged out of her house like an angry bull. When she saw the confrontation outside, she laughed.

"It appears the cat is out of the bag, Your Majesty," she sneered at the Wicked Queen. "Or rather, the killer is out of the Book."

"And who is this withered old grape?" Atticus asked.

"So another comes forward to mock the Old Mother. Enough!" Baba Yaga screamed, and her eyes turned black. The air around her crackled with magic.

"No! He's mine!" the Wicked Queen cried. She swung her arm across her body as if slashing at Atticus with an invisible sword. The result was immediate. A tidal wave of destruction sprang from her hand. It uprooted trees and threw earth skyward. When the debris settled, Atticus and Mirror remained unharmed.

The queen was shocked. "How?"

Mirror winked. "Now, that, I won't be telling."

Morgan stepped forward, hands extended, and rained blasts of lightning and plasma down on the two villains. Like before, Mirror and Atticus remained untouched. When she raised her hands for another attack, a blast of fiery flame sprung from Mirror's fingertips. The magic slammed into Morgan, and she flew backward several yards and collided with the side of Baba Yaga's shack.

"Now you've insulted my home," Baba Yaga growled. She reached into the folds of her dress and removed three slimy toads. They squirmed in her hands as she held them up to her mouth and whispered an incantation.

She dropped the animals onto the ground, and a disturbing transformation took hold. Their skin bubbled and their bodies stretched, growing several feet and twisting in unnatural directions. In a few short moments, three full-grown men stood in their place, each with the face and webbed hands of a frog. They were dressed in tunics and armor, and they clung to flaming swords. They sprang immediately into combat, slashing and stabbing at the villains.

Mirror sighed as if the sudden battle were a mild inconvenience. "Enough of this unpleasantness," he said. "We're all friends here, and I've come to make you the offer of a lifetime. I will leave this town and do no harm to those gathered here."

"You promised me the witch's head!" Atticus raged. "She imprisoned me in a nightmare for years. I will have my revenge!"

"And you will, Atticus, but only after I gain my freedom," Mirror said, then turned back to the group. "But I will do you no harm. All you have to do is lower the barrier. I know that it is within your power, Old Mother. After all, it was you who created it for the Grimm brothers in the first place. Why, I'm fairly certain that Jacob himself has the original copy of the spell. So, what do you say? Do we have a deal?"

"You are a curious thing, little mirror," Baba Yaga said as she stepped close to him. She studied Granny Relda's eyes as if she could see the creature hidden behind them. Then she smiled. What was it the old crone saw—some weakness?

"Curious?" Mirror asked.

"Yes—a mirror guardian who refuses to see that he is broken. The answer is always in the eyes," Baba Yaga mused. "Yes, I know how to beat you now. It's embarrassingly silly."

She cackled, and Mirror became enraged. He let loose a blast of raw energy that swallowed Baba Yaga whole. The magic melted the flesh right off of the old woman's bones. Her skeleton fell to the ground to join her collection of skulls.

"NO!" the Wicked Queen cried.

Mirror dusted off his hands. "I really didn't want there to be so much drama. Now, about my offer—"

To everyone's surprise, Baba Yaga's skeleton clambered to its feet. New muscles, veins, organs, and skin grew over the raw bones. In no time at all, the old crone was whole again.

Mirror cocked a curious eyebrow. "Now, that is a good trick."

"Get into my house!" Baba Yaga shouted, running for the door. Without hesitation everyone scrambled after her, leaving Mirror and Atticus behind. Once they were inside, Baba Yaga commanded her house to rise.

Sabrina felt the floor heave beneath her. The room tilted steeply to one side, and the group slid across the floor, crashing painfully in a pile against the wall. Then, the room tilted in the opposite direction, and everyone slammed into the other wall. "House, run!" Baba Yaga cried, and the house took off at an impressive clip. Its passengers bounced around like popping corn.

"I love this house!" Puck crowed.

"I hate this house," Sabrina groaned.

Baba Yaga darted to her window and screeched threats down at Mirror and Atticus. Then she reached over her head, and a spear made from fire and smoke appeared in her hand. She hurled it out the window, followed by another, and yet another. The Wicked Queen took the other window and began blasting long tendrils of lightning from her fingertips. Despite their best efforts to ward off the villains, a massive explosion rocked the house.

"Now do you see what we're up against?" the Queen demanded.

"We need you to join the coven," Daphne said, doing her best to keep her balance.

Baba Yaga turned to peer at the little girl. She then turned her attention to Morgan and finally to the Queen.

"This coven is imperfect. It calls for a crone, a temptress, and an innocent, does it not?" she asked, cocking a curious eyebrow at the other witches. "Which ones are you claiming to be?"

Morgan blushed. "Well, I'm not the innocent."

"So, Your Majesty is the one claiming to be pure of heart?" Baba Yaga cackled.

"It's the best we can do, Old Mother!" the Queen snapped.

"What's in it for me?" Baba Yaga croaked.

Sabrina was furious. "You get to live in a world that isn't ruled by a maniac."

Baba Yaga laughed. "The world is already ruled by maniacs."

"Fine, Old Mother. You want payment for your services? Name your price," the Wicked Queen said.

"Your eyes. When this battle is said and done, I want your eyes, poison maker."

No one in the house spoke. For a moment, all they could hear were the explosions outside.

Puck broke the silence. "That is so gross. I love it!"

Had Sabrina heard the old witch correctly? Had Baba Yaga just asked Bunny Lancaster for her eyes? Sabrina looked around the room and spotted a jar of what she had previously thought were hard-boiled eggs. Now, she realized that had been wishful thinking.

"You want her eyes?" Henry repeated.

"A witch's magic is in her eyes," Morgan explained, looking distressed.

"Every spell I've ever read, every experience I've ever lived, every vision I've ever seen—everything is held inside my eyes," the Queen added. "In essence, giving her my eyes is giving her my power."

"That's my deal, Your Majesty. This coven requires a crone, so you need me. Unless you want to dig up Frau Pfefferkuchenhaus's worm-eaten corpse."

Another blast rocked the house, and this one took the whole structure down. It stumbled and crashed into the forest floor. Sabrina grabbed her sister's hand just as everyone slid forward and slammed, once again, into the far wall. Elvis whimpered, trapped at the bottom of the pile.

"Get up, house!" Baba Yaga commanded, and the house obeyed, sending the people inside bouncing and tumbling again. It was a miracle that no one was hurt.

"Do we really have to do this?" Mirror called from outside. "I'm asking such a small thing!"

"Why offer them mercy?" Atticus complained to his partner.

"Atticus, have you never heard the saying that you can draw more flies with honey than with vinegar?" Mirror said. "A little negotiating can solve things the edge of a sword cannot. But if the Grimms are unwilling to listen to reason, I suppose we can try it your way."

"We have to fight them," Puck said, pulling his sword from his belt.

"They will strike you out of the air, fairy." The Wicked Queen blocked his path. "No, if we are to stand a fighting chance, we need the power of three. I will pay your price, Old Mother. I have made bigger sacrifices."

Morgan gasped. "Bunny, no!"

Baba Yaga's face twisted into a ghastly smile. She extended her hands, and the Queen took one. Morgan reluctantly accepted the other, and they formed a circle. There was a rumble, like a tiny earthquake, and Sabrina watched in disbelief as their hands turned to stone. They all looked toward the ceiling as if it were open to the universe beyond and said as one, "We are bound by coven."

The electricity in the air made everyone's hair stand on end. The stone fell away from the witches' hands, and the trio rushed to the open windows. Together, they chanted an ancient incantation, and a ghostly light burst from their chests and floated out the window. Sabrina watched the magic transform into a fifty-foot-tall giant made of mist and wind. The giant attacked Mirror and Atticus, snatching them in its fists. Atticus fought back with his sword, and Mirror launched a barrage of spells, but they could not harm the monster.

"We should go while they're distracted!" Henry shouted.

Baba Yaga ordered her house to run away, and it did, leaving the villains far behind them. From the window, Sabrina watched the two villains—one sporting the face of someone she loved.

5

OCTOBER 15 (PART 2)

Our attempt to boost morale around the castle has sort of backfired. Well, not sort of—totally. Mostly because our latest recruit terrifies everyone.

Baba Yaga has been walking around staring at everyone and licking her lips like we're all pieces of fried chicken. People have not been reacting well to her being around. The Pied Piper and Wendell barricaded themselves in one of the cabins. Puss in Boots hid beneath a shed and still refuses to come out. The Scarecrow burst into tears, ruining his face. He's had to paint on brand-new eyes and a mouth.

Ms. Lancaster is trying to assure everyone that the old witch is a necessary part of the plan to stop Mirror and the Scarlet Hand. I'm wondering what this mystery plan is, 'cause now that we have the coven, it's time for me to do my part of the prophecy—building an army (otherwise known as "leading everyone to their deaths"). I did a head count of my "troops" to see what I'm *working with, and the grand total is 24 people. That includes two very old men, a beauty queen, a little boy with a harmonica, some circus bears, a man made out of hay, a bird, a cat wearing boots, a feng shui consultant, and now a hungry witch and her walking house—all of whom are just waiting for me to let them down.*

Bunny says she's going to recruit some more help, but she's asking for something in return. She wants everyone who saw Atticus to keep their mouths shut about him. She says she doesn't want to make things any more complicated, especially with Snow, who already keeps her mother at arm's length. We agreed to keep Atticus a secret, but—in my opinion—Snow has a right to know he's escaped, and, more important, she has a right to know what her mother did to protect her from him.

Oh, and on a side note, Puck told my dad he's going to marry me and is now walking around discussing his plans for our wedding with anyone who will listen.

Worst. Day. Ever.

That night, instead of the hard floor in the Hall of Wonders, Sabrina and Daphne slept in one of the cabins on the grounds of Charming's castle. They'd pushed two cots together so they could sleep side by side. Elvis lay at the foot of the makeshift bed, eventually working his way up between them to hog the pillows.

It was a fitful night for Sabrina, filled with terrible nightmares.

In each dream, Mirror was strangling her and laughing. She woke several times, breathing hard and grasping at her throat. Daphne, a notoriously heavy sleeper, lay next to her, her little arms wrapped tightly around the Book of Everafter. Sabrina wondered if having such a dangerous magical item close by was causing her bad dreams. But she knew it was better to have the Book with them than to risk it falling into the wrong hands.

"Dreams can be terrible bullies," a voice said from the shadows. Mr. Canis had crept into the cabin at some point in the night and now sat in a chair, guarding them.

Sabrina nodded and stretched her arms toward the ceiling.

"You have my sympathies," the old man said. "They have tortured me every night for most of my life. I find meditation before bed to be the best tool for prevention."

"Are nightmares keeping you up, too?"

"I'm trying to be useful," the old man said, pointing at the Book of Everafter. "This camp is filled with untrustworthy people, including young Pinocchio. I wonder if I should take that book for safekeeping."

"Good luck prying it away from Daphne," Sabrina said. "She's been reading the stories one by one. She's convinced she's going to find something in one of them that will help. I keep telling her the Editor isn't going to let her change anything, but she's being stubborn about it."

"Very well," Mr. Canis said, throwing up his hands in surrender. "Sabrina, I'm not exactly the kind of person you would describe as comforting."

Sabrina laughed. "You don't say."

The old man ignored her joke. "But I want you to know that I won't give up on your grandmother. She is my oldest and dearest friend, and she has put herself in danger for me more times than I can count. Prophecy or not, I will work to free her, and I won't stop until she is safe."

"I know that," Sabrina said. "And I love you for it."

The two locked eyes, but it soon got too awkward, and they both looked at the floor. After a moment, Canis got up and left the cabin without another word. When he was gone, Sabrina put her feet on the floor and sat silently, listening to the wind in the trees and the world around her. Sleep was not going to come easily, again. Meditation might have helped, but what she really needed was some fresh air.

She snatched an extra blanket from under the cot, careful not to wake Daphne or Elvis. She wrapped it around her like a cloak, then stepped out into the frosty air. The moon hid behind storm clouds. The night wind rushed through leaves and branches, and it caught a strand of hair she quickly tucked back behind her ear.

Sabrina wandered around the grounds without a destination, content in her solitude. Eventually, she came across Briar's grave. Uncle

Jake sat in his chair, staring at the grave. He looked as broken as ever. She wanted to rush to him and tell him that she loved him and that he wasn't the only one grieving. But she suspected that, like herself, he wanted to be alone. She started to sneak away, but his voice called out, so she stopped. Sabrina quickly realized he was speaking to Briar. She listened as he told Briar about his day: the colors of the trees he saw in the forest, the crunch of the twigs and acorns under his feet, the tracks animals left as they prepared for winter, and the beauty of the red sunset. But mostly he talked about how hard it was not to share those things with her in person.

"I miss you, princess," he said.

Before Sabrina knew it, she was wiping tears off her cheeks.

"You got something to say to me, Sabrina?" Jake asked suddenly.

Sabrina started, surprised that Uncle Jake knew she was eavesdropping. She was embarrassed and ashamed, but she stepped forward nonetheless. "I didn't mean to spy. I couldn't sleep."

"I like to talk to her." Jake shrugged. "I like to think she can hear me, wherever she is. So I tell her how much I miss her, and I tell her about my plans to avenge her."

"By killing Heart and Nottingham," Sabrina said quietly.

"You don't understand, either." Jake gritted his teeth. "I can't let it go, Sabrina. They murdered her."

Sabrina looked at the ground. Her family had made it clear

that they all thought killing Heart and Nottingham was wrong, but part of her understood Uncle Jake's feelings. Still, she feared if she told him that, he would take it as permission. Mostly, she worried he would get himself killed if he tried.

"I've got to get back to work," he continued, then stood and scooped up his bow and arrows.

Sabrina followed him as he stalked toward the gate, then watched as the newly repaired drawbridge lowered. Just before he crossed it, Jake turned to her with a serious look in his eyes. "I heard the news about the prophecy," he said. "Good luck, 'Brina. That's a terrible burden to put on your shoulders."

"It's just a stupid prophecy," she said. "Two kids are really going to save the world?"

"Save the people you love," Uncle Jake said. "Who cares about the rest of the world?"

And then he was gone, leaving her alone with the murky moon.

Sabrina woke the next morning to someone pounding on the cabin door. Charming, Canis, and Mr. Seven were waiting on the other side.

"Someone's deserted," Charming announced, pushing his way into the cabin.

"Who?"

"Puss in Boots," Canis said with a grimace. "He slipped out early this morning."

Daphne rubbed the sleep from her eyes. "Did Baba Yaga threaten to eat him?"

Mr. Seven shook his head. "We fear he may have been a spy for the Scarlet Hand."

"Or he left because he's afraid my sister and I are going to screw everything up," Sabrina said.

Charming sighed but didn't disagree. "Sadly, he won't be the last to go. The mood in this camp is definitely dismal. But we can't afford to lose any more, so you and your sister need to get out of your pajamas and do something about this."

"And what do you suggest we do?" Sabrina grumbled.

"I have an idea." Mr. Seven stepped forward. "Our people have been suffering for a long time. It's exhausting to be afraid all the time, especially when it looks like things just get worse and worse every day. We need to do something to take everyone's mind off the gloom and doom. We should throw a party."

"A party? What do you want us to do—rent a bouncy castle and a cotton candy machine?" Sabrina asked.

"Actually, I was thinking we could host a wedding," Mr. Seven said.

"How romantic!" Daphne cried gleefully. "Who's getting married?"

Seven beamed. "Me."

When Sabrina looked over, Daphne was already biting down hard on her palm.

❧

Sabrina didn't know if putting on a wedding would boost morale in the camp, but it was definitely boosting hers. They'd decided to make the whole event a surprise for Morgan, and keeping the secret tapped into Sabrina's favorite skill: sneaking.

She was the Queen of the Sneaks after her time in the foster care system. She knew how to open a creaky window without making a sound. She knew how to slink across a room without stepping on a loose floorboard. She knew how to crawl out onto a roof, shimmy down a trellis, and tiptoe past a watchdog without making a peep. Pulling the wool over Morgan's eyes was her proudest sneak to date, and keeping the wedding plans under wraps reminded her that she was actually good at something. She had skills—occasionally illegal skills, but skills nonetheless—and she was determined to make the most of them.

In whispered conversations, she and Daphne gave everyone a job. Flowers, music, food, and—the most important job of all— keeping the bride busy until everything was ready. Since the castle was almost finished, its rooms also needed to be decorated. Morgan knew a simple spell for creating furniture from thin air, and Sabrina knew exactly whom to team her up with: Goldilocks. Goldie's obsessive eye for interior design and feng shui kept the two women running around until things were "just right." Under Goldie's supervision, Morgan would be busy all day.

Mr. Seven's plan worked! All the fear of the Hand was pushed aside, and the tiny community leaped headfirst into planning and preparation. It was the first time Sabrina had seen smiles on their faces since her arrival at the castle. She even caught Pinocchio humming the wedding march as he and Geppetto built a platform for the couple to stand upon when they exchanged their vows.

"A wedding under the stars is a lovely idea, Sabrina," Snow said as she approached carrying an armful of wildflowers.

"Your boyfriend gave me most of the ideas," Sabrina said. Actually, he had given her a five-page-long list of ideas. "He's quite the romantic."

"I've always thought so," Snow said, gazing across the courtyard. Charming was there, working with Nurse Sprat to draw up the seating chart. "I just hope he saves some of those ideas for us."

"Has he asked?" Sabrina said.

"Not yet," Snow said with a sad smile. "He will. But I'm getting tired of waiting. I might just have to ask him myself."

When everything was finished, the wildflowers lined a path to two beautiful wooden arches interwoven with red roses and white lilies. Chairs for the guests were wrapped in more flowers and ribbons. Mallobarb and Buzzflower hovered overhead, showering the space with magical glitter that erupted from their wands. It made the beautiful space look otherworldly, and the whole scene took Sabrina's breath away. She hoped it would have the same effect on the bride.

"Well, I better get ready. I have no idea what I'm going to wear. I didn't exactly pack for something this formal," Mr. Seven said as he paced back and forth in the courtyard. "I hope Morgan doesn't mind blue jeans."

Sabrina looked down at herself and gasped. She was a mess. Her shoes were ratty, and her sweatshirt was filthy. She couldn't show up to a wedding dressed so poorly. She rushed into the cabin that housed the magic mirror and darted into the Hall of Wonders.

Once in her room, she picked through a pile of dirty clothes on the floor, desperate to find anything that resembled a decent outfit. Most of her clothing had been lost when Granny's house was destroyed, so there wasn't much to choose from. She soon discovered that the only clean thing she had was her father's Red Hot Chili Peppers T-shirt from a concert in 1990. She slipped it on, then ran to the Room of Reflections to see how she looked.

A huge green stain from one of Puck's pranks had ruined the whole thing. She let out a groan of frustration. Sabrina had once been a card-carrying tomboy, but she was getting older, and her appearance was beginning to matter. She understood her situation, living in a war camp, trying to survive attacks from magical monsters. She knew a pretty dress or fancy shoes weren't a possibility, but couldn't she at least wash her face and comb her hair? Maybe wear a shirt that wasn't covered in glop? All she wanted was a little evidence that there were still some normal things left in this abnormal world. She couldn't do anything but cry.

"No one has anything nice to wear, honey," Fanny said as she and the other guardians appeared in their mirrors.

"I know," Sabrina said, wiping her tears on the tail of her father's shirt.

"Is this about Puck?" Donovan asked, and then mimed some exaggerated kissing.

"Don't tease the poor girl!" Titan roared.

"No!" Sabrina frowned. "It's not about Puck. Who cares what he thinks?"

"You do, Sabrina," Arden said. "There's no need for shame. Your feelings are totally natural."

Sabrina buried her face in her hands while the mirrors gave her well-intended advice about her first crush. It was mortifying. As she sobbed, she felt a hand on her shoulder.

"I'm OK, Daphne." Sabrina sniffed.

"No, you're not," a voice replied, but it didn't belong to Daphne. Sabrina looked up to find Red standing behind her. "None of us are OK."

Red took Sabrina off guard. Of all the Everafters, Sabrina was most uncomfortable around the little girl. It was hard to forget that Red had tried to hurt her family, even if she hadn't been in control of herself at the time. Sabrina knew it wasn't fair to hold a grudge, but she found it hard to let Red in nonetheless.

"Where's Daphne?" Sabrina asked.

"She's busy with Morgan's flowers," Red explained. "You know how she bites her palm when she's excited? I thought she was going to chew her hand off when Mr. Seven asked her to be the flower girl."

Red reached into her pocket and took out a brush. "Daphne put me on hair duty." She started untangling Sabrina's blond bird's nest of hair. "You know, there's a reason why the prophecy is about you."

"And why is that?" Sabrina said.

"Because of your gift."

"My gift?" Sabrina laughed.

"Yes. You're the brave one," Red said matter-of-factly. "Your mom is the leader, your dad watches over everyone, your sister makes everyone smile, and you—you're the brave one. You fight without hesitation. Mr. Canis says he's never seen you run away from anything."

"Mr. Canis hasn't been paying attention," Sabrina argued. "Listen, I'm not brave. I'm stupid. I get into a lot of trouble because I don't think things out, and I have a bad temper. Every time I turn around, someone has to save my butt."

"We all need saving sometimes."

"Did Mr. Canis say that, too?" Sabrina asked.

"No. I say that," Red said. "Look at Mr. Canis. He's feeling old. He's feeling useless, which isn't true at all. You inspired me to save him."

"How?"

"I made him my father. Now he has a purpose."

"So maybe that's your gift," Sabrina said. "You can make even the grouchiest person in Ferryport Landing care about you."

Together, both girls giggled.

"Sabrina, little Red 'as a way with a brush. Looking good!" Reggie said when Sabrina studied herself in his reflection. It was true. She looked a million times better, almost like a regular girl.

"Thanks," she said to Red.

"You're welcome. I enjoyed it. It was kind of like having a sister of my own for a while," Red said, then turned to go.

Sabrina snatched her hand. "Wait, your turn."

Red smiled and handed Sabrina the brush.

Sabrina slinked into the courtyard, hoping no one would notice her outfit. Now that her hair looked nice, her clothes looked even worse by comparison. She found a seat in the back next to her parents. Basil slept in Veronica's arms. She studied his face as if it were a work of art. The only time the little boy would sit still for her was when he was asleep, and Veronica took full advantage of the time.

"You look lovely," Henry said when Sabrina sat down next to him.

"Nice try, Dad," Sabrina replied.

He shrugged. "Kid, we all look like we've been through a war."

"We have," Veronica reminded him.

Sabrina turned in her seat to check out the other guests. Fanny was right. Most were dressed in nothing more than T-shirts and sneakers, but all had made their own best effort. Nurse Sprat and Snow White had stolen flowers from their chairs and woven them into their hair. Charming had pinned a rose to his ratty shirt. Henry took a couple of flowers off the back of his chair. He twirled one into his wife's hair, then another into Sabrina's.

"I trained you well, honey," Veronica said to him, leaning over to kiss him on the cheek.

"Has Morgan got any clue she's getting married tonight?" Sabrina asked.

Veronica grinned. "Not one."

Puck dropped clumsily out of the sky into the chair next to Sabrina.

"Where have you been?" she scolded. "You were almost late."

Puck held up a dead skunk. "I was shopping for the happy couple. I didn't check their gift registry, but I'm sure they don't have one of these."

"You got them roadkill as a wedding present?" Henry asked.

Puck seemed confused. "It's a wedding! Aren't you supposed to send the couple off with things they'll need for their home? Which reminds me, when Sabrina and I get married, it's customary in the fairy world for the groom and the bride's father to challenge each other in a fight to the death. I hope you'll put up a good fight, Henry. It can really ruin the mood if the bride's dad gets killed before we cut the cake."

"He's joking, right?" Henry said.

"Has anyone seen Uncle Jake today?" Sabrina asked, hoping to change the subject.

"I doubt he's in the mood for a wedding," Veronica said.

Sabrina's heart sank. In all the planning, she'd completely forgotten how sad the event might be for her uncle. She scanned the crowd, hoping to spot him, but he was nowhere in sight.

The Pied Piper and his son, Wendell, played an up-tempo march on their instruments, and the crowd stood to greet the wedding party. Daphne appeared first, and Sabrina's jaw hit the floor. The little girl was dressed in a beautiful silk dress covered with delicate lace. Her hair was clean and flawlessly styled. She strolled through the crowd, sprinkling rose petals behind her. When she got to the platform up front, she reached into her flower basket and removed a fairy godmother wand.

"Attention, everyone," Daphne said. "I thought and thought about what kind of gift I could give the happy couple, and this was my best idea. I hope you don't mind."

Daphne flicked her wrist and, with a loud *poof*, a purple mist filled the air. When it lifted, Sabrina looked down to find her raggedy clothes were gone, replaced by a creamy pink gown and white shoes. Her neck was draped with pearls, and her face and hands were scrubbed clean. When she glanced around at the crowd, she saw that everyone was dressed just as beautifully. Even her father's scruffy beard was gone.

"Wow!" Puck said.

Sabrina turned to him, hoping his compliment was aimed at her, but the boy fairy was admiring himself. His smart black tuxedo fit perfectly. His hair was combed and shiny. There wasn't a single fly buzzing around his head. In fact, he even had the pleasant aroma of soap around him. "This suit is going to look really great when I roll in those deer droppings I found by the front gate."

Sabrina sighed.

"Enjoy the clothes while they last, 'cause at midnight we all go back to being slobs," Daphne announced.

Everyone laughed and applauded as Mr. Seven appeared in a blue tuxedo, top hat, and tails. He greeted the guests and thanked everyone for coming. He thanked Sabrina for all her hard work and Daphne for the fancy suit, but he insisted the crowd hadn't seen anything yet.

He pointed to the back of the crowd. There stood Morgan le Fay. Her dress was the color of vanilla cream, and it was embroidered with seed pearls and tiny crystals. The train spread behind her for several yards, and her jet-black hair was woven with little white daisies. She was the most beautiful bride Sabrina had ever seen.

"She's breathtaking," Veronica whispered.

Her son stood by her side. Morgan looked bewildered, but Mordred was grinning widely enough for the two of them.

"What is going on here?" Morgan asked, her face bright pink.

"I'll let your fiancé explain," Mordred said. He led her down the aisle to the arches, where he placed his mother's hand into Seven's.

"What are you up to?" she asked.

Mr. Seven smiled. "I love you, Morgan."

The Scarecrow approached with a broad smile. "Thank you all for coming to this wonderful event. As the former emperor of Oz, I have the privilege and honor to officiate this ceremony."

"Ceremony?" Morgan asked.

"You did say you'd marry me, didn't you, Ms. Le Fay?" Mr. Seven asked.

"Yes!" she cried, and then bent down to kiss him as the whole crowd cheered.

"Let's save that for after the vows," the Scarecrow said with a laugh. He invited the crowd to join him in a prayer for the happy couple, then Seven and Morgan spoke of their love for each other. Morgan cried as she promised her life to Seven. Mr. Seven did the same, and when the Scarecrow pronounced them husband and wife, Morgan planted an even bigger kiss on the little man. The crowd roared with approval.

Confetti rained down, and music floated over the crowd. As the newlyweds made their way back up the aisle, everyone showered them with congratulations.

"You're a lucky man," Geppetto said to Seven.

"No, I'm the lucky one!" Morgan cried, swooping Seven into her arms for another kiss.

Charming called for everyone's attention. He held a glass of champagne in his hand, and Sabrina watched as several trays of bubbly magically floated through the crowd. "Just one more interruption, folks. This morning Mr. Seven came to me and asked me to be the best man at this wedding. Of course, he believed a wedding could be planned in one short day."

Everyone smiled knowingly.

"He also believed, for some reason, that I enjoy being in front of a crowd," he said, to cheers and laughter. "Well, let me tell you, this party has been incredibly inconvenient. After all, we're trying to build a castle, raise an army, and prepare for a war. Mr. Seven and his bride have been terribly troublesome."

Suddenly, the laughter died. Sabrina stared at Charming in disbelief. He'd always been selfish, but this was crossing a line.

"But that is love, isn't it?" he continued. "It's always inconvenient. It sweeps you up and steals your attention and slows down your work. Everything comes to a screeching halt! Everything, that is, except what really matters—true love. We've all been there. We know how it feels, how it looks. So when we see friends in love, we cast aside our work to celebrate. Because when we recognize love in the hearts of others, it reminds us of how important it is in our own. Mr. Seven, you are and have always been my companion, confidant, and friend. You make me a better man, and you remind me every day to celebrate the love in my own life."

Everyone turned to Snow. She was beaming, her face a rosy red.

Charming held up his glass. "So, my friends, on this lovely day, let us raise a glass and celebrate the maddening, all-consuming, terribly inconvenient magic called love."

The crowd raised their glasses and then burst into rousing applause.

Together, everyone cleared the chairs away to make room for singing and dancing and food. Where the feast came from, Sabrina could hardly guess, but somehow the runaways and refugees of Charming's army had prepared a lavish banquet.

Sabrina watched everyone let loose and enjoy the party. Charming whispered something into Snow's ear that made her giggle. Henry and Veronica waltzed around the courtyard, holding a sleeping Basil between them. Even Red dragged Mr. Canis onto the dance floor for a spin.

Sabrina was swept away by it all. The dread of the last few months and the threat of tomorrow were pushed into a far corner of her mind. As she watched the revelers, she realized the wedding was a celebration of life and its possibilities, even in the midst of all the madness.

"Dancing, ugh," Puck groaned, suddenly appearing beside her.

"Yeah," Sabrina said.

"Well, we might as well get it over with," he said, reaching for her hands.

"You know how to dance?" she asked, worried he was pulling a prank.

"I'm royalty. That's all we ever do."

He taught her an elaborate dance that seemed to be part waltz, part square dance. It was more theatrical than she'd expected, and it drew way more attention than she wanted. But soon everyone was mimicking their silly steps. Sabrina pushed her embarrassment aside and surrendered to the fun.

As the night marched onward, the crowd began to thin. People drifted off to their cabins and tents. The new Mr. and Mrs. Seven stayed late, thanking everyone for coming until they were banished to their honeymoon suite. Veronica carried Basil, and Henry carried Daphne, both asleep, back to their beds.

Soon the only people left in the courtyard were Sabrina, Puck, Geppetto, and Pinocchio. Sabrina was too hyped up from the night's events to go to bed, so she offered to clean up the mess. The other three helped her, though Pinocchio did quite a bit of grumbling. As they stacked chairs and picked up trash, Sabrina could still hear the music in her ears. Geppetto decided to leave the flowers out as a reminder to everyone of the joyful event, and then he said good night, reminding his son that tomorrow would be another busy day. Pinocchio groaned as he followed his father back to their cabin.

As she watched them go, Sabrina felt a warm, glowing light surround her. When it faded, she saw that her beautiful dress was gone. She was back in her filthy outfit, and she smelled. Puck's fancy suit had vanished, as well.

"It must be midnight," Sabrina said.

"Thank goodness," Puck said. "I didn't like feeling so clean."

"I wondered why you were helping clean up the trash, but then I saw you rolling around in it," Sabrina said.

"I'll never understand the desire to throw away perfectly good garbage," he said, then looked up at the moon high above. "So . . ."

"So?"

"Nice party, huh?"

"Yeah."

"It reminded me a little of Sven the Soul Eater's thirteenth wedding. Or maybe it was the fourteenth? It's hard to say. There were a lot. He kept eating his wives," Puck said.

"Well, that sounds very romantic," she replied, rolling her eyes.

"I will say this one was a tad boring. I've never been to a wedding that didn't have some kind of uncontrollable devastation. I was getting restless."

Sabrina wished Puck would just stop talking. He was going to ruin the night with his weirdness. She was about turn and leave him there when he spoke again.

"By the way, when I said 'wow,' I was looking at you."

Sabrina's face lit up in a grin. "Really?"

"Sure," he said, not quite meeting her eyes. "You're pretty, I guess . . . for a girl."

Who is this boy? He could drive her crazy with his pranks and teasing, but then, when she least expected it, he could be the sweetest and most thoughtful person in the world. He was maddening, but at the moment he was awfully cute. And she thought she might like to kiss him. The moment was kind of perfect . . .

"Um . . . kind of late, isn't it?" her father said, appearing from the shadows.

"Dad!" Sabrina cried. She could have died from embarrassment.

"All right, smell you later," Puck said. He flew off instantly to wherever he slept.

"You're a little young for a boyfriend," Henry said.

"DAD!"

"Get some rest," he said, turning back toward his cabin. "We're going to put an end to this war tomorrow."

Sabrina was mortified, but she headed for the cabin she shared with her sister. Surprisingly, Daphne was awake, and in a panic.

"Have you seen it?" she asked.

"Seen what?"

"The Book of Everafter. I think it's been stolen!"

6

THE GIRLS TORE THE CABIN APART SEARCHING
for the Book, hoping they'd just misplaced it. They
considered searching for it immediately but worried
their quest would attract unwanted attention. They decided to
track it down in the morning.

After a fitful night of tossing and turning, they got up early
to start looking. Sabrina and Daphne were both pretty certain it
had to be somewhere within the castle grounds. They divided the
camp in two. Sabrina would take the west side, and Daphne the
east. But as soon as they stepped out of their cabin, Snow White
was waiting.

"Are you ready for your training?"

"Huh?"

"Billy and I think it wise, in light of the prophecy, that you learn
to fight properly. He also thinks it might be good for everyone to

see you out here at the crack of dawn preparing for war. And who better to train you than me? Remember my self-defense class?"

Sabrina turned to her sister.

"Ummmm," the girls said in unison, trying to figure out how to get out of this.

"Don't worry," Snow said. "We'll eat breakfast after our first break."

"First break?" Daphne said. "As in, we'll be training so long that we'll need more than one break?"

"Don't be lazy, girls," Snow said, and then handed each girl a black pole. Each was thick, nearly four feet long, and polished smooth.

"What are these for?" Sabrina asked, doing her best to get a grip on the unwieldy object.

"Fighting," Snow said matter-of-factly. "They're called bō staffs, and I'm going to teach you how use them."

"This weighs a ton," Sabrina complained, trying to swing it over her head, only to drop it on the ground. "And it's clumsy."

"That's not the bō staff, that's you. Your muscles are weak, but you'll get stronger, and you'll get better at using the weapon," Snow explained. "Trust me, when I started learning martial arts, I had no upper-body strength, but now . . ."

Snow spun the staff at an incredible speed, twirling it around her head like the blades on a helicopter. She passed it from hand to hand, flipped it around her back, and finally landed in a crouch with the staff mere inches from Sabrina's nose. "I believe some would say that's 'very punk rock.'"

"My catchphrases are trademarked, Ms. White," Daphne said with a giggle.

"How is swinging a stick around going to help us stop a madman made out of magic?" Sabrina asked.

"Because when you hit someone with a big stick, even someone who is made out of magic, it hurts them a lot," Snow said.

The afternoon was painful. Ms. White's bō staff slapped against Sabrina's shoulders, knees, shins, and knuckles. Just holding her own weapon made Sabrina's shoulders burn like hamburgers on a grill. But defending herself from Ms. White's attacks was the most painful. Each blocked attack sent a jarring vibration through Sabrina's hands, up her arms, and into her neck and back. Sometimes those attacks were so painful that the staff fell out of her hands and bounced to the ground, crashing into her ankles and feet on the way down.

"C'mon, Sabrina," Snow cried. "I'm going easy on you. At least look like you're making an effort in front of the others."

An audience had gathered. Nearly all of the Everafter refugees were watching the sisters Grimm train. Some were smiling encouragingly, some were merely curious, but others were troubled by what they were seeing. Sabrina could almost hear their thoughts: *This kid is supposed to lead our army?* She wanted to shout that she hadn't chosen to be in the stupid prophecy in the first place.

"Well, that was a good first session," Snow said, collecting the bō staffs. "I'll see you back here at five."

"Five?!" Sabrina cried.

"Kids, you've got a lot to learn and very little time to learn it," the teacher said, then turned back toward her own cabin. Sabrina's glare could have burned holes into Snow's back as she disappeared.

"I need to be taken to a hospital," Daphne said, wincing at her bruises and strained muscles.

"I hear you, but we can't forget about the Book of Everafter," Sabrina said. "We can tend to our wounds after we find it."

Suddenly, Puck dropped into their path. He held three wooden swords in his hand.

"What's this about?" Sabrina groaned.

"I'm your next teacher. You can call me Mr. Puck," he said, handing each of the sisters a sword. "Today, I will teach you the art of swordsmanship—or, in other words, how to stab someone with a sharp, pointy thing."

Sabrina was so sore, she could barely lift the weapon. Daphne was struggling, as well.

"Listen, we've got a bigger problem," Sabrina said.

"Yeah, we lost something," Daphne added.

Puck didn't listen. Instead, he launched into an attack, forcing the girls to defend themselves. For ten minutes, Sabrina fought him off, but not before he used his wooden sword to smack her in her head, poke her in the belly, and crack her across the shins. Eventually, she fell to her knees and surrendered.

"Get up," Puck said as he stood over her.

"Puck, we're tired!" Daphne cried.

"Get to your feet," he demanded.

"What are you doing?" Sabrina asked as she gasped for air. She was surprised by his attitude—it was so serious and so mean. Where was the dancing boy from the night before? Where was the Puck she had wanted to kiss? She stared up into his eyes, hoping he could see how much she was hurting, but they were cold.

"You have this camp's attention," Puck said.

Sabrina looked to the crowd. They looked back at her like she was a turtle who had flipped over onto its back and could not right itself. To them, she was pathetic. She could hardly blame them. She wouldn't want her life put in the hands of a couple of little girls, either.

"They need to see that you can fight back," Puck continued. "They want to see that, when things get hard, you aren't just going to lie on the ground and whine. The party's over, Grimms. It's time to get serious."

He turned and stormed away.

Henry and Veronica approached. They helped Sabrina and Daphne to their feet.

"Girls, this isn't working." Henry sighed. "You don't have time to train properly."

"Duh!" Daphne cried.

"Don't panic. Your father and I have an idea," Veronica said.

The army was asked to gather in the courtyard. Sabrina stood before them all, painfully nervous. She didn't know how her parents' idea would be received, but she was relieved that someone—anyone—was taking charge.

"I hope everyone had a good time last night," Sabrina said to the crowd, "but now we have to get back to our plans for stopping Mirror. We're a small group—too small to defeat him. I think I know how to change that, but before I explain any further, I asked the Widow to fly down to the town and report back."

The huge crow pushed her way to the front of the crowd.

"It's a horror show," she squawked. "I can't make it sound any prettier than that. If you owned a business down there, it's time to fill out the insurance claim. The streets are a total disaster—completely overrun with the Hand. Those goons are using our home as their own personal playground. I saw two trolls tossing cars around like they were in a snowball fight. They're looting and destroying things just for the fun of it.

"And then there's Relda—I mean, Mirror. He . . . she . . . wow, this is confusing. Let's just say the Big Bad is camped out in the old police station. He's got his thugs running in and out of the place, ordering the members of the Hand to cause as much chaos as possible. Plus, there's this red-haired lunatic who seems to be Mirror's right-hand man. I've never seen him before, but he's got a sword as big as an oar."

"Red-haired lunatic?" Charming asked. "Is this someone new?"

Sabrina cringed. That had to be Atticus. She looked to the Wicked Queen, who was cringing, as well. Apparently, the witch had not yet told Snow or Charming anything about their past, or the vicious man who haunted it.

"How many members of the Hand do you think you saw, Widow?" Sabrina asked, quickly changing the subject.

"Two thousand . . . maybe more."

"Two thousand!" the Pied Piper cried.

"We'll be slaughtered!" the Scarecrow said.

The crowd broke into panicked chatter, but Sabrina continued, urged on by her parents' confident smiles. "It sounds like a lot, I know. That's why they're going to be super surprised when we beat them. And that's where my parents'—I mean, *my* idea comes into play. We need to recruit some more soldiers."

"And how do you propose we do that?" Buzzflower demanded.

"We need to ask the Scarlet Hand to switch sides," Sabrina said.

"That's insane!" Nurse Sprat cried. "They're a bunch of murderous maniacs."

"Not all of them," Daphne shouted over the din. The crowd quieted enough for Sabrina to continue explaining the plan.

"The Scarlet Hand has more than its fair share of evil Everafters, but the rest are just scared and desperate. They used to be our neighbors and friends, and they've turned to the Master for the sake of survival. They don't see an alternative, but we can give them one. If we can take them in, protect them, I think they'll join our fight."

"We believe most will jump at the opportunity," Henry added.

"That's a very big risk, Hank," Goldie said.

Henry nudged Sabrina to continue. "It is, but I think it has a very good chance of working, because we can give them a big dose of the truth. Mirror lied to them. He told them that they would all take over the world together, but then he tried to escape the town alone. He would have left them all behind, stuck inside the barrier. I'm betting they don't know that, and I think the news will make them pretty angry."

"What if they won't listen to reason?" Mr. Swineheart asked.

"We're going to use our secret weapon—my mother. She can reason with anyone," Sabrina said. "She managed to broker peace with King Oberon and Queen Titania back in New York City, and those two were impossible. If anyone can convince the Scarlet Hand to join us, it's her."

"Except for one thing!" Beauty said. "There are Everafters in the Hand that despise your family. More than a few would like to see you all dead."

"We won't win them all," Veronica said. "But we might win enough to make a difference. And maybe, once they see the rest of their comrades turning away from evil, the real diehards will realize they've pledged loyalty to a man who has already tried to betray them."

"It's worth a try," Sabrina said.

"It might save a few lives," Goldie added.

"And it might get us a proper army," Mr. Canis said.

Beauty stepped forward. "I'm in. I myself was once manipulated by Mirror. I didn't see another choice, but if someone had given me some hope—well, I'm sure I would have seized it. Besides, my husband and daughter are among those people, and I'm not ready to give up on them."

Morgan le Fay nodded. "Glinda of Oz was one of my best friends. I know she doesn't want this fight."

"My friend the Cowardly Lion would surely switch sides," the Scarecrow shouted.

"There are also a few people in their crowd we can already count on," Charming announced. "Robin Hood and his men as well as King Arthur and his knights have infiltrated the Hand. When the time comes, they will fight for us, but I'm hoping it won't have to come to that. I'd hate for them to be exposed as spies."

Sabrina couldn't believe the wave of enthusiasm rolling through the crowd. She had convinced the refugees to adopt her parents' plan.

"Then it's settled," she said. "We'll call for a meeting in the town square."

The crowd gasped.

"Didn't the crow just say the town square is a war zone?" Pinocchio said. "Are you trying to get us killed? Should we paint targets on our backs, too?"

"Hush up, boy," Geppetto snapped.

"We won't go in unprepared," Henry said. "The Pied Piper will be on crowd control. Baba Yaga, Bunny, Mordred, and Morgan will handle any magical attacks. Buzzflower and Mallobarb can create diversions if we need to escape."

"It's a suicide mission," Mr. Swineheart said.

"No, it's bold. I like it," Charming said. "I support Sabrina's plan."

Snow called for a vote. "All those in favor?"

Sabrina glanced at the crowd. Every hand was raised except Pinocchio's and, much to her surprise, Puck's. He was standing in the back of the crowd, arms crossed, glaring at her. Was he still angry about the sword fighting?

"Then it's settled," Canis said. "We should send word immediately that—"

"It is not settled. I won't participate in any truce with the Scarlet Hand," a voice called from the back of the crowd. Sabrina craned her neck and spotted Uncle Jake. "You cannot trust one of them. Not one!"

"Jake, they aren't all like Heart and Nottingham," Veronica said.

"Fine!" he growled. "Charming, this is your castle, but it's also

Briar's grave. Bring in all the trash you want, but if Nottingham or Heart set foot in this camp, I will kill them."

"Jake!" Henry cried, but his brother stormed away.

Jake's outburst didn't seem to change any minds. The crowd was still firmly behind Sabrina's plan. The Widow was sent out to call the meeting.

It was a long day, and nightfall crept up sooner than anyone expected. The girls limped back to their cabin on sore legs. There, they found the Book of Everafter, back in its hiding spot under Daphne's bed.

"You had me panicked about nothing!" Sabrina complained.

"I swear it wasn't there this morning," Daphne argued, eyeing the Book suspiciously.

Sabrina crawled into bed and pulled the covers over her head. She was too tired for mysteries, especially mysteries that weren't mysteries at all. "I think the only thing missing is a pair of glasses on your nose."

She fell asleep halfway through Daphne's defense.

Sabrina woke to the sound of loud voices. She sat up and listened, recognizing them immediately. Her father and her uncle were in the midst of an argument.

Her curiosity got the best of her, and she crept out of her cabin and toward the two men, who were standing near Briar's grave. Sabrina hid behind a stack of chopped wood so she could listen without being seen.

"Jake, this is a good plan," her father said. "You can't stand in the way. The girls' lives are in jeopardy."

"And whose fault is that? Sending them into that hornet's nest tomorrow is as good as aiming arrows right at them."

"Jake, you're not being fair," Henry said. "You can't paint everyone in the Hand with the same brush. They are not all evil. I know you're angry. I would be, too, but you are tumbling off the edge, Jake. This is not what Briar would want for you."

"Don't tell me what Briar would want for me!" Jake said, grabbing his brother by the collar and shoving him against the side of a cabin.

"You have to find a way to get control of this anger," Henry said, squirming to free himself.

"I intend to, Hank!"

Henry fell still, and there was a long silence.

"You're planning something, aren't you?" Henry said. "Jake, there are people who could get hurt if it blows up in your face, including my wife and kids."

"Then keep them away from me." Jake scowled, finally releasing his brother.

"You could make things a lot worse."

"How could things get worse?"

"We have to offer the Hand an alternative to the fear and violence. If you kill Nottingham and Heart, you'll be no better than Mirror in their eyes. It will be like taking a lit match to a stack of dynamite. People will get hurt, Jake," Henry said.

"Then you better get ready for an explosion, big brother," Uncle Jake said matter-of-factly.

Suddenly, Henry punched his brother in the jaw, and Jake fell to the ground. He lay there in the dust around Briar's grave. Sabrina gasped and smacked her hands over her mouth, hoping neither of them had heard. She had never known her father to be so aggressive. So many people told her stories of the impulsive and emotional young man Henry Grimm used to be, but she'd never believed them.

"Back to talking with your fists, Henry?" Uncle Jake said.

"My girls adore you, Jake. Doesn't that mean anything to you? You would put their lives in danger for your stupid revenge plot? Well, I won't let it happen. I won't let them get hurt because you're heartbroken. I'm sorry she's gone, Jake. We're all sorry. You have a right to want revenge, but you don't have a right to get it. If you try, I will hit you again. Stand up and find out if I mean it," Henry threatened.

"What's going on?" Goldie asked as she walked toward the two brothers.

Jake and Henry ignored her. "You weren't there, Hank! They

sent a dragon after her, and it swatted her away like she was nothing. You didn't hear the sound! You didn't see her eyes!"

Henry sighed and knelt next to his brother.

"I had a ring!" Jake continued. He buried his head in his brother's chest and sobbed.

Goldie knelt down beside them, but Henry waved her off.

"Goldie, this is family business. You should go."

She looked hurt. "But—"

"The three of us were a long time ago," he barked.

Goldie fought back tears and rushed toward her cabin. Henry
watched her. Sabrina thought she saw regret on his face.

When Goldie was gone, Henry turned back to his brother.
"Jake, I have a lot on my plate. My son doesn't know me. My
daughters are on the front line of a stupid prophecy. Our mother
is possessed. I need your help. When all this is over, we can talk
about Nottingham and Heart. We'll get justice for Briar."

Jake pulled himself to his feet and rubbed his sore jaw. "There
is no justice for Briar until those two are in the ground!"

"We don't murder people."

Jake frowned.

"Tell me you won't kill them!" Henry insisted, but Jake shook
him off. Jake sank back into his chair and looked out over Briar's
grave. Henry stood over him, watching for a long moment, then
finally headed back to his cabin. Sabrina stayed awhile longer,

quietly watching her uncle until he leaped from his chair full of fury and rage. He punched the cabin wall.

Blood trickled down from his knuckles. He stared at the wound for a long time, as if it might hold some answers, but then he slumped against the wall and down to the ground. He buried his head in his hands and wept. Sabrina wanted to go to him, to find a way to take his heartbreak away, but she knew he needed to cry. She slinked back to her cabin and found her sister and Elvis still sleeping. She sat on the edge of the bed in the dark and cried for her uncle and the lost love of his life.

October 18

Uncle Jake is gone again. Red says she saw him walk across the drawbridge and into the woods. He was carrying a bow and a quiver full of arrows strapped to his back. I guess he's determined to have his revenge.

It's a problem we don't need today. We're walking into an angry mob that wants everyone in my family dead. Even though it would ruin the plan, some part of me hopes we'll be the only ones who show up in the town square.

On a side note, Puck's sweet side has turned into a sour sack of socks. He keeps scowling at me and Daphne, and he won't speak to either of us. If I wasn't so tired and sore, I'd sit on his chest and demand an explanation.

Boys are moody.

And stupid.

❧

If someone asked Sabrina to list her virtues, patience would not be one of them. Waiting made her grouchy. She remembered one Christmas in particular when she was waiting to sit on Santa's lap. After seeing the mile-long line of kids in front of her, she darted to the front, stiff-armed an elf, and hopped onto St. Nick's lap. She shoved her wish list into his hands just as security guards yanked her away. Her parents were mortified, but Santa had her list, and that was more important than a photo opportunity.

So, waiting for the Widow to return to the camp was excruciating. Worse, there was no one to talk to. Her mother and father were busy writing Veronica's speech, her sister was giving Elvis a much-needed bath, and Basil was still not talking to anyone.

To take her mind off the wait, Sabrina kept herself busy with chores. She collected her family's dirty clothes and washed them in a bucket of water. There wasn't any detergent around, but she hoped the socks, jeans, and T-shirts might lose some of their stink if she rinsed them a few times.

After she hung everything up to dry, she offered Pinocchio help making the compost pile his father insisted he finish. Ten minutes into the task, his constant whining that he was "too smart for menial labor" forced her to leave.

She fed the horses, then the chickens. She watched Mr. Boarman milk a cow. She helped Mallobarb and Buzzflower hang a tapestry, then wandered through the castle to explore the rooms.

Unfortunately, nothing distracted Sabrina for long. Eventually, she gave up and marched off to see the magic mirrors. Maybe they had some news.

She found them waiting in their frames when she arrived. Reggie, Titan, Fanny, Donovan, and Harry were all smiling, but the rest eyed her warily.

"How was the wedding?" Fanny asked. "What did the bride wear?"

"Was there any dancing?" Donovan asked. "I was hoping someone would ask me to DJ. I have the most extensive collection of disco and funk records in the known universe. Half of my collection is of bands that are completely imaginary."

"Who caught the bouquet?" Titan roared.

"It was magical," Sabrina said. "But it's all over now. Drama has returned to Castle Charming."

She explained her family's plan to the mirrors—all about her mother's speech and the hope of building a bigger army.

"It sounds as if they've taken this out of your hands, girl," Reggie said.

Sabrina shrugged. "I don't mind. I just hope it works."

"The prophecy was for you and your sister," Arden said.

"I'm still involved," Sabrina said defensively, though she wasn't totally confident that was true. It seemed as if everyone had been bossing her and Daphne around even more than usual since the prophecy had been revealed. Plus, when she'd offered her parents a few ideas about the speech earlier that afternoon, they'd just ignored her.

"So, what can we do for you?" Harry asked.

"Can you show me Granny?"

The mirrors' reflections shimmered, then cleared to reveal Granny Relda wearing a filthy white dress. Her long gray hair was tangled, sticking out in all directions. Her eyes smoldered like black coals, and her face—once kind and amused—was twisted with bloodthirsty rage. Sabrina watched her with increasing horror. Granny's head cocked to the side as if she were peering back at Sabrina, and then she laughed. It was a low, foul, otherworldly sound.

"Stop!" Sabrina cried, tears in her eyes.

"We're sorry, honey," Fanny said as Granny vanished and the guardians returned.

Titan roared fiercely. "I swear on my life that our brother will pay for his crimes. We'll find a way to punish him and rescue your grandmother."

Sabrina prayed silently that Titan was right.

"Hey! The black chicken is back," Puck said, storming into the room.

"She's not a chicken. She's a crow," Sabrina said, wiping the tears from her cheeks before he could see.

"Whatever," Puck huffed. He stomped from the room, shouting behind him, "It's time to go!"

"He's grouchy," Fanny said.

Sabrina sighed. "Whatever's bothering him is just going to have to wait."

She said good-bye to the mirrors and hurried to the courtyard, where she found an eager crowd gathered around the Widow. Everyone wanted to know how the invitation had been received. As Sabrina drew closer, she noticed several unfamiliar birds with the big black crow.

"I invited everyone who didn't try to kill me, which wasn't many," the crow squawked to the crowd. "And I managed to find a few new recruits along the way. Allow me to introduce to you our new aerial spy network: the Silver Pigeon, the Gold Pigeon, the Clockwork Owl, and the Canary. The duck here is named Lenchen, and the big one with all the plumes is a firebird. Don't know his name yet, but the others say he is reliable."

The firebird squawked as if in agreement.

Beauty pushed to the front of the crowd. "Did you see my husband and daughter? Did you invite them?"

The Widow nodded. "I did. Now, whether they come or not is anybody's guess, but I have my doubts. Beast fired a crossbow at me. Real special guy you got there, Beauty."

"He's not really a bad person. He's just caught up with the wrong people," Beauty said.

"Beast would be a great recruit," Charming said as he handed a piece of paper to the Scarecrow. "I've made a wish list of some

Everafters who would be very useful: the Ice Queen, the Frog Prince, Glinda, and Big Hans are just a few. If any one of them shows a hint of coming over to our side, we need to make it happen."

"We better get going if we want to make it to the town square in time," Goldilocks said. She stood on the edge of the gathering, as far from Sabrina's father as possible. The previous night's encounter had clearly hurt her feelings.

Mr. Canis agreed. "We should get there early. We don't want to walk through a hostile crowd."

Veronica planted a kiss on Basil's forehead and turned to hand him to Red Riding Hood, who happily agreed to stay behind and look after him. "Be good, little man."

"Give your mommy a hug and say bye-bye," Red told the toddler, setting him down on the ground.

Basil turned and looked up at Veronica apprehensively. Then he wrapped his arms around her leg.

"Bye-bye," he said.

Veronica beamed.

The group filed into the woods. Charming estimated it would be a good two-hour hike to the town square. Unfortunately, the ground was muddy and messy from all the rain they'd been getting, and it slowed them down considerably. Puck suggested they all step into Baba Yaga's house for an easier trip, but no one was brave enough to try.

Mr. Canis hobbled forward to walk alongside the Grimms. "I don't like this plan," he growled. "We'll be out in the open and vulnerable to attack."

"We've got some of the most powerful witches and fairies in town on our side, Mr. Canis," Sabrina said, "as well as the Hamelins and Beauty. Plus, for brute strength, we've got the Three Bears. And Charming is no slouch."

"I can deliver a pretty mean kick to the kneecap, too," Daphne bragged.

"I think you're all entirely too overconfident," Canis growled.

"Plus, we've got Puck, who has a variety of, um . . . unique talents," Sabrina said.

Puck stomped forward, interrupting the conversation. "Exactly what am I supposed to do?"

"You're keeping an eye on the girls," Henry explained.

Puck groaned. "I have been in the middle of a hundred wars, many of which I started myself. Why waste my skills on your rug rats? Can't we just lock them in a playpen until it's over?"

"A playpen?" Sabrina said.

"Yeah, like babies," Puck said, stomping ahead of the group.

Finally, they reached the center of town. The Widow's description of the destruction didn't do it justice. Streetlamps were uprooted, broken electrical wires popped and snapped on the ground, huge slabs of concrete were completely missing from sidewalks and streets, and the smell of burning rubber nearly overwhelmed Sabrina. Worse, as Mr. Canis had feared, the army was late for the meeting. The Scarlet Hand waited for them in the middle of Main Street. Charming and his people walked through the angry crowd to get to what was left of the gazebo. Sabrina fully expected to be attacked.

Mayor Heart, Sheriff Nottingham, Glinda, the Three Blind Mice, the Beast and his daughter, Natalie, the Ice Queen, and the White Rabbit were all there, as well as a mob of ogres, imps, trolls, goblins, orcs, leprechauns, and brownies.

But worse were the faces in the crowd that Granny Relda had once called friends: Mowgli, Baloo, Jack Pumpkinhead, Hansel and Gretel, Old King Cole, and Old Mother Hubbard each had a bright red handprint painted on their chests. If the meeting had a silver lining, it was that Mirror and Atticus were nowhere to be seen.

Mayor Heart roughly shoved her way to the front of the crowd with Nottingham in tow. Heart was in a ball gown decorated with lace hearts. Nottingham wore his usual leather pants and cape.

"You're late! Say what you've come to say!" Heart barked through her electronic megaphone. "Your bird said it was important, and it better be. If you waste our time, I can't guarantee your safety."

Her crowd cheered and laughed. Many shook swords and knobby clubs in the air.

Henry gave Veronica a thumbs-up, and she stepped forward, fully vulnerable. Panic rose in Sabrina's throat as she imagined the endless number of attacks that could strike her mother down. Why had they put themselves in such danger? What were they thinking?

"May I have your attention?" Veronica asked.

The crowd ignored her, so she asked again, with similar results.

Finally, Heart blasted an angry "PIPE DOWN!" through her megaphone, which quelled the crowd. "Let her speak!"

"Why don't we just kill her and the whole family?" a troll called.

"You know full well why we can't!" the mayor cried. "The Master has claimed their lives for himself. No one kills them but him."

The crowd's boos and jeers infuriated Canis. He clenched his fists and looked ready to pounce, but the mob was not as intimidated by him as they once were. For once, Sabrina missed the Big Bad Wolf.

Unfazed, Veronica looked out on the crowd. "Thank you for coming. I won't waste your time. My name is Veronica Grimm. I was considered an asset to Oberon and Titania's kingdom in Manhattan. I can be of help to you, as well."

"Can you bring down the barrier?" Chicken Little squawked from the front of the crowd.

Veronica shook her head.

The audience booed loudly again. A few bottles were flung at Veronica and shattered at her feet.

"Don't worry, Grimm. When the crowd gets ugly, I'll be here to save your butt," Puck said to Sabrina. "Like always."

"What's the matter with you? You've been such a crybaby for days," Sabrina snapped.

"I'm just bored with saving your life. If you think I'm going to keep doing this after we get married, you can forget it."

"First, we are not getting married, ever. Second, if you're so put out, feel free to stop. I don't need your help."

"Trust me, you do."

"Trust me, I'm fine. Find something else to do with your precious time. That nose of yours isn't going to pick itself."

"I would love nothing more than to give my nose all the attention it deserves, but if I did, you'd be dead within minutes," Puck said. His head suddenly morphed into that of a lion, and he roared angrily.

Sabrina roared back, though it didn't have the same effect. Worse, she suddenly realized the entire crowd was watching. She was mortified. Puck had an almost magical ability to get her to make a fool of herself.

"As I was saying," Veronica said, turning her attention back to the crowd, "we have come here with an offer—"

Heart's laughter interrupted Veronica. "Are you suggesting we surrender?"

"No. We want you to join us. Abandon the Scarlet Hand and help us defeat Mirror."

There was a moment of silence, and then laughter broke out. It was so loud that it hurt Sabrina's ears.

Veronica frowned, but she waited patiently until the crowd calmed. "Many of you have been pressured to join the Hand, either through violence or threats. You feel you have no other option—no place you can turn to for protection. We will take you. You don't have to live in fear any longer, and you don't have to continue doing things that you know in your heart are wrong!"

More bottles came flying toward Veronica. Mordred stepped forward and cast a shield to protect the group.

"Your Master has turned his back on you," Veronica shouted over the din.

"Who are you to question the Master?" Heart barked into her megaphone.

"He is a liar," a voice said, and the crowd fell silent. Sabrina turned and was shocked to find Uncle Jake moving through the mob.

"Watch your tongue, Grimm, or my blade will remove it," Nottingham raged.

"Two years ago, your so-called savior kidnapped my brother and his wife. He cast a spell on them that put them to sleep. Veronica was pregnant, and while she and my brother were asleep, a baby grew. Once it was born, Mirror stole him in hopes of taking over his body. He wanted to put his spirit inside the child. Now, why would he do that?"

"He needed the body of a human being to escape the barrier, you fool!" Heart snapped.

"How would that help you?" Jake asked as he climbed the steps to the gazebo. He turned and looked out over the small army, all staring back with angry eyes. "How would that help any of you?"

"Once he's on the other side, he can find a way to remove the barrier entirely—the one your family built for us!" Nottingham howled.

"Is that what he told you? Nottingham, you're a smart man. How could Mirror turn it off from the outside if he couldn't turn it off from the inside?" Jake said to the crowd. "There's no magic button out there. He played you all for fools. He's not going to set any of you free."

The crowd murmured. They looked around at their companions for answers, but no one had any counterargument to offer. Sabrina was flabbergasted. What had happened to her uncle's broken heart and anger? Where was his hostility and talk of revenge?

"Mirror told me himself that he had no plans of freeing you," Sabrina said. "He just used you to get what he wanted."

"You lie!" Nottingham growled. "The Master will free us all, and together we will wipe out your foul, inferior race. This world will belong to Everafters, as it was intended."

"I know you don't all believe that," Veronica said, scanning the crowd. "I can see it in your faces. You know right from wrong. Many of you don't want to be part of this. My family is extending an olive branch. If you were forced to join the Hand, you can walk away from this. You can join us."

"Don't listen to these liars," Nottingham said. "They're Grimms. They want to keep us in this cage like dogs! The Master opened our eyes to their deceptions. For too long, we have not been in control of our own destinies, and this family, who now stands here begging for mercy, is to blame!"

"Pipe down, Sheriff. The Grimms make a good point. The Master said if we helped him with his plans, he would free us," the White Rabbit argued. "He said he was all-powerful. But we are still trapped here, and so is he."

Nottingham seethed. "I've heard enough! These people cannot be trusted, and I, for one, think it's time they paid for their lies. The spell that keeps us here says that when the last Grimm dies, the barrier falls. If we kill them all now, we'll be free."

The crowd grew more excited.

"Except that killing us won't get you what you want, you morons," Jake shouted. "Your Master is inside my mother's body. Yeah, you didn't think that one through, did you? Are you going to kill him to win your freedom? You're stuck! Just like him!"

The crowd fell silent.

"There's only one person in the world who can set you free," Jake continued. "Me!"

"You?" the Frog Prince cried. "What are you talking about, Jacob?"

"Many years ago, my brother fell in love with an Everafter. To give them a chance at a happy, normal life, I found the spell Jacob and

Wilhelm used to create the barrier. I stole it from their accomplice, Baba Yaga, and I used it to turn off the barrier for a moment."

"What is he doing?" Mr. Canis asked Henry. "He's ruining everything."

"You lie!" Nottingham shouted.

"It's true," Goldilocks said as she stepped forward. "Jake let me out. I lived outside of Ferryport Landing for fifteen years before I came back to help save Henry and his wife."

Jake reached into one of his jacket pockets and took out a weathered, yellowing piece of parchment. He unfolded it and held it up so everyone could see. "I can do it again, but only if you give up your loyalty to the Scarlet Hand and help us free my mother from Mirror's control."

Nottingham snatched Heart's megaphone, clearly preparing to unleash another tirade, but the mayor stopped him.

"Sheriff, let him finish," she demanded, then turned back to Jake. "How do we know we can trust you?"

"You might not like my family, Your Majesty, but we've always been honest," Jake said. "When I tell you I will end your suffering, I mean it."

Sabrina watched the crowd, fully expecting them to attack Jake and seize Baba Yaga's spell out of his hand, but the angry faces were changing. Much to Sabrina's surprise, many members of the Hand were quietly considering his offer.

"My brothers and I will join you," called a voice from below.

The Three Blind Mice pushed their way forward, their canes clicking on the ground with every step. As they made their way to stand with the family, a number of threats were hurled at them.

"Traitors!"

"You have signed your own death warrants!"

If the mice were bothered, they didn't show it.

"That's an excellent start!" Veronica exclaimed, ignoring the fiery cries. "Who else will join us?"

"Can you protect me?" the Cowardly Lion asked.

"Ab-absolutely," Sabrina sputtered before the gigantic beast.

"Then you have my claws," the Lion replied, then leaped forward to join the mice.

"Good to have you, old friend," the Scarecrow said, rushing to pat the Lion on his massive head.

"Where's my daughter?" Beauty coolly asked her husband.

"She's safe," Beast said.

"Is she here?"

"No. You don't have to worry."

"Don't tell me what I have to worry about, James. You don't get to do that anymore," Beauty snapped.

"They've turned you against me!" he roared.

"No, you did that when you decided to help these criminals. You can do what you want now, but you won't do it with our daughter," Beauty said.

The Beast growled. "Beauty, why can't you be reasonable? These people you befriended have brought us nothing but misery. What happened to the woman who would do anything for our freedom?"

"That woman realized she's also someone's mother," Beauty said. "One of us has to teach Natalie right from wrong. Turn away from this madness, and you can help me."

"I won't," the Beast snarled.

Several goblins and a troll pushed through the crowd. A handful of lambs, a couple of robotic men, and Little John followed, taking their place among Charming's troops.

Nottingham planted himself before the rest of the members of the Scarlet Hand, blocking others from joining the growing army.

"You fools! This is the Grimm family," he said. "They have caused all of our suffering."

"And I can fix it," Uncle Jake said, extending his hand toward Mayor Heart. For a moment, she looked as if she was ready to take it, but Nottingham pulled his dagger.

"Lies!"

Charming unsheathed his own sword and pointed it at Nottingham's face. The sheriff stumbled backward, afraid.

"My quarrel is with the Grimms!" Nottingham shouted.

"Then your quarrel is with all of us," Charming said.

"I will kill you, Charming," Nottingham seethed.

"I hear your words, Sheriff. Do you have the courage to back them up?"

"If it's courage you seek, little brother, I have it in spades," said a strange, deep voice at the back of the crowd.

"Oh, no," Daphne whispered.

"Atticus," Sabrina gasped. She turned to the Wicked Queen. Bunny stepped in front of Snow. Mr. Seven joined them.

Charming scanned the crowd, then watched a man with a mane of greasy red hair push through the mob.

"Who are you?" Charming called.

"Don't you remember me?" Atticus cried. "You should! You destroyed my family and stole my rightful seat at our father's side. But your most wicked crime was stealing my wife's heart while I was away."

"I think you've got me confused with someone else," Charming said, turning his sword in Atticus's direction.

"Oh, no. I definitely have the right person." Atticus leaped into the gazebo. He stared at Charming for a long time, his face contorted with hatred. For the first time, Sabrina could see the resemblance between the two men. They had the same eyes and jawlines. But while all of Charming's features combined to make him handsome and approachable, Atticus's were twisted, rough, and cruel. "You really don't remember me? You did your work in the Book of Everafter well, Your Majesty."

Charming turned his attention to the Wicked Queen.

"Do you know this man?" he asked her, but Ms. Lancaster didn't respond. She watched Atticus as if he were a venomous snake waiting to strike.

Atticus reached for his sword but then seemed to think better of it. Instead, he turned to the members of the Scarlet Hand. "The Master has sent me with a message, people. He is very disappointed in you. He has worked so hard to set you free, and the moment there is a minor setback, you run to the enemy. It's treason. And, if it were up to me, I would walk through this crowd taking fingers and noses and hands as punishment. Lucky for you, the Master's got a much kinder heart. He's offering you a second chance. Turn away from the Grimms, or blood will spill. Personally, I'm hoping you pick the latter."

"Who do you think you are?" Snow White demanded.

"Who am I?" Atticus said, then snatched her by the wrist and pulled her close. "Surely you remember me. Don't tell me you have forgotten the face of your own husband?"

"Do something," Sabrina cried to the Wicked Queen.

"Let go of me," Snow said. "You've lost your mind."

"Get your hands off of her," Charming said, leveling his sword at Atticus's head.

The foul man laughed, and with a sudden burst of ferocity, he slugged Charming in the nose. The prince fell backward, blood spraying from his face. Atticus drew his sword and towered over the fallen man. He looked as if he were ready to stab the prince, but Snow stepped between them.

"You've made a mistake. This man is not your brother. I am not your wife. I've never seen you before in my life," she said, calmly but fiercely.

Atticus slapped her with the back of his hand, and she fell to the ground. "You filthy harlot! How dare you argue with me? You are my property!"

"That's enough!" Mr. Seven said, cutting in.

"No, it's not enough. Not enough at all," Atticus said, and without a second thought, he thrust his sword into Mr. Seven's belly. It slid through him and out his back. With a jerk, Atticus pulled his blood-soaked weapon free.

"Nooo!" Morgan le Fay cried. As Mr. Seven fell to the ground, she raised her hands above her head. A ball of vicious red energy formed between them.

"Morgan, no! Save your magic for Seven! Get him to safety," Henry barked, leaping into action. He raced forward and punched Atticus in the face with all his strength. The villain staggered but quickly righted himself. He swung his sword toward Henry's head, but a blast of white energy slammed into Atticus's chest and ruined his aim.

"I told you once that I would kill you if you touched my daughter again," the Wicked Queen said as she stormed toward Atticus.

Her hands were growing red like lava. She let loose her power again and sent Atticus flying through the crowd, knocking people aside as if he were a runaway bowling ball.

While the queen stalked her prey, Sabrina rushed to Morgan's side. The poor woman hovered over her husband, sobbing. "I don't know any healing spells!"

Her son, Mordred, stood nearby, looking just as helpless.

Goldie and the Three Bears rushed forward. "What can we do?"

"Find Beauty and try to calm this mob down before anyone else gets hurt," Sabrina said. "We need to get Mr. Seven back to the castle."

Goldie crawled onto Poppa Bear's back, and they charged into the madness.

"Puck!" Sabrina cried, spotting him in the crowd. "Get Canis and the rest of my family to safety."

She expected an argument, but Puck took one look at the blood pooling around Mr. Seven and darted off to do as he was told.

"What should we do?" a voice asked. Sabrina turned and found the Frog Prince, his wife, and their daughter, Bella—all members of the Scarlet Hand. At first Sabrina pulled away, but then she realized they were being sincere.

"Help anyone who is in danger of being trampled by this crowd," Henry said as he and Veronica rushed to join them.

Bella and her father sprang into the air and leaped into the crowd, hoisting people off their feet and then jumping them to safety.

When Sabrina turned to see if there was anyone else in need of help, she found Nottingham hovering over her with his dagger and twisted smile. Mayor Heart stood by his side, watching the action with bright eyes.

"One Grimm down, six to go," he hissed as he thrust his blade at Sabrina.

"Not today, you psycho," Uncle Jake said, punching the villain in the belly and then kneeing him in the face. Nottingham fell over, gasping for air. His dagger slipped from his grasp, and Uncle Jake snatched it up. He stood over the struggling villain, his hand squeezing the dagger's handle until his knuckles were white. For a moment, the dark, tragic expression he had worn for many days returned. Sabrina was sure Jake was going to kill Nottingham. Then, with a flick of his hand, he threw the blade to the ground.

"The offer still stands, Your Majesty," he said, extending his hand to the former queen. "Mirror is no friend of yours."

Sabrina couldn't believe what she was seeing. How had her uncle had such a dramatic change of heart so quickly?

"He's trying to free us," Heart argued.

"No, he's not, and deep down you know it. He's going to do what's right for him, and he's going to leave you all behind. I'm not asking you to do the right thing, Your Majesty. Just do the right thing for you."

Heart eyed him suspiciously, then snatched up her megaphone and dashed back into the mob. Jake looked disappointed.

"Looks like some of us are still loyal to the cause." Nottingham laughed from the ground.

An explosion shook the gazebo, nearly knocking everyone off their feet. The Wicked Queen's battle with Atticus was escalating. The witch blasted him repeatedly with magical attacks, and he slammed into bystanders as if he'd been fired from a cannon. Nothing Ms. Lancaster did, however, seemed to hurt Atticus, and after every assault he sprang to his feet and rushed forward with his sword.

"Bad news, Your Majesty," he bellowed. "That book you tried to bury me in was full of magical weapons. I managed to acquire a few over the last four hundred years, including this suit of armor enchanted by Merlin himself to protect King Arthur. As long as I wear it, no human can kill me. Now put away your card tricks. I'm here to settle a different score."

Ms. Lancaster's body glowed like a sun, and she rose off the ground, floating over the dumbfounded crowd. Her eyes went black, and tiny bolts of lightning buzzed around her body.

"Card tricks? You don't get a name like the Wicked Queen doing card tricks," she cried, then shot a green rocket of mist at Atticus. It sent him crashing to the ground.

"Woman!" he said. "You're not listening. If you could kill me, you would have done it already. You would have done it instead of locking me in your book."

"Mother, what is he talking about?" Snow demanded. "What book?"

"Not now, honey, the grown-ups are talking," the witch said, then stretched out her arms. She cried "Gladius!" and a flaming sword appeared in her hands. Leaping forward, she struck at Atticus, who blocked her attack with his own sword. He was a master swordsman, and his attacks were forcing her farther and farther back. Each strike of blade on blade sent red-hot sparks flying in all directions. The two pushed at each other until their noses were as close as their swords, and then, with a vicious kick, Atticus sent the Wicked Queen flying backward into a lamppost, knocking her dizzy.

"I need a sword!" Charming shouted as he watched the maniac stand over the fallen woman.

"Coming right up," Daphne said, and dug the fairy godmother wand out of her pocket. With a flick of her wrist, Charming was in a full suit of armor with a sword in his hand.

"I didn't need the armor!" Charming complained, pulling off the helmet and tossing it aside.

"Sorry, the sword comes with the outfit," Daphne said.

Charming raced forward, stepping between the witch and Atticus.

"Ah, baby brother has come to play the hero," Atticus said.

"I don't know who you are, pal, but you're not taking another step toward the lady," Charming said.

"That suits me just fine. It's you I want to kill anyway," Atticus said matter-of-factly.

The men chased each other around the square, sword fighting and landing terrible punches with their free hands. They fought into the crowd, unconcerned about the people around them. One swipe of a blade went past Sabrina's head. She felt it slice off a chunk of her hair. The next one looked as if it might take her head clean off, but before it landed, she was whisked into the sky. She was with Daphne, high over the crowd, held aloft by Puck.

"And again, I'm saving your lives," Puck said. "I rest my case!"

"Fine. Sometimes I need your help," Sabrina said.

"Sometimes?"

"Don't push it, dog breath," Sabrina said.

"There's Mom and Dad," Daphne said. "Put us down with them."

Their parents were part of a group gathered around Mr. Seven. When they landed, their mother pulled them into a tight embrace. Sabrina noticed the tears in her eyes. Goldilocks was standing nearby, crying, as well.

Mr. Seven lay on the ground with Nurse Sprat hovering over him. He looked exhausted. A bandage was wrapped around his belly, but a red stain was leaking through it. His wife, Morgan le Fay, sat next to him, holding his hand. He leaned up to her with some pain and kissed her. "I love you, Morgan."

The enchantress wiped his hair out of his face. "I love you, too! Everything is going to be fine. We'll just postpone the honeymoon for a few days."

"Tell Mordred I want him to look after you," he said.

"You're going to look after me, darling. That's your job," she replied.

"I tried everything I can," Nurse Sprat said. "Nothing is helping."

Snow White pushed through the crowd. The beautiful teacher knelt beside her friend and took his hand. "Take care of Charming, Snow," the little man said. "He needs you more than even he knows, especially now."

"I will," Snow said through her tears. "But why now?"

The Wicked Queen joined them. She looked exhausted from her fight. She knelt down to Seven and nodded grimly.

"The crowd has joined William. Together, they are fighting Atticus off," she said, then looked hopefully at Sprat. The nurse shook her head. There was no saving Seven.

The little man locked eyes with the queen. "I've done everything I could to protect him from the truth, Your Majesty," Mr. Seven said. "But it seems it has come knocking nonetheless."

"What are you talking about?" Snow asked.

The queen sighed and leaned down to Mr. Seven. "You have done your job well. You were the right choice."

"I appreciate your saying so, Bunny," Seven said. "It was an honor."

Charming stepped forward. His face was bruised, and blood leaked from one ear, but he was otherwise unharmed.

"The coward ran off," he announced, kneeling down beside

Mr. Seven. "Are you going to lie here all afternoon? There's a war going on, you know."

"William Charming, you are my friend," the little man said.

Charming's face turned red, and he fought back tears. "Don't get all mushy on me now. You're going to recover, and it will be very awkward later."

"It has been my pleasure to look after you," Seven continued.

"Is that what you've been doing?" Charming said with a chuckle.

Seven nodded. "Try to be strong, Billy. She did what she did out of love," he said, leaving the prince confused.

Then Seven turned back to his wife. "You are the most beautiful person I have ever seen, Morgan. And I have been alive a very long time. I'll be waiting for you. We'll have that honeymoon. I promise."

A grin spread across his face for the last time. And then he was gone.

Morgan shrieked in agony, and Mordred did his best to comfort her. Charming took his friend's hand and quietly prayed. Sabrina and Daphne cried and cried until there were no more tears to spare. Even Mr. Canis shed a tear for Mr. Seven.

When Snow could finally speak, she took her mother's hand, looked her in the eyes, and said firmly, "You are going to tell me the truth now."

The queen nodded. "Yes, I am."

7

OCTOBER 18 (PART 2)

We buried Mr. Seven next to Briar Rose's grave. Morgan sobbed, and Mordred supported her. Her love for Mr. Seven had been short-lived but very intense, and I feel terrible for her. It doesn't help that the flowers from the wedding are still hanging on everything. No one has the heart to take them down.

Everyone said a few words about Mr. Seven, even Daphne, who cried and cried. Everyone, that is, except Uncle Jake. This loss seemed to open fresh wounds inside him. He stood in the back of the crowd, more upset than ever.

Charming spoke kindly of his old friend. I wish I'd had a tape recorder so that I could play it back and listen again, but I'll write down what I remember. He said, "Seven was a giant of patience and consideration. He was as quick with a smile as he was with a caring ear. He took care of me for many years, and I am, admittedly, a difficult man to handle. He was my friend, my counsel, and my brother. Good-bye, old friend."

When it was over, the Wicked Queen took one of the white roses from Briar's plot and planted it on Seven's grave. The bud sprouted hundreds of new flowers, each blooming in the moonlight.

Everyone is heartbroken, and they are afraid. No one ever expects to suddenly lose a friend, especially at the hands of someone like Atticus. The troops are shaken, even the new members who abandoned the Hand to join us. No one is sure exactly what to say to boost morale. It's probably my job, but I'm too curious about what Ms. Lancaster is going to tell everyone about Atticus and the Book of Everafter. Daphne and I know some of the story, but not all of it. I worry how her revelation is going to go over with Billy.

"He's not crazy or confused. He's your brother," the Wicked Queen said.

"That's impossible!" Charming said. "I'm an only child."

The witch shook her head. "No, not originally."

Charming's face was twisted in confusion.

"Mother, what are you telling us?" Snow asked.

The witch took a deep breath. "What I'm going to tell you is complicated, and you must pay close attention. This is the story of your life, William—the story of your real life. A long time ago, your parents, King Thorne and Queen Catherine, had two children—"

Charming jumped forward. "Woman! I told you—"

"Shut up!" Ms. Lancaster snapped. When Charming fell silent again, she continued. "The firstborn was a boy named Atticus, and he was the heir to your father's throne. You were the second son, not the heir but still a prince. As was the custom in those days, your father and I arranged a marriage between our children designed to help increase the wealth and the power of both families. Snow was promised to Atticus—"

"But I grew up in a village," Snow interrupted. "I was carried away by my father's loyalists to protect me from you."

"Can I finish?" Bunny sighed impatiently. "I promise I will explain everything! Now, as I was saying, Snow and Atticus were to be married. When I consented to this arrangement, I didn't know that Atticus was cruel, vicious, and mentally unhinged. He killed a stable hand for fun when he was only twelve and was known for torturing animals—but, by the time I learned this, he and Snow were already married.

"I did what I could to keep Snow safe. I sent spies to the castle to watch him, to see if he turned his sick rage on my daughter. When he did, I got involved. William, I went to your father and begged him to intervene, but he refused. He used his own wizards and witches to fight off every attempt I made to rescue Snow. Atticus continued to abuse her in unspeakable ways, and there was nothing I could do to stop him. When we all moved to America, to this small town, I saw Atticus's cruelty clearly. It felt like it was being rubbed in my face every day. Yet I was still helpless. That is, until the day I went into the Book of Everafter."

"The book of what?" Charming said. Both he and Snow

looked at the Wicked Queen like she had lost her mind. "What is this bedtime story you're spinning, Bunny?"

Sabrina could tell the witch was losing patience with their interruptions.

"The Book of Everafter is a collection of every fairy tale ever told, from Little Red Riding Hood's to, well, yours. The difference between a regular book and the Book of Everafter is that it lets you go into the stories and walk around. You can visit where you came from."

"We've been inside it," Daphne said, hefting the book into Charming's lap. Bunny had asked her to bring it to the meeting. "It was kooky."

Charming cracked the book open. He flipped through the pages but looked no less confused.

"It also lets Everafters do something else," the witch continued. "It lets them change their stories to something more pleasant. If the change sticks, it alters history. It not only changes the events within the book, but it also changes how the real world experiences and remembers them."

"You rewrote our story?" Snow gasped, finally grasping her mother's meaning.

"Yes, to save you," Ms. Lancaster said. "The world now knows Snow's story as 'Snow White and the Seven Dwarfs,' but the original tale was called 'The Murderous Blood Prince.'"

Charming's face went hard and cold. "Exactly how did you fix it?"

"I tried to add events into the story that would destroy the evil in your brother and make him a hero instead, but nothing I tried worked. I wrote a mentor who taught him honor and kindness, but he slit the man's throat. I gave him a loving fairy godmother, and he pulled her wings off and threw her into a fire. No matter what I tried, I couldn't extinguish the darkness inside him. Snow's life never got any better, so I did what writers call a page-one rewrite. I erased Atticus entirely from the story—or at least I tried to. I managed to force him off the page, into the margins, so to speak, but his presence was still there. He could no longer hurt my daughter, but his shadow hung over everything. It was the best the Book would allow."

"When we went into the Book of Everafter, we were told to stay out of the margins," Sabrina said. "When we did venture there, we encountered Atticus."

"The Book's magic is very fickle. It wants what it wants. Taking Atticus out caused the whole story to collapse, so I had to rebuild it. But that proved more difficult than I anticipated. What happened to Snow with Atticus was so intense that it echoed throughout the new story. I tried a variety of approaches. I wrote a version where Snow spent the entire story dancing on flowers. I gave her a kingdom made of starlight that no evil could touch. I even tried to make her into a maiden on a sea voyage. But no matter how perfect it was, the story always ended with an unexpected tragedy. Snow was always harmed or, worse, killed. Maybe that was Atticus's influence rearing its ugly head. Maybe it was the Book's magic. Or maybe it was just happening because I'm not that great a writer. But, luckily, it dawned on me that I couldn't save Snow. I needed someone else to help me, someone to rescue her. After I made him into a proper suitor for my daughter, William Charming was perfect for the job, and—"

"Made me?" Charming interrupted again.

"Edited you," the witch clarified. "William, you weren't what anyone would call princely at the time."

Charming looked at her in disbelief.

"You were a hopeless womanizer with a compulsive tendency to spend too much money. You drank too much wine, and, well, you were lazy. But, you had a good heart. With a little fixing up, you were the perfect match for Snow. I rewrote you into a dashing hero on a white horse. I made you regal and dignified, romantic and strong. But, unfortunately, even you were not enough. Tragedy came upon my daughter again and again and again until I stumbled upon the flaw in my tale—without a villain, the Book was forced to harm my daughter itself.

"I don't pretend to understand exactly how it works, but I knew enough about the magic by then to know I needed a villain I could control—someone who wasn't bent on killing Snow—so I did the only thing I could think of. I wrote myself into the Book as the Wicked Queen. As the story's dark witch, I could manage the tragedy and control the pain. And it worked! The Book was satisfied—even with my character's ridiculous motivations. I mean, what kind of witch gets upset because her daughter is more beautiful? But it didn't seem to matter to the Book that nothing the Wicked Queen did made sense. The story had a dashing hero and a villain, and my daughter was safe."

"I'm still a little confused," Daphne said. "What did Mr. Seven have to do with all this?"

"I needed someone to keep an eye on William. I was worried that the changes I made to him might start to unravel. So I asked the Seven Dwarfs to be his guardians. Only Seven volunteered. It created a terrible rift between him and the others, but he agreed that what I had done was for the best."

"You changed history to save me, but you lost your daughter," Snow said. "I have hated you for hundreds of years."

The witch nodded. "A small price to pay to keep you safe."

Snow's gaze drifted off, as if she were reliving her entire life. A tear rolled down her cheek. Then she crossed the room and took her mother's hand.

Charming, however, was not quite ready for a family reunion. He stood, flustered.

"What am I?" he whispered.

"What do you mean?" Bunny asked.

"I'm an invention. I'm . . . I'm a fairy tale!"

"Billy, that's not true," Snow said.

"Do I even really love your daughter?" Charming cried, ignoring his girlfriend. "Or is that part of your story? It sure explains an awful lot: my failed marriages, my obsession with rebuilding a kingdom for us. I built this castle to fight the war, but I've been fantasizing about living in it with Snow. Is any of this real or not?"

The Wicked Queen looked to the floor. "I don't know if it's real or not, William. All I can say is, it's what I wanted."

"Well, I suppose it's time for this puppet to cut his strings," he declared, then stormed out of the cabin.

"Billy!" Snow chased after him, and Sabrina and Daphne followed. They watched him stomp across the courtyard toward the front gate. "Where are you going?"

"I don't know," he said.

"You can't leave," Snow said. "We need you. You're our leader."

While the drawbridge lowered, Charming turned to her. "I can't trust my feelings for you, Snow. I can't trust why I'm here. I don't know who I am."

"You're William Charming!" Snow said. "You're the man I love!"

"You're in love with a person who doesn't exist. In a town full of people who aren't supposed to be real, I'm the one who's a fantasy." He walked across the bridge, then disappeared into the forest.

The cold, misty damp returned the next morning. The gray sky was low and constricting, like an outgrown jacket. The weather did nothing to cheer the suffering group of people.

The Pied Piper slouched on a bench sipping from a mug of coffee. Nurse Sprat was too tired to say good morning. Everyone moved slowly, as if each step were painful.

If there was any good news, it was that Mordred and the Three Pigs were finished with the castle construction, and—aside from a few evil doors that slammed in people's faces—it was ready. Finding rooms for everyone kept people distracted from Seven's death and Charming's departure, but when everyone gathered in the castle's dining hall for breakfast, the sour mood returned.

Geppetto stood. "I've decided to dismantle the cabins," he announced. "This is a big castle, and we're going to need wood to keep it warm, especially since colder weather is coming. Right after breakfast, we can get started."

"We can't stay here, Geppetto," the Frog Prince croaked. "We need to find a place to hide."

"Hide?" the Three Blind Mice cried. "We were told we would be safe here if we joined you."

"And you would have been if more of you had turned your backs on the Scarlet Hand," the Scarecrow said. "We only changed the minds of about a hundred people, so our plan was a failure. We don't have the numbers to go up against Mirror or that Atticus lunatic. They'll find the castle soon enough, and we need to be gone before they arrive. I suggest we scatter. It will be harder to find us all if we go in different directions."

The Cowardly Lion roared in agreement.

"I hate to admit this, but I think you're right. Even Charming has left, and he's the most stubborn, prideful man I've ever met," Nurse Sprat said. "This was his plan—this whole army—and now he's gone."

Mallobarb agreed. "Maybe the prince had the right idea. Maybe we should just get lost."

"Don't talk like that. William will come back," Goldie said.

"And what if he doesn't?" a troll growled. "I took a big risk turning my back on the Hand. When they find us, they will be especially hard on those who betrayed the Master."

Puck kicked Sabrina's leg under the table. "Say something," he muttered under his breath.

"Like what?" She shrugged.

"Give them a pep talk," he shot back. "The prophecy isn't about Charming. It's about you and your sister. You're their real leader."

"But I think they're right," Sabrina admitted.

Puck slammed his hand down on the table, and it rattled as if it had been struck with a sledgehammer. Everyone turned their attention to him. "It doesn't matter if Charming comes back!" he shouted to the crowd. "We don't need him anyway. Most of us know all about the prophecy from the Council of Mirrors. Sabrina and Daphne Grimm are destined to fix this, so stop your bellyaching about the prince."

The crowd just stared at Puck for a long moment, then responded with boos and jeers.

"They're little girls!"

"Children cannot save us from the Master!"

"Sit down and shut up, fairy!"

Puck looked ready to explode, but a commotion outside captured even his attention. Trumpets were blasting. It was the signal to warn that someone was approaching the castle. Everyone raced outside to watch as the drawbridge descended to admit a crowd of Everafters. They marched into the courtyard, led by Uncle Jake.

"We have some new recruits," he crowed.

But Sabrina and the others were hardly excited. The crowd was made up of Cinderella and her husband, Tom, both quite elderly; their mice servants; Chicken Little; a potbellied robot from Oz named Tik-Tok; a gigantic caterpillar; the Cheshire Cat from Wonderland; followed by the incredibly thin Ichabod Crane. Rapunzel was with them, as well as fewer than a dozen Munchkins—all well on in years. The Old Woman Who Lived in a Shoe had brought along all of her filthy, shoeless children. Rip van Winkle hobbled in on his cane before falling asleep standing up. Surveying her new recruits, Sabrina felt the pressure of the prophecy even more.

"This army gets bigger and stronger with every second!" Puck cheered, but no one responded. They seemed just as disheartened as Sabrina.

"It also gets more pathetic," Pinocchio grumbled. His father glared at him, and the boy flushed with shame.

"It's time to tell everyone your plan," Puck said, pulling the sisters to the side.

"We don't have a plan," Sabrina whispered.

"Duh! But they don't need to know that. Just fake it 'til you make it! That's what I do. Most of the time, I have no idea what I'm doing, but if I told everyone that, they wouldn't put their faith in me."

"Actually, it's pretty obvious that you never have any idea what you're doing," Daphne said.

"Listen, these people need heroes, and whether it makes any sense or not, you're it," Puck said. "As a ruthless villain, I know very little about being a do-gooder, but I do know that heroes are never unsure of themselves. You have to be confident, even if you're just pretending. If someone asks you a question, answer them—even if you don't know what you're talking about! If they ask you if the moon is made out of cheese, the two of you say, 'Absolutely! I've been there! It was delicious!'"

"So being a hero is all about being a good liar?" Daphne asked.

Puck winked at her. "Now you're getting it!"

"I'm not going to lie to them. We're in a life-or-death situation. They deserve to know the truth," Sabrina said.

Puck looked angry enough to pull out his own hair. "I can't be-lieve you. You know what? I'm seriously reconsidering marrying you." His wings popped out of his back, and he was in the air and gone before Sabrina could inform him, once again, that they were never getting married.

Geppetto led Pinocchio to Sabrina. "My son and I will prepare some rooms for the new arrivals."

Pinocchio rolled his eyes. "Papa, now that the army is growing, maybe we can delegate my chores. Many of our new soldiers can split wood and heat water for washing."

"Everyone works," the old man said, looking at his son with disappointment. "That's part of being an adult. You want to become a man, correct?"

"But aren't there many different types of work?" Pinocchio argued, his voice growing shriller with each passing second. "Should those with a genius-level intellect dig ditches alongside the ancient and feebleminded? I should be assigned to tasks that take advantage of my learning and world experience. Take Mr. Canis, for instance. He is really quite old, past the point of usefulness, yet he's still involved in making decisions in this camp. He should be making beds and—"

Geppetto grabbed his son by the ear and dragged him toward the castle.

Unfortunately, Mr. Canis heard every insulting word as he and Red approached. The old man's face fell.

"Come along, little one," Mr. Canis said to the little girl. "There are beds to make."

Red slipped her hand into his. He looked down at it but did not pull away. Together, they wandered toward the castle.

As the day passed, more recruits trickled into the camp. Among them were Robin Hood and his band of Merry Men. King Arthur and his knights followed. The king informed Sabrina and the others that a wave of paranoia was infecting the Hand. Everyone was accusing one another of being a spy. Since Arthur, Robin, and all their men actually were spies, it had seemed wise to leave Mirror's army before fingers were pointed at them.

Sabrina watched the recruits settle into the camp. She was happy to see some actual soldiers walking around the castle, but their little army was still no match for the one Mirror had built.

"Ready for your next lesson?"

Sabrina looked up to see Daphne and the Scarecrow approaching. "I thought we were done with lessons," she said. "Since we're both sort of terrible at fighting."

The Scarecrow shook his head. "I'm not here to teach you how to fight. I'm going to teach you military history and strategy. You may not know this, but I was once the emperor of Oz. I had to defend the city from attacks."

"How did that go?" Daphne asked.

"I was overthrown by an army of little girls carrying knitting needles," the Scarecrow admitted. "But right now, I'm the best you've got."

The girls and the Scarecrow found some privacy in the Room

of Reflections. The guardians watched from their mirrors while the Scarecrow paced back and forth, leaving strands of hay in his wake.

"All right, girls. We've got to cover ten thousand years of war in one afternoon," he said, and then turned to the mirrors. "I'm hoping you can help."

Sabrina and Daphne paid close attention as the Scarecrow used the mirrors to illustrate important military campaigns throughout the history of the world. Each mirror became an audiovisual display, showing portraits of military leaders and grand paintings of battlefields.

The Scarecrow lectured about Caesar's invasion of Gaul in 58 BC, a major domino to fall in Rome's conquest of the globe. Then, a painting of Genghis Khan appeared in the mirrors as the Scarecrow discussed the Mongol invasion of China in the thirteenth century. The girls learned of the invasion of Germany in 1630, led by Gustavus Adolphus of Sweden, and how his combination of artillery, soldiers, and horses became the template for modern war strategies. In a few short hours, the sisters Grimm covered the campaigns of storied military leaders like Alexander the Great, Hannibal, Frederick the Great, and Napoleon.

Then, the Scarecrow shifted gears to talk about strategy. He specifically discussed how small groups of soldiers managed to defeat huge armies, pointing to the Battle of Thermopylae, when a few hundred Spartans beat back hundreds of thousands of Persian troops. He pointed to the American Revolution, in which the military fought off a much bigger invading force by using forests and rivers to their advantage. By the time he was finished, Sabrina's head was spinning.

"Any questions?" the Scarecrow asked.

The girls never got to respond. The door to the room flew open, and a group of men pushed their way inside. The first was King Arthur, followed by Sir Galahad, Sir Lancelot, and a dozen other knights. Robin Hood was right behind them with his Merry Men. All of them were arguing angrily as they jockeyed to be at the front of the strange parade.

"We heard war planning is going on in here," King Arthur said.

"Not at all," the Scarecrow said, but he was shouted down by the others.

"We demand to participate!" Robin Hood cried.

Henry pushed his way into the crowded room. "What is this about?"

"You have placed the fate of this army in the hands of little girls!" Sir Lancelot roared.

"It's madness!" Little John added.

"What can children know about planning a battle?" Sir Galahad asked.

"We'll take over from here," King Arthur said.

The paintings in the mirrors vanished, and the guardians returned.

Arden shook her head. "These little girls will save the world, gentlemen. It is prophecy."

King Arthur's face turned beet red. "The prophecy is bogus! We've seen what the Master and his Scarlet Hand are capable of, and two little girls are not going to challenge him."

"Arthur, you're not needed in here," Henry said. "The Council already told us, the girls will lead the rest of us. I don't like it any better than you do, but—"

"Your family is filled with insolent whelps," Arthur interrupted. "You Grimms think you know better than the rest of us. You think you're so wise. Well, look around, Henry. How are your big ideas working out for you now?"

Henry stepped toward Arthur until they were nearly nose to nose. "I said, get lost."

"Dad, let them stay," Sabrina implored. "Let them all stay. Arthur is right. We don't know what we're doing. And if anyone in the camp has real military experience, it's him. I think Arthur and Robin and their men can be a big help."

"Thank goodness, there is some sense in this family after all," the king said, turning back to the mirrors. "I need to see maps of the town!"

His request magically materialized in the reflections.

"Now, it's obvious to me what needs to be done," Arthur continued. "We use the element of surprise and attack a small group of the Hand in the very center of town. When the rest of the goons hear about it, they will come running to help. But we'll be ready for them, picking them off one by one."

"Henry, you and your girls can go. We'll let you know if we need you," Robin said.

It was clear they weren't wanted, so Sabrina, Daphne, and Henry stepped out of the Room of Reflections, and into the Hall of Wonders. There, they found Pinocchio waiting for them. He was sitting on the floor, close enough to have heard the conversation.

"They're morons," Pinocchio said. "The plan is pure gibberish."

"And you can do better?" Sabrina said.

"Of course I can," Pinocchio said. "Even a monkey could tell you, it's better to stay hidden and in small groups. The army should lure the Hand into the woods and then use the trees as cover. It's the same strategy General Marion used during the American Revolutionary War. His men attacked from the swamps of South Carolina. They called him the Swamp Fox, and—"

"And we should trust you to have our best interests at heart because . . . ?" Sabrina interrupted.

Pinocchio flushed, but instead of lashing out, he got to his feet and walked away. "Well, I tried," he called over his shoulder.

"He might be right," Henry offered.

"But we can't trust him, Dad," Daphne said.

He nodded. "Arthur and Robin Hood are both very smart. I'm sure they can come up with something to help us win."

"Better them than a couple of little kids," Sabrina said.

Henry took them to their room and tucked them into bed. He kissed them each on the cheek and told them not to worry.

Since the Council had spilled their silly prophecy, Sabrina had felt as if she were carrying the weight of the world on her shoulders. In some ways, it was nice to have some grown-ups taking charge. That night, she got her first good sleep in days.

The Scarecrow came by very early the next morning. He led the girls back to the Room of Reflections.

There, they found the knights and Merry Men, still making plans. They were told that Robin Hood's strategy from the night before was considered the best of several approaches. Robin explained the plan in detail, but Sabrina didn't understand most of it, only that she had no physical role in the battle. All she had to do was present the plan to the army. Arthur felt that would be enough to please the prophecy.

After breakfast, Sabrina stood before the camp and explained what the adults had spent the night planning. King Arthur interrupted her several times to explain the more complicated details. Sabrina marveled at his command of the crowd. Like Charming, he had a natural charisma that made people want to follow him. When he finished, the crowd cheered. She watched them disperse—eager to get started on preparations. They would leave the camp at dinnertime to head back to town and confront the Scarlet Hand.

All of their faces were full of hope. All of them, that is, except Puck. He stood off to the side, arms crossed, face etched with disappointment.

"Would you let me know exactly when it's my time to come and rescue you from this fight so that I can be ready?" he snapped.

Sabrina threw her hands up in the air. "What is it with you lately?"

Puck's wings fluttered like a hummingbird's. "Never mind," he said, rising off the ground.

"No! You get back here!" she cried, snatching his leg before he could fly away. Sabrina was tired of Puck's nasty attitude. She wanted an explanation.

"Let me go," he demanded.

"Not until you tell me why you're so moody," she said.

Puck tried to shake her off, but he couldn't. "I'm warning you!"

"Not a chance," Sabrina said, and then she was rocketed into the sky. She hung on to Puck's pant leg with all her might.

"You had your chance, loser," the boy said as they sailed over the castle and out into the woods.

"Puck! Put me down," Sabrina cried. She looked down. She was too high to survive the fall if she lost her grip. "I can't hold on for that long!"

"Wah! Wah! Wah!!!! It's just like you to need someone to save you," Puck mocked. "Poor donkeyface can never do anything for herself."

Sabrina's aching arms gave way, and she fell. The air whipped through her hair. A tree limb smashed into her leg. She was sure that she would hit the ground next, but then something had her—something strong. She looked at Puck as he set her on the ground. He looked angry.

"Don't you ever do that again! Are you trying to kill yourself?" he yelled.

"I told you I couldn't hold on," Sabrina said. "What's wrong with you? Why are you being so mean?"

"What's wrong is how you just gave up," Puck said.

"Huh?"

"Every time I think you're going to stop being pathetic, you just throw in the towel," he said.

"Sorry to be such a disappointment," she replied.

"Ever since you slithered into my life, you have done nothing but complain about your lack of control: 'No one listens to me. No one pays attention. Everyone treats me like a baby.' Boohoo-hoo! They treat you like a kid because every time you get a chance to grow up, you choke!" Puck cried.

"Look who's talking!"

"I'm a trickster! I'm supposed to act like a child! You, on the other hand, don't want to grow up because you like having everyone look after you. Look what's happened since you came to town. You've come face-to-face with every kind of monster there is, and—"

"And I've lived to tell the tale!" she shouted.

"Because someone else had to save you, Sabrina. It's been

me, or Canis, or your grandmother, or your uncle. But now, when you've got a real chance to actually take charge, you hand it over to those nutters Arthur and Robin Hood!"

"I know you can't possibly understand this with that tiny pea brain of yours, but we're in the middle of a war. I need help from people who know what they're doing. I can't run around using your 'fake it 'til you make it' approach. People will die," she snapped, and then she turned to head back to the castle.

Puck leaped over her and blocked her path. "I'm sorry, but you were at the whole mirrors-speaking-prophecy thing, right? They said you will lead this army. Not the king. Not the thief. You! I don't like it any better than you do, but you're the star of this show."

"But I don't know how to lead an army!" Sabrina argued.

"When it comes to saving the world, no one knows what they're doing. But heroes don't dump their responsibilities onto someone else. Have you forgotten that the old lady is out there in those woods? Are you going to put her life in the hands of people who don't care about her?" Puck asked. "Sabrina, it's up to you."

Sabrina pushed past him. "You think everything is so easy, but it's not, Puck."

"The old lady would expect more from you!" he shouted after her.

8

OCTOBER 20

As I write this, I'm sitting in the courtyard, watching the troops prepare. I'm super worried about this plan. Pinocchio's words still ring in my ears, as do Puck's.

But I don't know what to do. And, because I don't know, I think putting the decision in more experienced hands is the right thing to do. My family and I are going to watch the battle unfold from the Room of Reflections. Canis will be joining us, since Robin Hood flat out told him that he's too old to join the fight. He's not happy about it. If the Wolf was still inside him, I don't think Robin's head would still be attached to his body. I hope all these people come back. They've become my friends and family. I fear for every one of their lives.

As planned, Baba Yaga's house stormed the town square, providing the ultimate distraction. Word spread fast among the members of the Hand. The villains raced to confront it, shelling it with rocks, sticks, clubs, and magic. Sabrina and her family cheered as they watched through the magic mirrors.

Baba Yaga, the Wicked Queen, and Morgan le Fay defeated dozens with magical assaults. Robin Hood's men rained arrows down from atop buildings. The Pied Piper and Beauty lulled beasties away from the fight. Goldie and her bears stampeded approaching trolls. Even Puck transformed into an African elephant and used his tusks to swat aside approaching members of the Hand.

It appeared that Arthur and Robin's plan was going to work, but then things changed very quickly. A mass of trolls, goblins, and ghouls swept into Main Street like a deadly tsunami, all of them wearing red handprints on their chests. They destroyed everything in their path. They were followed by a wave of knights and princes and witches, all fighting on Mirror's behalf. Soon, there were nearly three thousand members of Mirror's army in the square, and Sabrina's feeble forces were overcome. Within a few short minutes, Sabrina's entire army was scattered, chased away by members of the Hand.

People died in the battle. Sir Kay was struck with a hammer by an enormous piglike creature. Mallobarb was killed by a stray arrow. Tik-Tok was trampled. When he fell over, a mob stomped and smashed him until there was nothing left of him but springs and sprockets. Sabrina and the others watched in helpless horror.

Veronica took Daphne, Basil, and Red out of the room so they wouldn't have to witness any more tragedies. Sabrina stayed behind. Mr. Canis placed a reassuring hand on her shoulder, but she shook him off. This was all her fault.

"I should prepare the infirmary for the injured," Nurse Sprat said. Others went along to help her, and soon Sabrina was alone with her uncle and Pinocchio.

"This isn't your fault, Grimm," Pinocchio said. "They knew you were unsure of what to do, and they took advantage of you. You can't let them steamroll you next time."

"Next time?" Sabrina said. "There won't be a next time. You saw what happened. We can't win this."

"Yes, we can," the little boy said, turning to make his way to the door. "When you're ready to get serious, come find me."

Sabrina turned to her uncle. "Any advice?"

"I wish I had some for you, 'Brina. This is a disaster, and I think we can forget new recruits for now. I have to find another way to get—" Uncle Jake suddenly stopped himself.

Sabrina was suspicious, but she didn't press Jake on his meaning.

"I should go help get things ready for the wounded," he said, and then left her alone.

Sabrina continued to watch the chaos for a while longer, until the images of the battle dissolved and the guardians of the mirrors reappeared. They watched her with pitying eyes.

"Now what?"

"Excuse me?" the fish-faced guardian gurgled. Her name was Namoren, and she looked after an undersea kingdom called the Trench of Wonders. Up until that moment, she had never spoken. Now, her words were angry and frustrated. "We told you what to do the first time, and you ignored us. Now your friends are dead!"

"It's too much responsibility!" Sabrina cried. "Why am I the only one who can save the world?"

"There are so many variables," Donovan offered.

"Many paths to the future, all intertwining, all shifting," Arden added. "Your refusal to embrace your destiny has made this particular path even more difficult."

"So if I had just done what you told me, no one would have died?" Sabrina asked.

"Child, you are trying to save the world. Of course people are going die," Titan said.

Tears flooded down Sabrina's cheeks. "I don't understand what my sister and I are supposed to do. You know the future! Just tell us what to do, and we'll do it. We'll do anything!"

"Oh, Sabrina, we're sorry, but that's forbidden," Harry said from his Hotel of Wonders. "We can only tell you the future, not how to get there."

Sabrina leaped up and lunged at Harry. "You have to give me something to work with!"

Harry shook his head.

She darted to Arden's mirror and pounded on it. "How do I save everyone?"

"Do what you have always done," Reggie said from his place on the other side of the room.

"What is that supposed to mean?" she demanded.

The faces faded from the mirrors, and in their place, she saw something she did not expect: herself. Each of the mirrors showed a different moment of her life. In one, she was helping Daphne out of the second-floor bedroom window of Granny's house. In another, she was locking Mrs. Robinson in the closet so that they could escape her foster home. Sabrina saw herself racing through subterranean tunnels hunting for her family with nothing but a shovel and a broken arm. She saw herself accidentally killing a giant. She saw herself clutching Oz's hot-air balloon as it dragged her off the Empire State Building's observation deck. She saw herself helping everyone break Mr. Canis out of the town jail, destroying the bank with the Horn of the North Wind, fooling the Headless Horseman with his own head, sneaking past Ichabod Crane as she and Daphne tried to free Jack the Giant Killer, and shoving Puck into a swimming pool. She even saw herself tiptoeing past Ms. Smirt's office at the orphanage.

"Why are you showing me this?" Sabrina asked. "I don't understand."

"THIS IS THE GIRL WHO SAVES THE WORLD," the mirrors answered as one. "SABRINA GRIMM, QUEEN OF THE—"

"Sneaks!" she gasped, finishing their sentence. "This is what makes me special? Being sneaky is what will help me save my grandmother and stop Mirror?"

The faces returned, all of them nodding. Reggie gestured for Sabrina to approach him, smiling from ear to ear. "The rules say telling you is a no-no, but if I were a betting man, I'd put all my money on 'yes.'"

"In your life, you've mastered the great art of deception," Titan said.

"You have the rare ability to pull the wool over anyone's eyes," Donovan added.

"Plus, you often make people regret taking you for granted. You have a gift for the unexpected, for taking your opponents by surprise," Harry said. "You've used it a million times to keep your sister safe. That is the skill that sets you apart from others."

"And your heart, honey," Fanny said. "You don't let a lot of people visit it, but once they are inside, you love them with all you are. Those are the things that will win this war, save the world, and rescue your grandmother."

"It's time you let the Queen of the Sneaks do her job, sister," Donovan said.

She wiped her tears on her shirt and nodded. "OK. I get it."

☙

When her army returned, Sabrina already knew what needed to be done. Much to everyone's surprise—especially Arthur and Robin's—she took charge, and the others listened.

The wounded were tended to in Sprat's infirmary, and the dead were prepared for burial. She stopped the knights from digging their graves inside the camp and insisted they be laid to rest in the forest instead.

"Why?" Friar Tuck asked as he prepared a sermon for their last rites.

"Because we won't be here much longer," she told him, but she refused to say any more. Sabrina wasn't going to let the adults bully her any longer.

As the sunset's orange glow lit the horizon, Sabrina's army said good-bye to the bravely fallen: Mallobarb, Tik-Tok, Sir Kay, Sir Gawain, the Silver Pigeon, and Will Scarlet. When they left the graves, the troops reassembled outside the castle. Sabrina called for everyone's attention. Their exhausted, beaten-down faces made her hesitate, but only for a moment. What Sabrina was about to tell them might push some over the edge. But for the first time in a long time, she felt she was doing the right thing.

"You deserve an apology. The mirrors told me to lead you, but I was afraid. I haven't fought in any wars, so I put my responsibility in the hands of a few well-meaning people. They failed, but I don't blame them. They were doing what they thought was right, too. Unfortunately, this prophecy is not about them. It's about my sister and me. It's ironic, because ever since my sister and I showed up in this town, I've complained that no one takes me seriously—"

"I can vouch for that," Daphne added.

"But I wasn't taking myself seriously, either. I couldn't think of anything special about my sister and me that would help us stop Mirror and the Hand, and then some friends helped me see myself clearly. Once upon a time—before any of you met the sisters Grimm—Daphne and I had a reputation as very successful juvenile delinquents. We were good at moving quietly, good at running and hiding, and good with keys and locks. We were good at getting each other out of tough situations, and we were very good at tricking people."

Daphne looked up at her, confused but eager to hear Sabrina's plan.

"What I'm saying is that Daphne and I are experts in the art of shenanigans," she continued.

Daphne grinned so wide, Sabrina worried her face might split in two.

"It's about time!" Puck cheered. For the first time in days, he smiled at her. It was oddly comforting.

The Cowardly Lion growled. "What do you have in mind?"

"Well, my military strategist has a brilliant plan," she said, locking eyes with Pinocchio. He gave her a curious look, then returned her knowing smile. "Meanwhile, you should all pack your things. Pack everything you can carry. We're abandoning the castle."

"Abandoning the castle? That's crazy," the Widow squawked. "This is the only safe place for us."

"Not anymore. If the Hand isn't on their way, they will be soon enough."

The crowd broke into worried chatter.

"Where will we go?" Cinderella asked.

"Into the forest," Sabrina replied.

"And what are we going to do in there?" Goldilocks asked.

Pinocchio lifted his hand for attention. "We're going to lay traps, build cages, and create every obstacle we possibly can to make the Hand's lives miserable. We'll attack in small groups, capturing one or two of them at a time. Then we'll slink back into the trees and disappear."

"But there are thousands of them," Little John said. "We'll never catch them all."

"Soon, there won't be thousands of them anymore. I know this is not easy for you, but you're just going to have to trust me," Sabrina said. "Where are our birds?"

"On patrol," the Widow said.

"When they get back, I need them to deliver a message. And, Scarecrow, I want you to write it," Sabrina said.

"Of course. What would you like it to say?"

"It's another offer to the rest of the Hand to join us. Let them know this is the final time we're reaching out. It's their last chance."

"Do you think any of them will listen?" Beauty asked. She was clearly still holding out hope for her husband and daughter.

"If they don't, they're going to regret it."

Henry eyed Sabrina curiously. "What are you two planning?"

"Don't worry, Dad. We're good at this stuff," Daphne crowed.

As the hours passed, the small, tired army packed. Sabrina instructed everyone to keep both magical and non-magical weapons on their persons, no matter how cumbersome. Carrying food was also encouraged.

"Can you get your coven to pull it off?" Sabrina asked her sister after the two went over the plan in more detail.

Daphne rolled her eyes. "Daphne's Fabulous Ladies of Magic can do anything. I just need to get the spell from Uncle Jake. Apparently, you have to hold it in your hand to make it work."

"We can't screw this up," Sabrina said.

"You worry too much," Daphne said. "My girls put the *pow* in *powerful.*"

That night, Sabrina couldn't sleep. She sat by the window in her room and watched the sky, waiting for the Widow to return from delivering her message. The more time passed, the more nervous she got. Eventually, she gave up on sleep and went outside for some air. She found her father at a picnic table in the yard, clearly nervous himself.

"Can't sleep?" she asked him.

He shook his head. "I'm worried about you and Daphne and Basil, worried about your uncle, my mom, all these people . . . Your mother kicked me out of bed. I was keeping her awake."

Sabrina sat next to him and rested her head on his shoulder.

"Can't be easy for you, either," her father said. "Responsibility is hard, huh?"

Sabrina nodded. "I don't know how you and Mom do it. You must go out of your mind worrying about us."

"That's probably the best way to describe it. There are times I'm so angry, I want to pull my hair out, and other times I'm so scared, I have to go somewhere and cry."

"I guess we haven't exactly made it easy."

Henry laughed. "That's the understatement of the year."

"I'll do better," Sabrina promised.

"You're doing fine, considering the circumstances. In case you didn't know it, a girl your age isn't supposed to be planning a military campaign," Henry said. "Just do me a favor, and remind yourself every once in a while that your family loves you."

Sabrina nodded. "You do the same. Oh, here she comes."

The Widow landed on the picnic table. "Well, I spread the word, but I wouldn't get your hopes up. Most of them just laughed.

They reminded me that they're winning the war, but I reminded them that they're fighting the Grimms. That gave them something to think about. If I knew what you were planning, I might have been able to craft a better argument."

"Not yet, but soon," Sabrina promised. "Why don't you go and get some rest? Tomorrow is going to be a busy day."

The Widow wobbled toward the castle, but she stopped for a moment to look back at Sabrina. "Hey, kid. We're all behind you."

Just then, Daphne raced past the Widow, and she came to a screeching halt in front of Sabrina.

"Uh, I need to talk to you," she said, locking eyes with her sister.

"About?"

"It's . . . um . . . about our messy room," Daphne said.

"Huh?"

Daphne yanked Sabrina out of her seat. "Sorry, Dad. Sabrina's a slob, and I'm sick of it."

She dragged Sabrina halfway across the courtyard before she would explain anything.

"What is this about?" Sabrina demanded.

Daphne frowned. "Someone stole the Book again!"

"No one stole it." Sabrina sighed. You just misplaced it, again."

"I didn't misplace it!" Daphne cried. "Someone took it!"

Sabrina rolled her eyes. "Listen, I need some sleep. When you find wherever you hid it, let me know. Or better yet, maybe you should be extra careful and lock it up so that you don't lose it for good. It's dangerous, Daphne! And if someone actually did get their hands on it, they could do a lot of damage."

"I'm being careful!" Daphne shouted as she went back into the castle.

The next morning, Sabrina took a long bath, knowing it might be the last one she would get for a while. She washed her hair and face and brushed her teeth. She put on her ratty T-shirt, jeans, and trusty sneakers. When she stepped outside, she found the rest of her family helping the Everafters load carts with their meager belongings.

When it was time to roll out, the troops marched over the drawbridge and into the forest. Buzzflower hovered overhead, zapping each of them with purple dust from her wand. They vanished right before Sabrina's eyes.

"There's too much stuff," Robin Hood complained. "We need to travel light."

"We're storing it in the woods," Sabrina explained. "When the birds did their flyover, they found a cave near the base of the mountain. It's well hidden and deep enough to keep everyone's things safe. We're sending all the young children and elderly there, as well, at least until this is over."

"You make it sound as if this will all be over quickly," Hood commented.

"Fingers crossed," Sabrina said.

Snow White approached. "I just don't understand the plan."

"It's better that you don't," Sabrina replied. "Just keep your bō staff at the ready."

"Are you going to blow this place up?" Mr. Boarman asked. "Seems like a waste."

"Who told you that?" Sabrina asked.

"Puck."

"We aren't blowing anything up." Sabrina shook her head. "Mr. Boarman, can you remind everyone who's still here to listen for the signal? When they hear it, that means it's time to go. They'll only have five minutes after the signal to get out of camp. And if they don't, they're in for a world of trouble."

Red and Canis rushed forward.

"A world of trouble?" the old man asked.

Sabrina nodded. "Mr. Canis, I need something from you, and it's not going to make you happy. I need you to go with the children to the cave."

She could feel Canis's disappointment come off him in waves.

"This isn't babysitting," she continued. "You have to keep them safe and calm. My baby brother will be with you. There is no one in the world I trust with him more than you."

"I'll help," Red said.

"Very well. I guess I won't be needing these weapons."

Canis sighed, and he dropped his backpack from his shoulders. A jar rolled out onto the ground. Inside was a terrible black shape, snapping and scratching at the glass, desperate to escape. The evil spirit known as the Big Bad Wolf was trapped inside that jar. Canis scooped it up and put it inside his long coat, as if it were nothing. Then he turned to Red. "Gather the little ones, child, and any slow-moving animals that can't fight."

Red smiled, though she looked just as nervous as Sabrina. She ran off to complete her task without a word.

"You're good for her," Sabrina said to Mr. Canis. "You're like the father she never had. It would be sad for her to lose you."

The old man lowered his eyes.

"He had his uses," he muttered, speaking of the incredible strength and power that the Wolf gave him.

"I'd take you before him, a million times over," Sabrina said, and then she watched as Canis hobbled off after Red, making his way carefully with his cane.

By midafternoon, the birds had returned to report that the supplies and children were safe in the woods. Sabrina could move forward with her plan.

Arthur and Robin dutifully checked the castle room by room for any useful weapons or supplies that might have been left behind. Others searched the few cabins that remained. Sabrina walked around the grounds, poking her head into the blacksmith tent. She found a hammer that might be helpful and set it in the last cart to leave the grounds. The kitchen was completely empty, as was Nurse Sprat's medical tent.

Sabrina found her uncle and Morgan standing over the graves of the ones they loved. Daphne had told them everything the girls were planning. It seemed only fair.

Morgan noticed Sabrina standing behind her. "I see how this is necessary, and I support your plan, Sabrina, but . . . it's more than I can . . . It's just so wrong," she said.

"I'm sorry," Sabrina said. "I knew you two would suffer the most from what we're going to do."

"I feel like I'm abandoning her," Jake whispered, as if he were afraid Briar Rose might hear.

He leaned down to pick a rose off of Briar's grave and slid it into one of his shirt pockets. He closed his eyes tightly, as if preparing to jump out of a plane. "OK, I'm ready. Let's do this before I change my mind."

Sabrina took his hand. "I think she would understand."

The trio headed to the courtyard, where Sabrina found the army—her army—waiting. She climbed up on a little chair and looked out across the crowd of faces. Many of them had never held a sword or a bow. Some had never even been in a fistfight, but they were the bravest people she had ever met.

"Thank you for being patient. I know you're all a little freaked out because I've kept what we're doing a secret, but you can't be sneaky if everyone knows what you're up to. So, let me explain my plan," Sabrina said. "We're going to lure the Hand into this castle—as many as we can. You're going to fight until you hear the signal. Then, you're going to run! Get away from the castle, off of the grounds, as far away as you can. You all know where the gathering site is—meet there if you get separated from the others. That's when our war really begins. I wish you all luck. Daphne, are the witches ready?"

Daphne pushed her way through the crowd. "They are."

"All right, Buzzflower, drop the cloaking spell," Sabrina called.

"Drop the spell? The Hand will be able to see the castle. Are you sure?" the fairy godmother asked.

Sabrina nodded. The crowd murmured anxiously, and Buzz-flower looked uncertain, but she waved her wand in the air. Suddenly, the sky went from blue to sparkly purple. Tiny crystals drifted down from above, like snow.

"Here we go," Henry said.

Sabrina took her sister's hand. "Any luck with the Book?"

Daphne shrugged. "I told you, I didn't misplace it. Someone stole it, I swear."

Sabrina fought back a wave of panic as she scanned the crowd again. *Is Daphne right? Did one of our own steal the Book of Everafter?* On the one hand, there might be a traitor in their ranks who intended to use the Book to hurt their effort. On the other hand, it might be even worse to leave it behind here, inside the camp. Neither was a great option, but there was nothing they could do about it now.

Sabrina turned to the crowd. "Open the gates!"

"Wait? Really?" Puck cried.

"Yep," she said.

"That's insane," he said. "I love it."

"You're just going to let the Hand walk through the front door?" the Cheshire Cat asked.

"She knows what she's doing!" Veronica said, trying to calm the crowd.

"Get ready!" the Widow called. "They'll be here any second."

"How do you know?" Beauty asked.

"Because Sabrina told me to tell them where they could find us."

"She did *what?*" Snow cried, holding her bō staff above her head.

Sabrina could already feel the rumbling of approaching feet and the clanking of eager swords. The first wave of attackers rushed through the gate and let out a mighty war cry.

"Fight until you hear the signal!" Sabrina shouted, and jumped off her chair. She gathered her family and crouched behind a hay cart.

The first wave of the Hand was met by Arthur's knights and Robin Hood's Merry Men. Sword clanged against sword, shield slammed against shield.

The next attack came from the Ice Queen. The temperature dropped wildly, prickling Sabrina's skin. The witch waved her hand at a few of Arthur's knights, and they were immediately encased in solid blocks of ice. Luckily, Mordred was ready, and he quickly warmed them with a wave of heat. They were soggy but alive.

The third wave was a motley crew of monsters of all shapes and sizes. They viciously swung clubs and hammers. Two Merry Men were killed in a few short moments, and dozens more creatures piled through the doorway with every passing second.

"Widow, how many more are coming?" Sabrina shouted to her eye in the sky.

The crow was circling the battle. A moment later, she landed at Sabrina's side, looking troubled. "At least a thousand in sight, probably more on the way."

"Good. It's working just the way I hoped," Sabrina said.

Puck was in the middle of the action, and Sabrina kept a particularly close eye on him. The boy was arrogant—much too confident in his own abilities. He fought like war was just play, and though he slashed and poked and leaped about with a smirk on his face, his opponents aimed to kill. She cringed just watching but then reminded herself that Puck was nearly four thousand years old. He was a pro at staying alive.

Sabrina's attention was torn away from Puck as another wave of villains stormed the castle, this one made up of magical animals. She saw the Six Swans and Hans the Hedgehog, Shere Khan, and

the Ugly Duckling. Large creatures with the bodies of bears and the faces of cats leaped into the fighting with merciless ferocity. She remembered seeing them in Oz when she and Daphne had visited the Book of Everafter.

They were followed by a wave of strange Everafters Sabrina had never seen before. There was a woman who carried her head in her hands, a cat who appeared to be made of crystal, a girl with a body of patchwork quilts, a stampede of intelligent horses, and a fleet of table forks that leaped about, stabbing at everything within reach.

The next wave carried wizards, witches, and mechanical men. They raced across the drawbridge and joined their comrades. A cheer went up among the villains as if they'd already won the battle. Sabrina couldn't help but smile. That was exactly what she wanted them to think. *Keep coming*, she thought to herself, *every last one of you.*

She turned to Daphne, and the little girl smiled back. "Shenanigans?"

Sabrina nodded, then shouted to her troops, "RETREAT!"

"What are you up to?" Henry asked.

"You don't want to know yet, Mr. Grimm," Pinocchio said with a smug smile as he approached.

"Time to go!" Sabrina shouted. She darted through the courtyard and across the drawbridge with her father, her sister, Pinocchio, and Uncle Jake in tow. Jake punched and kicked anyone who got too close, knocking some assailants into the moat. Along the way they collected the Cowardly Lion and the Scarecrow, Boarman, Swineheart, the Pied Piper, and Wendell. Goldilocks and her bears joined their retreat, followed by Rapunzel and Chicken Little.

They were nearly across the courtyard when Uncle Jake came to an abrupt stop. On the ground lay Mayor Heart, injured. He looked at her in disgust, but then he reached down and helped her to her feet.

"I-I won't go quietly," Heart stammered.

"You're not my prisoner, at least not yet. But I suggest you come with us right now," Jake said.

"Jacob, what is going on?" Henry asked. "Leave her! Heart can't be trusted!"

Jake turned back to Heart. "Are you coming, Your Majesty?"

She nodded to Jake, and he helped her escape into the woods.

More of Sabrina's army trickled out of the castle grounds. Robin Hood and Little John helped an injured Friar Tuck limp across the drawbridge. The Cheshire Cat was behind them. The Frog Prince followed with his wife and daughter in tow.

"How many more are in there?" Sabrina asked.

"I don't really know," the Frog Prince replied.

Beauty darted through the gate with tears streaming down her face.

"Beauty?"

"My husband won't listen to reason," she sobbed. "I begged him, and Natalie won't leave his side!"

"We could force them," Sabrina offered, turning to the Wicked Queen.

"You'd be a fool to go back in there, child. I'm afraid they're lost to us now," Bunny said sadly.

From inside the castle walls, a cheer rang out. As Sabrina had hoped, the Hand wanted to demoralize their enemies by celebrating their conquest of the camp immediately.

"I can't believe we just let them take the castle!" King Arthur shouted as he charged through the gate. "We're completely defenseless now."

"They didn't take the castle. We gave it to them," Sabrina corrected, and then turned to her sister. "Let's do it."

Daphne nodded. She turned to the Wicked Queen, who was just crossing the drawbridge along with Baba Yaga and Morgan. "Girls," said Bunny, "let's have some fun."

Bunny, Morgan, and the old crone turned as one back toward the camp and unleashed spells that kept the Hand from following Sabrina's army. The magic slammed into members of the Hand like a tidal wave, keeping them trapped inside the castle grounds. Meanwhile, Daphne took a yellowing piece of paper from her pocket and unfolded it.

"That's not what I think it is, is it?" Henry demanded.

"It's Wilhelm's barrier spell," Daphne said, marveling at the paper. It was written in a language Sabrina couldn't read. Daphne approached her coven and gave the spell to Morgan. "OK, just like we planned: You read it, Ms. Lancaster handles the stones, and Baba puts on the light show."

"Wait! Where's Puck?" Sabrina yelled. Panicked, she searched the crowd around her, desperate for a sight of his filthy hoodie or his unruly mop of hair, but he wasn't there. She searched the sky, but he wasn't there, either. Without a second thought, she ran for the gates.

"Sabrina, no!" Henry cried out after her.

"I can't leave him! Daphne, get the spell ready!"

"I'm going with you!" Beauty shouted, and ran after Sabrina.

Beyond the gates, the two found an ugly celebration, so they were able to slip by unnoticed. They pushed through the crowd, weaving in and out of monsters, until they stumbled upon Puck. He was still fighting a disgusting-looking creature with a pig snout and huge tusks. The beast had his foot planted on Puck's throat and would not let him up.

"Oh, hey," Puck said when he saw Sabrina. "Sorry, I'm a little busy right now."

"Is this yours?" the creature snorted at her.

"Yes," Sabrina said.

"Then fight me for him," he grunted.

The creature swung at her, but she dodged his attack at the last possible second. She noticed a nasty red wound on his rib cage, fresh and bleeding. She remembered her father's lesson about using her opponent's weaknesses against them. Without another thought, she leaped and kicked at his ribs. The brute bellowed and fell to one knee. With all her might, Sabrina punched him in the side of the head. He fell over, unconscious, and set Puck loose.

"Well, how's that for a change of pace? You saved me. What is that, your one to my seven zillion saves?" Puck mocked her.

"You're hilarious," Sabrina said flatly.

"Grab on and I'll fly us out of here," he said.

"Wait, where's Beauty? She was right behind me five seconds ago."

Sabrina scanned the crowd, but only for a moment. Puck grabbed her by the waist and rocketed skyward, narrowly dodging the spears and arrows flung at them from below.

"Seven zillion and one," Puck crowed.

"Do you see Beauty anywhere down there?" Sabrina asked. "We can't leave her."

"There!" Puck shouted, pointing to the castle gate. Beauty and the Beast were arguing. Beast had his wife's arm clenched tightly in his hairy claw. She was sobbing.

"We have to help her," Sabrina insisted.

"Um, isn't your sister about to—"

"Just do it."

Puck floated back to the ground, mere feet from Beauty.

"How could you turn your back on us?" the Beast growled.

"The Master lied to you. He lied to all of us. I'm trying to help our family," Beauty said. "Where's Natalie? She needs to come with us now."

Sabrina stepped between them. "Listen, pal, despite your stupid furry face with the fangs and your crappy attitude and the fact that you might be evil, she loves you. She's been trying to save you, but since you're too thickheaded to listen to her, then listen to me. Didn't you notice how little we fought back when you and your goons broke through the front gate of our camp? That's because we wanted all of you ugly punks to come right on in. Because at this very moment Baba Yaga, the Wicked Queen, and Morgan le Fay are outside recreating the magic spell that put the barrier on Ferryport Landing. Except the new one is going to be a lot smaller. In fact, it's going to be pretty much the exact same size as this camp."

Suddenly, the Beast's face fell. He understood Sabrina's plan. He understood that the Scarlet Hand was in a lot of trouble.

"So, you can stay if you want, but if you hated being trapped in a little town for two hundred years, imagine eternity in a castle infested with trolls, goblins, witches, and monsters—oh, and no indoor plumbing. You've got thirty seconds to decide."

"Twenty, actually," Puck said.

"Please, James," Beauty begged.

"I'd rather our daughter be trapped in here with monsters than let her be raised by a traitor like you," the Beast growled, and then he turned toward his comrades. "It's a trap! Everyone, out of the castle, now!"

Puck grabbed Sabrina in one arm and Beauty in the other. They shot into the air and over the wall, landing among the waiting army.

"Take me back," Beauty pleaded. "My daughter is in there."

Sabrina looked to the Wicked Queen. She shook her head. There was no more time.

"Cast the spell," Sabrina told Daphne.

"All right, ladies. It's time to put the Hand in time-out," Daphne called. Morgan read the magic spell, a collection of dark incantations in a foul, frightening language. The Wicked Queen tossed a handful of flat, oval stones into the air, and they hung suspended before her eyes. She moved them around, as if working some elaborate puzzle only she could see. Baba Yaga raised her hands and squatted down like an angry monkey. She shrieked and bellowed as if demanding the spell to work.

The sky grew purple with heavy clouds. Above the castle, Sabrina saw the beginnings of a dome of energy, materializing from the top down. The faster Morgan read, the more Bunny fiddled with her rocks, and the louder the old crone shrieked. As the minutes passed, more of the dome appeared.

The Hand was heeding the Beast's cries for retreat. He and his daughter Natalie led many toward the drawbridge. The Six

Swans, Sheriff Nottingham, Shere Khan, and the entire nation of Lilliputians, as well as the glass cat, Bungle, Mowgli, and Humpty Dumpty made it across without harm. But the second wave wasn't so lucky. Led by the Ice Queen, they tumbled backward halfway across the bridge as if they had crashed into something. The Ice Queen stood with her hand out, pushing against something no one could see. She raged and blasted at the invisible obstacle with hail, but her magic had no effect whatsoever.

"What have you done?" the Ice Queen cried to those on the other side.

"I think they call it winning a war," Henry called, beaming with pride at his daughters.

"So, what do we do with these?" King Arthur asked, leveling his sword at the small group of escaped Hand soldiers.

"We let them go," Sabrina said, turning to the Beast. "Get lost! And tell Mirror two little girls beat his big dumb army. Tell him he's next."

Nottingham was enraged by the defeat. He pushed through the other escapees, charged toward the woods, and confronted Mayor Heart, who stood alongside Sabrina's troops. "What are you doing with these traitors?"

"They saved me," Heart said. She seemed frightened by Nottingham's anger. Sabrina couldn't remember ever seeing Heart this afraid.

"Saved you?"

Uncle Jake stepped between them. "Relax, Sheriff, the lady is injured. She's not herself."

Nottingham drew his deadly dagger.

"She's about to feel even worse!"

Jake swung, landing a painful blow to the sheriff's chin. Nottingham fell to the ground hard and lay still.

The Beast turned to his wife.

"How could you do this?" he asked.

"I could ask you the same question," Beauty said. She watched him heft Nottingham onto his shoulder and slink into the woods with their daughter in tow.

"Natalie! I love you!" Beauty called out after them.

Natalie turned to her. The girl's face was awash with confusion. It was clear that she felt torn between her parents, but she kept walking. Soon, she and her father vanished into the trees.

The other Hand soldiers filed past Sabrina's army, looking sheepish and embarrassed. A few snarled threats of revenge, but most were too demoralized to say a word.

"Oh, no! Mom!" Mordred cried, rushing back across the drawbridge. Somehow, in all the chaos, Morgan had slipped through the newly formed barrier without anyone noticing. She was trapped.

"We'll get you out!" Mordred promised. "Don't worry. I'll make the other witches break the spell."

"I just couldn't leave him, honey," Morgan said with a soft smile. "I couldn't bear to think Seven was in here all alone."

"But the castle is filled with maniacs!" Mordred cried.

"Honey, don't worry about me. I'm a pretty powerful witch. I'll have everyone behaving in no time."

Mordred locked eyes with Sabrina, and then he stepped through the barrier to stand beside his mother.

"Mordred, no! They need you!" Morgan cried.

"I'm not leaving you," he said, grabbing her hand. Then he turned his attention back to Sabrina. "I'm sorry, but you've got all the magic you'll need."

"I'll visit her often," Morgan called to Uncle Jake, referring to Briar.

"Thank you, Morgan," Jake said. "Take care of your mother, Mordred."

"We should check on your mother and the children," Henry said to Sabrina.

Daphne said her good-byes and thanked Morgan for being a part of the coven. Then, along with the others, she headed into the woods. Sabrina took one last look at the castle before following. It wasn't the end of the war, but it was a pretty big win. Maybe the Council of Mirrors had been right all along.

9

FTER REUNITING WITH ALL THE OTHERS, THE
army marched single file toward Mount Taurus. Soon,
they got to a clearing Pinocchio said was perfect for
pitching camp. But most of the army was still in the dark about
the next phase of the plan.

Luckily, nearly everyone was pleased with how things had gone
so far, so they eagerly went to work setting up a campsite.

Mayor Heart, exhausted from the hike, slumped down against
a tree. Uncle Jake knelt beside her and offered some water. She
drank greedily until Jake's canteen was dry.

"He tried to kill me," she wheezed, panicking. "Nottingham
tried to kill me."

"He's a violent man with a very dark past. I'm glad I was there
to stop him."

The queen looked up at Jake, and her eyes narrowed.

"And why, exactly, did you help me? You should have left me

to die, especially after the unfortunate incident with that woman," she said dismissively.

Sabrina overheard the comment and was enraged. *That woman?!* Briar's death wasn't some unlucky accident! Heart and Nottingham had sent dragons to kill her. Sabrina fully expected to see her uncle strangle Heart right then and there, but he remained calm. Where was his maddening need for revenge? How could he show compassion to a woman he'd once wanted dead? His sudden change in behavior made no sense to her.

"Letting him kill you is not what Briar would have wanted," Jake said to the queen.

Heart's face softened. "Well, of course she wouldn't want that. She was a . . . she was a kind soul. I suppose I owe you a great debt of thanks."

"That's not necessary. But there is one thing you could do that would make me very happy," Jake replied, and then reached into his jacket. When he withdrew a dagger, Sabrina panicked. Jake was going to kill the Queen of Hearts, in broad daylight! She rushed to stop him but was surprised when her uncle placed the knife in the queen's palm. "Stay alive. I don't think we've seen the last of the sheriff."

Heart stared at Jake in utter shock, but then her face split into a smile.

Sabrina set her pack on the forest floor and scanned her

surroundings. Their new camp was up high on a hill. Pinocchio claimed it was harder for soldiers to fight their way up an embankment. Plus, approaching troops would be easier to spot.

"It's a good camp," Pinocchio said, suddenly appearing next to her. "At least for the night. We'll have to find a new one in the morning and the next morning and every morning after that until we get the job done."

"We?" It was the first time she'd heard him express a sentiment that wasn't selfish.

He shrugged. "We."

He walked a few paces to look over the valley. Sabrina followed.

"Your father should be proud," she said, even though the words sounded funny to her.

"You should tell him that," Pinocchio said. "He still thinks I'm a spoiled brat."

"You are," she said. "Or were. I guess we'll find out. But I do know that people change. I've done it a few times myself."

Pinocchio nodded, then pointed to the horizon. On the edge of town, Sabrina saw the same black-and-purple storm that had been brewing for days. Mirror was still trying to break through the barrier, and his failure was sending him into a magical tantrum.

"The rest of the Hand morons are simple," Pinocchio said. "Mirror's going to be a real challenge."

A chill ran down Sabrina's spine. "Any ideas on what we should do?"

"I'm afraid my knowledge of military strategy doesn't cover scenarios in which the enemy is an all-powerful magical entity inhabiting an old woman's body."

He left her side as Mr. Canis approached.

"It appears your plans were a success," he said.

"Thanks. Everyone did a great job."

"Child, there is something I must tell you. You really should have told me what you were planning. If I had known what you intended to do, I would have stopped it. The risks are too great."

"I'm not following what you're saying, Mr. Canis," she said, bristling a little. "I know it's hard listening to a kid, but—"

"I have every faith in you, Sabrina Grimm. It's the barrier spell. Are you planning on using it again?"

She shook her head.

The tension in Canis's shoulders relaxed. "Good. It would be a tragedy if you and your family were trapped inside your own cage."

"Don't worry. The spell only works on Everafters. We could just walk right out, since we're human," Sabrina said.

Canis seemed to wrestle with something, but he just nodded and smiled. "Of course, you are correct. Red and I will be meditating if we are needed."

Sabrina watched as the old man hobbled away.

∾

Once the camp was set up and everyone was fed and rested, Sabrina gathered her troops around her. As she stood before the crowd, she realized everyone's worry and fear had dissolved. In fact, they were looking at her with a newfound respect. She was no longer at the kids' table—for better or for worse.

"Thanks to everyone's hard work, we managed to trap a majority of the Hand. We lost a few of our people—a terrible tragedy, and we will mourn them when we can—but for now we must prepare for the couple hundred goons still roaming these woods. They are looking for us, and they are angrier than ever. When they find us, we have to be ready."

"Ready how?" Snow White asked.

"My sister and I have faced a lot of weirdos in our day, and we've always managed to outsmart them. We're going to do the same thing here, but to be successful we have to do something unexpected. That's why I'm putting my faith in the king of the unexpected. Puck, this forest needs the Trickster King treatment."

The crowd let out a collective groan.

"Oh, yeah?" Puck said as he pushed to the front of the crowd. "What do you have in mind?"

"Think of these woods as your own little playground of mischief. I want traps and bombs and glop grenades and even flying horses with stomach issues. I want you to booby-trap every inch of the forest."

"Sorry, Grimm." Puck smiled. "The Trickster King doesn't do

a greatest-hits show. I've got all new pranks. And I guarantee, the losers who come after us will wish they'd stayed at home."

"Are you sure about this?" the Cowardly Lion asked. "That boy doesn't exactly care who gets pranked. How can we be sure we won't all end up in some pit full of jelly or in a nest of fire ants?"

"I know Puck can be immature and unpredictable, but that's exactly why he's the man for the job. And we're going to help bring his twisted visions to life, too. Mr. Boarman and Mr. Swineheart will work on designing any machines he needs. Geppetto and Pinocchio will help build the intricate parts. Unfortunately, the rest of us have the worst jobs. We have to collect the ingredients he wants, and from my experience, that's not going to be pretty."

Puck laughed. "You've got that right! Some of the stuff I want will scar you for life!"

The community went to work helping Puck with his bizarre plans. It took all day and much of the evening to build some of the things that came out of his wild imagination. Plus, since they were going to be moving camp every day, the army needed to booby-trap a huge area of the woods so that they could keep catching goons along the way.

They assembled spring-loaded catapults, cannons that shot all sorts of muck and filth, cages that dropped from above, and trip wires that set off explosions. Puck wanted to dig ditches and fill them with angry badgers. He wanted to hoist logs high into trees so that they could swing down and pulverize approaching villains.

He asked the witches to create magic spells that turned ordinary shrubs into poisonous plants. He asked the Pied Piper and Wendell to force a furry army of deer, rabbits, possums, squirrels, and chipmunks to obey Puck's every command. But what the boy fairy was most excited about was the possibility of gaining access to his enchanted bedroom.

"When the old lady's house imploded, the door was destroyed," he explained to the Wicked Queen. "But the room was made out of magic, and it still exists . . . somewhere. And it's got all the special supplies I need. Plus, I sort of miss my chimpanzee army. They could really come in handy right about now."

The Wicked Queen promised she would do her best.

By the time the moon shone bright overhead, Puck's demented traps were scattered throughout the woods. Everyone was exhausted, and more than a few were deeply troubled by some of Puck's special assignments. But, when all was said and done, Sabrina could sense that morale was high—the army felt as if they stood a chance against the rest of the Hand.

That night, Sabrina lay in a sleeping bag, with her sister curled beside her. Puck lay in a tree branch above them, looking out on the woods and grinning proudly.

"You should get some sleep," Sabrina said.

Puck shook his head. "I'm too excited. It feels like Christmas Eve—like I'm going to wake up and find something big under the tree. I'm just hoping it's smelly."

"Puck, I know I don't say this enough, but you're an awesome villain," Sabrina said.

"Charmer," he whispered.

Sabrina closed her eyes. She woke hours later to the sound of someone crying. Daphne was sound asleep, undisturbed by the sobbing, as was Puck. Sabrina carefully climbed out of her sleeping bag and followed the sound until she found Snow.

"I'm sorry. I didn't mean to wake anyone," Ms. White blubbered when she spotted Sabrina.

"Are you all right?" Sabrina asked, kneeling beside her.

"I'm just worried about Billy. I thought he'd come back for the fight. When he didn't, I sent some birds to search, but they say he's nowhere to be found," she explained. "Oh, Sabrina, what my mother did to our lives . . . I'm worried it has totally broken him. He's a proud man. He must be so confused."

"Let's go find him," Sabrina said.

A smile broke out over Snow's tear-stained face. "Can we?"

Hand in hand, the duo crept back through the camp and found the magic mirror propped against a tree. Elvis lay on the ground in front of it, acting as guard dog. He opened one sleepy eye when Sabrina and Snow entered the reflection but did nothing to stop them. They rushed to the Room of Reflections and found the guardians waiting in their frames.

"Hello!" Harry cheered. "It's so good to see the both of you."

"Hello, Harry. Good to see you in one piece," Snow said.

"What can we do for you?" Arden asked.

"Yeah, honey. We can help with anything you need," Fanny said.

"We're trying to find someone," Sabrina explained.

"Well, you know how it works," Reggie said. "We'll make some time if you make a rhyme."

Snow sniffed. "Mirrors, mirrors, hanging there, where's my prince with the awesome hair?"

The mirrors chuckled, amused by her silly poem, and then they showed her an image of Charming sitting on the edge of a rocky cliff high above the Hudson River. He looked so depressed. Sabrina wouldn't have believed he was capable of such deep sadness.

"Where do you think he is?" Sabrina asked.

"Not far," Snow said. "It's called Douglass's Peak. I used to go there when I wanted to be alone. I wonder how he knew."

"He and I looked in on you from time to time," Harry said, his face reappearing in his frame. "Not in a creepy way. He just wanted to make sure you were safe."

"I have to go to him," Snow said. "I love him, and I want to help him with this."

"Let's go find him," Sabrina said.

"Your parents will kill me if I take you along." Snow sighed.

"Then let's make sure they don't find out."

⁊

"It was love at first sight for us—at least, that's what we always thought," Snow explained as they made their way down an old trail littered with fallen limbs. "He swept me off my feet. I agreed to marry him after two weeks, but when it was time to walk down the aisle, well, something wouldn't let me. For decades, I thought that was because I was unsure of who I was and what I wanted. But now, I'm beginning to suspect it had something to do with Atticus. His 'echo,' as my mom calls it, kept me feeling like a damsel in distress. Maybe he's really the reason I learned how to fight. Maybe some part of me remembered that old life. There was always a voice in my head telling me to stay independent, to never rely on a man to save me, and Billy—well, he's the kind of guy who's made for rescuing fair maidens. I loved him, but I didn't want him to save me. I needed to see if I could do it on my own. I could have picked a better time than our wedding day to tell him. I only wanted a little more time to find out who I was, but he was so humiliated.

"But he never gave up on me. His love for me survived three marriages and hundreds of years. And now, I'm afraid he thinks those feelings are nothing more than my mother's inventions."

"Are you sure he's wrong?" Sabrina asked.

"He has to be wrong. What we feel is real," Snow said with resolve.

They found Charming where the mirrors had shown him,

sitting on the edge of a rocky cliff. He was unshaven and looked as if he hadn't slept in days.

"It just dawned on me that he might not want to see me," Snow whispered when they reached the tree line.

"Wait here," Sabrina said, and then she walked over and sat down next to Charming. He didn't seem surprised. He looked at her but stayed silent. For a long time Sabrina did the same. She wasn't exactly sure where to begin. What kind of pep talk do you give someone who just found out he's not real? Daphne was the one with the knack for making people feel better. She would know what to say. She would just open her mouth and let the words come out. Well, it was worth a try.

"Nice view, huh?" Sabrina said, gazing at the river. The water below was calm, and the moon painted it a soft blue. On the far banks, there were a couple of fancy houses. Sabrina wondered if those people ever guessed at the crazy things that happened in the little town on the other side of the river.

"What do you want?" Charming grunted.

"Nothing. We never get a chance to just sit and talk."

"Go away. I don't feel like talking."

"Then don't talk. I'll just sit here and enjoy the scenery," she said. She took off her shoes and swung her stockinged feet back and forth through the cool air. She looked up at the sky, then at the trees around them.

Sabrina knew her presence was annoying Charming. She

worried she might push him too far, and he'd push her off the cliff. "You know, normally, I would run to the other side of town to avoid having a conversation with you—especially about feelings—but I'm trying to turn over a new leaf. So, we're going to be friends. And, as friends, we're going to share stuff with each other." Sabrina took a deep breath. "I'll start. I'm running your army, and it's really scary. I don't really know what I'm doing. I'm afraid I'm going to get everyone killed. You should come back. Oh, and Snow is really worried about you. OK, now your turn."

Charming sighed in surrender. "Is she with you?"

"Snow? Yeah, she's hiding in the bushes."

Charming glanced over his shoulder into the woods. "I don't want to talk to her."

"Because you blame her for what her mother did?"

"No." He shook his head. "It's complicated."

"I know. I don't understand most of it, but I do have to wonder why you're so mad. It's not like the Wicked Queen turned you into some weirdo. She made you pretty awesome. You're brave and smart and strong. Your girlfriend is smart and gorgeous. Sometimes, I wish someone would remake me."

"But none of those things are real, Sabrina. I'm not brave because I have courage. I'm not smart because of experience. I'm not strong from hard work. I haven't earned any of my qualities. Even my hopes and dreams aren't mine—wanting to build that stupid castle, rebuild my kingdom, marry Snow, everything! These goals have consumed me for hundreds of years, and for what? They're not even what I really want!"

"How can you be sure?"

Charming looked back out to the river, as if the answer might be bobbing in the water. "I'm not sure, and that's what's so maddening. There is nothing I can be certain about anymore—not even Snow. Especially not Snow."

"You don't love her anymore?"

"Oh, I love her, all right—with everything inside me. But I have to ask myself if that love is an invention, too. Bunny wanted me to love her daughter, so she wrote it into the story. Did it work? I have carried a torch for Snow for almost five hundred years, never questioning how I truly felt. And now, I can't trust that it's real. I can't trust any of my own feelings anymore."

"Seems to me that if you feel it, then it's real," Snow said as she approached.

Charming climbed to his feet, and Snow rushed to him, wrapping her arms around his neck and kissing his cheeks.

"Billy, we can work this out," she continued.

Charming pulled away. His face was twisted with confusion and pain. "I can't be with you, Snow."

"You—what?" Snow cried, heartbroken. But, after a moment, she lost her temper. Her cheeks turned bright red, and she yelled in Charming's face. "William Charming, I will not have it!"

Both Charming and Sabrina took a step back, surprised by her anger.

"I know life has thrown you a curveball—"

"It's a bit more than a curveball," Charming said.

"Well, get over it!" she cried.

"Good-bye, Snow," he said, then turned and walked into the trees, vanishing into the forest.

"Billy! Billy!" She called after him several times, but he did not return.

"Don't worry. The man can't stop thinking about you. He's not going to give up on you after five hundred years," Sabrina said.

"I don't know, Sabrina. This time, it's different," Snow said, her whole body trembling. "This is really big."

Sabrina woke to shouting. She opened her eyes to find that everyone was rushing from the campsite into the woods.

"What's going on?" Daphne asked, climbing out of her sleeping bag.

"I think one of Puck's traps caught its first mouse," Henry said, appearing beside them with Basil in his arms. "Why don't you go take a look? I'll take Basil and prep a secure room in the Hall of Wonders."

Sabrina and Daphne chased after the rest of the army. Soon, they came across Jack Pumpkinhead, dangling upside down, a vine wrapped around his feet. His giant head was as red as the handprint painted on his shirt.

"Let me down, traitors," he demanded.

"Welcome, Jack," Sabrina said. "And congratulations, you're our first prisoner of war."

"When I get down from here, I swear you'll pay," Jack raged.

"I never get tired of hearing empty threats," Sabrina mocked. "Cut down this walking pumpkin pie."

"Wait! It's not finished," Puck said. A moment later, a dozen chimpanzees dropped down from the treetops. Each wore a soldier's helmet and held a fat Wiffle ball bat. They swung at their captive as if he were a piñata.

"So, I guess Ms. Lancaster found Puck's bedroom," Sabrina said to her sister.

"Yep. For better or for worse," Daphne said.

Over the course of the day, Puck's traps snatched up more members of the Hand, one by one. Hansel fell into a pit filled with honey (and, to no one's surprise, fire ants). His sister, Gretel, was chased through the woods by a pack of zombie chipmunks. Bo Peep was hoisted skyward by enormous helium balloons that were then popped by tiny arrows. She fell onto a well-placed hornet's nest. A couple of goblins found themselves caught in the hungry jaws of a giant Venus flytrap. Surprised cries rang out from the woods every few minutes. Each time, Puck clapped with glee.

By nightfall, thirty of the Master's troops were locked in the Hall of Wonders. But there was no time to celebrate. Sabrina's army needed to move on to their next camp. Sabrina examined a map of the forest, and, with help from the mirrors, her father, and her uncle, she found a great site farther up Mount Taurus. It wasn't far from where the Ferryport Landing Asylum had once stood. The army packed their belongings, and they were all pitching tents in their temporary new home by midnight.

The next day started with more captures. The Patchwork Girl from Oz was the first victim. Sabrina had never met her, but Scarecrow, who had once been in love with her, told Sabrina that she was made entirely of old pieces of blankets. Unfortunately for the Patchwork Girl, she tripped a wire and was then doused with gallons and gallons of sewage. Sabrina was sure the smell would never come out.

"I wonder if you can dry-clean a person," Goldilocks said through her pinched nose.

Puck's pixie minions also helped bring in some prisoners: Big Hans and Little Hans, Babe the Big Blue Ox, Jack and Jill, Solomon Grundy, and a cyclops as tall as a house got the worst of their painful stings.

By nightfall, thirty-five more members of the Hand were locked in the Hall of Wonders.

In the morning, they abandoned camp once again and found a new site near the banks of the Hudson River. By noon, twenty-

five more villains were captured by one of Puck's unpleasant surprises—animal bites, toxic waste, angry bumblebees, and even a
few very intense pies to the face.

"At this rate, we'll have every bad guy under lock and key in no
time at all," Daphne said when she and Sabrina met in the Room
of Reflections.

"You should be very proud of yourselves," the guardian named
Archie said. He was a beaver who wore a short sword on his furry
back. "You fight with great honor. You do justice to your family
name."

"Thank you," Sabrina said. "Unfortunately, after we capture all
the bad guys, we'll have to deal with the two worst of the bunch."

Archie's reflection changed to show the girls the wicked storm
still hovering over town. Black-and-purple clouds rumbled with
threatening thunder.

"Rest easy that our brother and Atticus will not come to these
woods," Titan said. "They are smart enough to know that you are
dangerous. If you want them, you're going to have to go after them."

Sabrina nodded, feeling deflated. "We just don't have a clue
what to do when we find them. I was hoping the Council might
have some ideas."

"Your best chance is to kill the First. He is trapped in a feeble
body. If you kill her, you kill him," Arden said.

"Shut your mouth, girl!" Fanny cried in horror. "That feeble
body belongs to their grandmother."

THE COUNCIL OF MIRRORS

"I understand it is not the best choice for the girl," Arden said. "But it may be her only choice."

"As long as Atticus wears the armor he stole from the Book of Everafter, he's unstoppable," Donovan said. "No mortal man can kill him. You've got to find a way to get it off of him."

Suddenly, the mirrors began to shake. The guardians inside them were thrown about as if they were on board a ship in rough seas. Startled, Sabrina and Daphne took a step back.

"What's happening?" Daphne cried.

"I don't know," Sabrina admitted.

"Run!" Harry cried.

"He's coming, Sabrina!" Fanny warned. "The First is coming!"

All the guardians vanished. In their frames, Granny Relda's face appeared, twisted with mocking hatred. A wicked smile stretched across her face. Sabrina understood Mirror's plan—and knew how truly selfish it was—but she was still stunned to see such evil emanating from him.

"Hello, girls," Mirror sneered. "Surprised to see me? Turns out, if I exert enough energy, I can hear and see everything you say when you're standing before my brothers and sisters. So, yes, I've known your plans all along!"

Daphne gasped. "That makes no sense, Mirror! If you knew we were going to trap your goons, why didn't you stop us?"

Mirror chuckled. "Well, one, they were getting in the way. Two, a lot of them are pretty smelly. I could get them to burn the whole town to the ground, but a little body wash was out of the question. And three, I didn't want you or the rest of your family to be injured. You see, girls, my troubles aren't about you. Well, at least they weren't until now. It appears the three of us are going to have a showdown."

Sabrina was shocked. Of course he knew the prophecy.

"I wish it didn't have to be this way, Sabrina," Mirror continued. "I do have a soft spot for you and your sister, but despite my efforts to be reasonable, the two of you keep getting in my way."

"Reasonable? You call stealing our grandmother's body reasonable?" Sabrina snapped.

"Trust me," Mirror said, gesturing to Granny Relda's face. "This wasn't part of the plan. Being inside Relda Grimm is exhausting. Not only is her body old and creaky, she's fighting me tooth and nail every step of the way.

"So, I'm back with one last peace offering, in hopes of making all of our troubles go away. Just use the spell that creates and destroys the magical barriers to let me out of Ferryport Landing. I'll find someone more suitable to house me, you get your grandmother back, and—hey—you've already locked up all the bad guys. It's a win-win-win. What do you say?"

Sabrina shook her head. She tried to think of something brave and confident to say to him, but nothing sounded very good in her head.

"We're never going to let you out!" Daphne said. "You're a bad person, and you can't be trusted."

"Now, that makes me sad." Mirror frowned. "Well, girls, you've forced my hand. If you won't give me the spell willingly, I'm going to have to take it from you."

The surfaces of each mirror bubbled and churned. Lightning shot out from the reflections. Sabrina grabbed Daphne's hand and pulled her away, just as an explosion went off near their feet. Both girls were knocked to the floor. As Sabrina struggled to stand, she saw long, jagged cracks appearing in the reflections. Then, all twenty-four of the guardians reappeared, howling in a chorus of pain.

"Don't give up, girls! The First can be defeated!" Titus shouted.

"Trust in each other!" Donovan cried.

There was a sudden moment of total stillness, and then the mirrors shattered. The broken shards were like bullets crashing around the room. Sabrina threw her body over Daphne's, trying to protect her sister as best she could. She felt the glass slice into her arms and legs and back, each shard a tiny red-hot brand.

When it was over, Sabrina and Daphne were lying in a sea of glass. Daphne was sobbing but uninjured. Sabrina, however, was bleeding. Her arm was impaled with a large piece of glass. She took a deep breath, preparing to pull it out. But when she tried, the glass melted in her hand and seeped into the wound.

Sabrina felt an odd tightening in her chest, followed by a nervous energy. She recognized the feeling immediately—it was the way her body responded when she was around magic. And now, some of it was inside her.

Daphne didn't notice. She was too busy hugging her sister with all her might. The little girl was trembling. Sabrina got them both to their feet, and they raced out of the Room of Reflections.

When they got out into the woods, the army was nowhere in sight. "Mom! Dad! Puck! Uncle Jake!" No one answered. Where was her family? Were they wounded?

Sabrina and Daphne ran through the deserted camp. Footprints led them up a hill and then down a steep embankment, but still they found no signs of life. In the distance, Sabrina could hear screaming, and when she looked at the ground—blood! They followed its trail through a patch of trees until they suddenly found themselves face-to-face with Atticus. Next to him were two enormous trolls, each standing nearly eight feet tall and packed tight with muscles. They were terrifying creatures, but not nearly as fearsome as Atticus.

"And here are the little brats causing all the trouble," Atticus said, and then turned to the trolls. "What are you two empty-headed fools waiting for—an invitation? I'll handle these two. Get going."

The trolls grunted and lumbered off into the woods, leaving Atticus alone with the girls.

The villain raised his sword and pointed it at Sabrina, then Daphne, as if trying to decide whom to kill first.

"You know, you haven't made that thing living inside your grandmother very happy. You should hear his temper tantrums. He rages even when the body's asleep. It's very unsettling."

"Sorry for the inconvenience," Sabrina said. She found a long branch and scooped it up, remembering what Snow had taught her about the bō staff. She spun the branch around with all her strength and hit Atticus in the side of the head. It didn't seem to harm him at all. Sabrina hit him again, with the same result.

"It's the magic armor," Daphne reminded her.

Sabrina brought her branch down once more, but the evil prince caught it and wrenched it from her hands. Then, with a ferocity she did not expect, he slapped her across the face. She fell back against a tree. He stood over her, jabbing the steel tip of his blade into the side of her neck.

"I'll kill you!" he bellowed.

10

L EAVE HER ALONE!" DAPHNE SHOUTED.

"And how do you plan to stop me?" Atticus mocked, but his voice was drowned out by a loud growl. Elvis charged out from behind a tree and stood at Daphne's side. There was a threatening anger in the dog's face—he was ready to pounce.

Atticus laughed. "If you can't hurt me, why do you think a mutt will have any luck?"

"Don't call him a mutt! He's sensitive. Get him, boy!" Daphne cried.

Elvis leaped forward and chomped down on Atticus's groin, where there was no armor to protect him. He fell over into the leaves, moaning. Daphne snatched Sabrina's hand, and they ran with Elvis deeper into the woods.

It seemed as if they were running forever. And, luckily, it also seemed as if Atticus had not followed them. After some time,

Sabrina finally felt it was safe to stop and catch their breath. Finding her family and the army was the only thing on her mind. She knew that shouting for them had been a big mistake—it had led Atticus to her. If only she could find someone, maybe Puck. He'd know what was going on.

A queasy feeling grew in her belly, a yearning, hungry sensation—and then, suddenly, she could see Puck. Not with her eyes, but inside her mind. He looked panicked as he stomped through the woods. He was looking for help. She didn't know how, but she knew exactly where to find him.

"This way," she said, grabbing her sister's hand and running down a thin path that led along a ridge. A few moments later, they met Puck.

"Where is everybody?" Daphne asked.

Puck's face was ashen. "Come quick! It's Geppetto."

The girls followed him until they found Pinocchio. The boy was kneeling next to his father. Geppetto lay on the ground with a ragged wound in his chest, probably from Atticus's sword. His face was calm, his eyes closed. Pinocchio held his hand and wept.

"Papa?" he cried. "Papa, please be OK."

But he wasn't.

October 23

It seems as if every time I open this journal, I have to write about death.

I hate these pages. I hate this pen. This is not supposed to be a record of the people who have died because of me.

The Frog Princess (who I'm told was really named Sharlene), Sir Lancelot, Friar Tuck, and Geppetto were all killed fighting Atticus and his trolls.

Poor Pinocchio. He blames himself. He thinks it's his fault, since he was the one who opened the Book of Everafter and set Atticus free. Uncle Jake tried to console him, but he didn't have much luck. The boy is devastated.

Sadly, we have another tragedy on our hands. Atticus's trolls took Snow White. Ms. Lancaster is beside herself with worry and anger. She wants to go after him, but Baba Yaga warns her that she doesn't have the power to stop him. They need a full coven to confront the prince, and with Morgan trapped in the old castle, their bond is broken. The council said we would need the coven to stop Mirror. I worry we've done something to ruin our chances.

We left the graves in the woods and moved our camp. Mirror destroyed the Council of Mirrors, so I assume he can no longer see or hear us. I've asked everyone to destroy any mirrors they might be carrying. I can't take the risk that he might be able to see us through regular mirrors, too. The Room of Reflections has been locked tight and is off-limits to everyone, even me.

Especially me. Something is happening. I'm sick, though sick doesn't feel like the right word, exactly. I feel weird. When the mirrors exploded, a piece got into my blood, and I can . . . this is going to sound strange, but I can feel it swimming around in there. I think it helped me find Puck, but the side effects are terrible. I started out feeling dizzy and tired, but now . . . well, I feel like I'm dying. My eyes are blurry, and my head is pounding. I just want to lie down, but I can't. Everyone is counting on me.

Sabrina stood before her army, their faces etched with fresh grief. She tried to stand strong. She knew that she could not let them see how terrible she felt.

"The Hand is all but defeated. It should be cause for celebration, but I'm afraid I have bad news. Mirror has been watching us," Sabrina announced. "He knew all about our plans from the beginning. The only reason we were able to trap the Hand inside Charming's castle is because he let it happen."

"So he can see us?" Goldilocks asked.

Sabrina shook her head. "Not anymore. The mirrors were destroyed, but the tricks and traps we've laid aren't going to work on him. We have to do something else. I wish I could say the hardest part of this fight is behind us, but it's not. Atticus and Mirror are next. I think we need to handle Atticus first. He took Snow."

"He tore through us, Sabrina," the Frog Prince said. "Nothing we did could stop him. He's a monster."

Mr. Canis stepped forward. In his hand was the glass jar that held the spirit of the Big Bad Wolf. "Perhaps it's time our side had a monster."

"Absolutely not!" Henry cried. "You are not letting that thing loose again. Canis, you spent hundreds of years trying to get rid of it, and now you want to subject yourself to that misery again?"

"What I want and what must be done have always been at odds, Henry."

"Having the Wolf running around is no better than having Atticus at large," Mayor Heart said.

"I have managed a level of control over him," Canis argued.

"Which you lost," Mr. Swineheart squealed. In his anxiety, he transformed into his pig form.

"There are ways to stop him," Canis said impatiently. "I'm aware that the Horn of the North Wind vanished when the Hall of Wonders was looted, but our friend Beauty may have some influence over him."

"I could try," she said, though she didn't sound very confident.

"This is crazy," the Pied Piper said. "I have power over most animals, but I know from experience I have no control over the Wolf."

"This is not your decision to make!" Canis bellowed. Everyone stood agape at his boiling anger. "I know you've all found it perfectly convenient to have me babysitting or guarding your belongings, but I have never been someone who stands aside and lets others do what I must do myself. My dearest friend, Relda Grimm, needs help. The only way to get to her is to take Atticus out of the picture. I'm not here asking for permission. I'm telling you what I'm going to do!"

Red broke into tears and ran from the camp.

"Canis, I'm disappointed in you," Veronica said. "That little girl is counting on you. Don't you have a responsibility to her? She's already been abandoned so many times. Are you going to abandon her, too?"

Canis lowered his eyes and flushed with shame. "I'll go and speak with her." He hobbled after the little girl.

"So," Puck said. "This is getting interesting."

"Canis wants to feel useful," Uncle Jake said.

"He's going to get someone killed," Henry argued.

"Isn't there someone else who should be here, being useful?" Cinderella asked. "Where's William?"

Without warning, Sabrina's stomach did a flip-flop, and she doubled over. A clear vision of the prince forced its way into the center of her thoughts. He was curled on a dirty mattress inside the former mayor's mansion.

"Sabrina, are you OK?" Veronica asked.

Sabrina nodded, but Baba Yaga and the Wicked Queen eyed her curiously. They knew something was wrong. "I'm just a little tired," Sabrina lied.

"Finding Billy is a good idea," Daphne agreed. "He would want to know Snow is in danger."

"Before we get ahead of ourselves, do any of you want to quit?" Sabrina asked. She looked out at her army, searching their dirty, tired faces for hints of fear and doubt. "I wouldn't blame you. I don't really know how to stop Atticus or Mirror, and we might all die. This is going to be hard."

Beauty stepped forward. "I admit that my rage at being trapped in this town has caused me to do things I regret. But there has always been something about your family that I've deeply respected—your steadfast principles! Wilhelm taught his children to stand for something, to protect our community, even when we didn't want it. Douglas taught Sterling, and Sterling taught Spaulding, and Spaulding taught Josef, and so on and so on. Well, that integrity used to drive us crazy. Now, I marvel at it. I envy it. I will do anything to emulate it, so that my daughter will know what it means to be a good person. I will die to protect you."

"I will lay my life down for you," the Wicked Queen said.

"You can count on my son and me," the Pied Piper said.

"You have the birds," the Widow crowed.

"You have my men," Robin Hood said.

"And mine!" King Arthur shouted.

"It was never a question," Goldie said. The roars of three fierce brown bears echoed her promise.

"I will fight," Pinocchio said through his tears. "I will fight."

All present made the promise, though Mayor Heart did so reluctantly. At the end of the chorus of cheers, the only person who hadn't spoken up was Puck. The crowd looked at him for his answer.

"Yeah, I got nothing better to do," he said.

That afternoon, Sabrina, Puck, and the Wicked Queen set out to find Charming. The witch planned to force William to come back to the army, but Sabrina urged her to hear Charming out before using magic on him.

The group hiked toward the old mayor's mansion. Puck was perplexed as to how Sabrina knew where to find the prince. She considered telling him the truth, but she didn't want him to worry. So she claimed it was just a hunch. Unfortunately, there was no denying something was wrong. Sabrina was suffering from both fever and chills, and she needed to stop several times to shake off dizzy spells and nausea. It was getting harder and harder to concentrate, and she kept seeing a red handprint flash in her mind's eye.

"What's wrong with you?" Puck asked. "You're starting to look a little green."

"I'm just tired," Sabrina lied again.

Puck spun around on his heels and transformed into a donkey. The queen helped Sabrina climb onto his back, and she got a good look at the jagged scar on Sabrina's arm where the magic mirror had cut her. Bunny looked at Sabrina meaningfully but said nothing.

The trio arrived at the mayor's mansion to find the front door wide open and all the windows broken. It was obvious the place had been recently looted by the Hand. There were huge holes ripped in the floors and graffiti painted on the walls. Sabrina hardly recognized the place.

Puck morphed back into his true form, and the group climbed the once-grand staircase. Inside Charming's former office, the prince slumbered, just as Sabrina had seen in her strange vision. He looked and smelled as if he had been drinking.

"Wakey-wakey, eggs and bakey," Puck called.

Charming lifted his head as if it were filled with rocks. He groaned when he saw the visitors. "I told you to leave me alone."

"That's not an option anymore," the Wicked Queen said. "Atticus has Snow."

Charming shook his head, as if trying to wake himself up. "What? When?"

"A few hours ago," Sabrina said.

"We would have come sooner, but we weren't sure you were finished with your pity party," the queen snapped.

Charming growled. "How dare you, Bunny? You meddled with my life—my memories, my identity—and you think I should just snap out of it? You try being a fictional character for a minute!"

"I've been a fictional character just as long as you have, William. Have you forgotten that to keep Snow safe, I had to rewrite myself, too? I turned myself into a villain and gave up my daughter! She has feared me for decades. Do you think it was easy, being scorned by the person I love more than anyone in this world?"

"That was your choice!" Charming cried.

"Stop acting like a child. It's not like I turned you into a fool. I just embellished qualities you already possessed. I made you more courageous and resilient. I gave you the attention of the most beautiful woman in the world. Was it really that intolerable?"

"I want it to be real," Charming said, staggering to his feet. He stepped forward, nearly tumbling into the trio. "Don't you understand?"

"This fighting is wasting time," Sabrina said. "We need a hero, and, Billy, that's what you are."

Charming shook his head. "Tell Bunny to open her magic book and write herself a new hero."

"You know what, William? You're wrong. You're not fictional at all, and you never have been," Sabrina said. "She wrote you to be a hero, but you're actually a jerk."

"What?"

"She just said you're a jerk," Puck said. "I know because she calls me one all the time."

"I don't need this," Charming said, turning toward the door.

"She's right, William. I rewrote you to be the ideal man, but you're nothing more than a grouchy, impatient, arrogant crybaby."

"Which proves you are your own person," Sabrina said.

"OK, I get it. I've heard enough insults for one day."

"No, you don't get it," Sabrina said. "You constantly turn from a perfect prince into a sour old lemon. If Ms. Lancaster didn't write that into Snow's story, it must be coming from you. You're a real person, William—warts and all."

Charming turned back and stared at the group for a long time. "This is the worst pep talk in the history of the world."

Puck laughed. "It really is."

"Is it working?" the Wicked Queen asked.

Charming nodded.

"So, are you ready to put away the sad face so we can go save the love of your life?" Sabrina asked.

Charming snatched his sword off the ground. "I am."

"Great, we got the band back together," Puck said. "Now, where do we find Atticus?"

Once again, Sabrina felt her mind take over. She staggered and fell as visions of Charming's brother crashed through her head. Atticus was camped in a house that sat on a rocky cliff overlooking the Hudson River. Atticus stood over Snow White, who cowered at his feet. Sheriff Nottingham stood nearby, laughing at the scene.

Puck helped her to her feet. "All right, Grimm. What's going on with you? And don't tell me you're tired one more time."

"She's fine," the Wicked Queen lied for Sabrina. "Don't worry about her; she's under my care."

"We have to get the others and hurry," Sabrina said. "He's at Devil's Peak, and he's hurting Snow."

❧

The road leading to Atticus was twisted and dangerous, running parallel to the river's choppy waters below. Charming insisted on leading the charge and demanded that everyone walk as quickly as possible.

It was easier said than done. Canis stumbled along as fast as his old bones would allow. On the other hand, the Queen of Hearts wasn't exactly in a hurry, and she whined incessantly the whole way.

"This is a very steep road," Heart complained. "Perhaps I should stay here and wait."

"We've heard enough of your excuses, Mayor. Stay or continue on, but please shut your mouth," Pinocchio snapped. The boy kept pace with the prince. A simmering desire for justice seemed to fuel his every step.

Uncle Jake, however, treated Heart with patience. "I would recommend you rest, but Nottingham is still lurking somewhere in these woods. I know it's physically demanding, but it's safer if you stay with the group."

Heart grumbled but continued the climb, wheezing like a tired pig all the way to the top. Once there, they heard screaming.

"Snow!" Charming cried, and raced ahead.

"Charming, no!" the Wicked Queen said. "We need a plan!"

Sabrina's brain buzzed with possibilities. There were so many options, all laid out before her. Each vision revealed a new prospect—a final outcome—but there were thousands, and many ended in the deaths of people she loved. How could she know such things? She guessed it had something to do with the broken mirror swimming in her veins.

"We need to circle around and try to get behind Atticus," Prince Charming said. "It may be the only way to save Snow."

Everyone scurried through the bushes. All the while, Sabrina watched Charming. He was so eager. It was clear it was taking all his strength not to run headlong into a confrontation with his brother.

"Are you ready for this?" Daphne asked him.

Charming still looked tired, but his eyes were clear. He nodded.

"I am here, Atticus!" Charming shouted, and he stepped out of the bushes. Suddenly, new possibilities spun around in Sabrina's mind, sending the future in a new direction. The whole experience gave her a tremendous headache.

"Billy! Don't come any closer. He's going to kill you!" Snow shouted from somewhere within the house.

"Shut up!" Atticus roared, and Sabrina heard a wicked slap.

"It's a cowardly man who beats a woman, brother," Charming said.

"So, you remember me now, do you, William?"

"No, but from what I understand, that's for the best. I wish I could remember the satisfaction of stealing your wife. You aren't worthy of her," he taunted.

"You should not be so insulting, little brother."

Suddenly, an arrow shot through an open window and pierced Charming's leg. He fell over, clutching the wound and cursing. There was blood everywhere. The prince pulled the arrow out with his bare hands, but he could barely stand.

"And it's a cowardly man who attacks from behind closed doors," Charming shouted.

Atticus kicked open the door and then stormed out, dragging Snow behind him. Snow's face was bloody and her clothes torn. Nottingham followed, his sword drawn.

"I'll let you have a look at me, William. If you're satisfied, I suggest you leave while you still can. I won't tolerate your interfering with my family reunion. My wife and I have a lot of catching up to do."

Charming drew his sword.

"Oh, baby brother. I thought you were the smart one. You don't want a fight with me. It won't be like the roughhousing we used get into on the castle lawn. Father and Mother are not here to attend to your bloody noses and boxed ears."

Atticus pushed Snow to the ground and rushed at Charming, his sword held high. Their blades met with a savage crash, shooting sparks in every direction. They fought for dominance until Atticus kicked Charming in his wounded leg. William fell to one knee with a cry but quickly hobbled back to standing. Atticus showed no mercy. He punched Charming so hard on the side of the head, it nearly took him off his feet again. Charming stumbled but stayed upright. He swung wildly, missing his brother completely. Atticus laughed at his clumsiness, then slashed his own sword. The tip sliced Charming's shirt open, and blood seeped onto the cloth. Charming collapsed, clutching his wound.

"You were never very bright, Billy," Atticus said, turning his back on his brother. Atticus dragged Snow over to where Charming knelt. "Look at him, my love! This is who you chose over me? He's a runt. My father should have drowned him in the castle pool."

Mr. Canis stepped out of the woods. He opened his pack and reached inside, then turned back to the group, panicked. "Wait! It's not here. The jar is missing."

And that was when Sabrina saw Red. She was carrying the deadly jar in her hands. Before Canis or anyone could stop her, Red unfastened the cork that kept the monster inside. The black spirit that had been trapped inside rushed out with a triumphant roar, circled the little girl, and flew into her open mouth.

"I did not see that coming," Puck said, and quickly stepped out of Red's path.

"Red, what did you do?" Daphne cried.

But the girl did not answer. She was busy going through a

horrifying transformation. Hair sprouted from her skin, her hands elongated into sharp claws, and a long, bushy tail grew. When the metamorphosis was complete, the creature towered over everyone at a staggering nine feet tall.

"Look who's back," the Wolf howled. "What's for dinner? Oh, I know. Him!"

The Wolf leaped at Atticus, knocking him to the ground.

"You are as foolish as you are ugly, beast," Atticus said. "As long as I wear this armor, no mortal man can harm me."

"I am no man!" the Wolf cried, ripping Atticus's breastplate from his body and throwing it into the woods. "Now, let's get this little clam out of his shell."

Realizing the truth in her words, Atticus shrieked in fear and backed away from the creature. The Wolf stalked him, tearing off his leg guards and shoulder plates one at a time.

"Is that all that's inside?" the Wolf complained. "Why, there's hardly any meat on him."

Atticus scrambled to his feet and swung his sword in desperation, managing to slash the Wolf's arm. The small wound only made the beast laugh.

"I love it when my food fights back."

Without hesitation, she leaped onto Atticus, knocking him to the ground. She climbed on top of him, yanking off the rest of his armor. Soon, the magical defense was completely gone, and Atticus was just a man.

"Let him be, Wolf! Atticus is mine!" Charming said, struggling to his feet.

"No, he's mine!" the Frog Prince yelled. "He killed my wife."

"Get in line!" Pinocchio called as he struggled to lift Atticus's fallen sword.

"NO!!!!" the Wicked Queen boomed, and with a clap of her hands the entire army fell to the ground. The witch floated into the air and hovered over Atticus, her eyes glowing white like stars and her hands as red as magma. "I warned you not to touch my daughter," she said, her voice like thunder. "I told you what I would do."

"She's my wife! My property!" Atticus shouted. His face was defiant, even in the face of certain death.

"You should have stayed inside the Book, Atticus Charming," the witch said as energy grew in her hands. She was going to unleash her magic on the villain. But before she could, a sword impaled Atticus from behind. He looked down at the tip, panicked, and then squirmed like a worm trying to free itself from a fisherman's hook. Behind him stood Snow White. Her face was bloodied and bruised, her hands wrapped around the hilt of the sword.

"No," she said. "He's mine."

Atticus fell face-first into the dirt and lay still.

"Oh, but dinner's always so much tastier when it knows it's being eaten," the Wolf said, turning up her nose at the dead villain. "I was much more interested when he was squirming." The Wolf stomped toward the crowd, only to have spindly Mr. Canis block her path.

"Well, look who it is," the Wolf growled. "Step aside, old man."

"No," he said defiantly.

"I'll tear you apart."

"You'll try," he said. "Red! Red, can you hear me?"

The Wolf laughed. "She's not listening."

"Red, I know it's dark where you are, but you can find the light. You just have to follow my voice," Canis said. "Come to me, sweetheart."

The Wolf let out an angry howl and doubled over as if in pain. Then, she slowly transformed back into Red Riding Hood. When she was herself again, she raced to Canis, buried her face in his chest, and sobbed. He wrapped his arms around her tightly.

"I didn't know it was like that for you," Red said through her tears. "My demon wasn't that angry. It was just confused. The Wolf is so vicious."

"I'll help you control it," he promised. "I'll be by your side."

Suddenly, Sabrina's head pounded more intensely than ever, and she saw images flashing rapid-fire before her eyes: Uncle Jake's face, Nottingham's blade slashing at arms and legs, a cliff over a rocky beach.

She came back to herself and looked around at the gathered crowd. Nottingham had slipped away in the fight. Uncle Jake had done the same. Worse, the Queen of Hearts was missing, too. Were Nottingham and Heart still working together to kill her uncle? Sabrina felt weak at the knees.

Henry rushed to her before she could fall to the ground. "Sabrina, what's wrong?"

But she couldn't answer. The visions took over again, and all she could see was her uncle watching Mayor Heart and Sheriff Nottingham stabbing at each other with daggers. He wasn't in any danger at all, but the two villains were trying to murder each other.

"You betrayed me, Heart, and you will pay," Nottingham said as he poked at his former ally.

The queen shrieked and slashed back. "You're a lunatic! Can't you see the writing on the wall? The Hand is over. The Master can't open the barrier. All of his promises were lies. The Grimms have offered us an alternative. Since when do you turn down an opportunity?"

"An opportunity? You're a traitor!"

"Please, stop fighting!" Jake cried. He took a folded piece of paper from his pocket and held it out to the villains. "Here, just take the spell."

Nottingham snatched the paper from Jake and tried to unfold it, but Heart seized it from him.

"No, he promised it to me!" she cried.

"It's mine, you disgusting pig!" Nottingham shouted as she snatched it back.

Heart tackled him, and they rolled on the ground, wrestling and cursing, edging closer to the cliff's edge. They were so busy fighting each other that they didn't notice.

"I should never have made you my ally in the first place," Nottingham said. "The Master told me you couldn't be trusted."

"You and your precious Master," Heart sneered. "He cares nothing for you or anyone else." She finally kicked Nottingham off of her and seized the paper. She unfolded it and stared in confusion. "What is this?" she cried, outraged.

Nottingham snatched it back from Heart once more. He examined one side of the page, then the other. Then, he crumpled it into a ball and tossed it off the cliff. "It's a blank piece of paper. This is a trick!"

Uncle Jake took two daggers from his pocket and approached the cliff's edge. "Yes, it is. I knew the two of you would turn on each other if you had the chance. I wish I'd thought of it earlier. If I had, maybe Briar would still be alive."

"You manipulated us?" Nottingham asked in disbelief. Then, in a fit of rage, he wound up to toss his blade at Jake. Just before he released it, the ground crumbled, and both he and Heart fell off the edge of the cliff.

Uncle Jake rushed to the edge. Nottingham and Heart clung

to roots to keep from plummeting a hundred feet to the jagged rocks below.

"You planned this all along!" the queen raged.

"I did," Jake admitted.

"Killing us won't bring her back, Jacob!"

"No, it won't," Uncle Jake said as he knelt down. Sabrina hoped he was about to hoist them onto safe ground, that his plan was to scare them but keep them alive. Instead, he reached into another one of his jacket pockets and removed the enchanted white rose he'd plucked from Briar's grave. It looked as fresh and alive as if it had just bloomed. He dug a tiny hole in the soil and set the severed stem inside. Then, he gingerly packed soil around it.

"What are you doing, you fool?" Nottingham shouted. "This is no time for gardening. We're going to fall—help us!"

Uncle Jake gazed lovingly upon the rose. As before, the flower quickly sprouted many more buds. The roses grew around Jake's feet, down the cliff, and through the desperate fingers of Nottingham and Heart. The stems wove through their arms and torsos, ran down their legs and around their feet. Thousands of fresh flowers appeared, causing a tiny ripple, then a huge wave in the cliff side, making it impossible for the villains to hold on any longer.

Nottingham and Heart fell. White petals followed them down until they were caught on the rocks. The villains' broken bodies were quickly swallowed by more flowers that grew right up to the shore of the Hudson River, as if the earth demanded their ugliness be replaced with something beautiful.

Sabrina's mind focused on her uncle's face as he looked out over the edge. He said nothing, and his expression revealed no satisfaction from the deaths. He took a single rose from the abundant garden around him and placed it in his pocket.

A blistering fever swept over Sabrina as the vision faded and her present time and place came back into view. She felt as if her blood were on fire. The world got fuzzy and dark. The last thing she saw before she collapsed was her father's worried face.

"Sabrina, what have you done?"

11

SABRINA GRIMM WAS NO STRANGER TO NIGHT-
mares. Long before she came to Ferryport Landing,
she'd suffered through many a bad dream, tossing and
turning as her imagination spun out one horror after another. But
her mind had never concocted a terror quite as horrible as Baba
Yaga hovering over her and pulling on her tongue.

"The child is infected," the old crone announced.

Sabrina shook Baba Yaga off of her and sat up.

"With what?" her father asked, panicked.

"Magic, of course," Baba Yaga said. "Did you think I was giving her a checkup for chicken pox?"

"Are you saying magic is making her sick?" Daphne asked. She
placed her hand on her sister's, and her eyes grew big. "Yes, I can
feel it. But how?"

"When the mirrors exploded, a piece of glass cut into me,"

Sabrina explained. "I haven't really felt like myself since, but I'm OK. No one needs to worry."

"This is not good," Mr. Canis said. "Sabrina is magic intolerant. We've had to keep her away from enchanted items ever since she arrived in Ferryport Landing."

"Is this true?" Veronica asked.

"Yes, I sort of get power hungry around it. But I'm fine, really," Sabrina said as she tried, unsuccessfully, to stand. "I have it under control. I just feel like I've got the flu or something. We've got to keep moving."

"You're not going anywhere, Sabrina," her mother said. "You need to rest while we figure out a cure."

"Waste of time, woman," Baba Yaga said. "She'll be dead soon."

"She could die?" Daphne cried.

"I didn't say she could die," the old crone croaked. "I said she will die."

"That's nonsense. All we have to do is get it out of her, right?" Puck asked.

"It's not a splinter, fairy," Baba Yaga said. "The magic is inside her—deep in the tissue. It isn't coming out."

"So, there's nothing we can do? Letting her die is our only choice?" the Wicked Queen asked.

"The best thing to do, poison maker, is to put her to work.

She's got the stuff magic mirrors are made of floating around inside her. I know you understand. It's your handiwork, after all. Her magic rivals that of the monster inside Relda Grimm. I say we send her out to kill it while she's still breathing."

"You're saying my sister has power like Mirror?" Daphne asked the old crone.

"Yes, they share the same abilities, and hers grow every second," Baba Yaga said. "Bah! If we stand around here yammering for much longer, she'll explode like a bomb from all the buildup. Let's use her while we can!"

"Um, hello, I'm right here!" Sabrina said, surprised and irritated that she was, once again, being ignored.

"There's a chance she could burn herself out," Ms. Lancaster said, waving Sabrina's comment away like it was a gnat.

"A slim chance," Baba Yaga argued.

"What are you talking about?" Henry demanded. "What do you mean, burn herself out?"

The Wicked Queen turned to Sabrina but spoke to all those gathered. "If you give in to its power and let it take over, then push it to its limits, you might be able to drain the battery, so to speak."

"So she has to get crazy with the magic?" Daphne asked.

"Real crazy." The witch nodded.

"OK, that sounds like a plan," Uncle Jake said. "Sabrina, all you have to do is use it all up. Unleash it all on him."

"I can't," Sabrina said. "That's Granny Relda's body. I might kill her."

"Child, haven't you seen what Mirror's done since taking over your grandmother's body?" Canis said. "I doubt she will live no matter what you choose to do. But, if you can defeat Mirror, that might be her only chance to survive."

Sabrina didn't want to die, but if she could save her grandmother, it would be worth it.

"I need your help getting to Mirror," she said. "He's waiting on Route 9 near the barrier's edge. I can see him in my mind. He knows I'm watching, and he's calling out to me, demanding we bring him Jacob and Wilhelm's spell."

"Then give it to him," the Scarecrow said.

"Just let him out," the Lion agreed.

"You don't understand," Daphne said, taking the real spell from her pocket. "We can't let him out. He could take over the world. Innocent people will die."

Sabrina could see all of the possibilities once again. She could see the future Mirror controlled. She watched him step through the barrier, then sweep across North America, Europe, Africa, and Asia, until there was no one left to fight him. She watched a stampede of panicked humans running from giants and dragons. She saw monsters running amok.

"Dad, I think you, Mom, Basil, and Uncle Jake should leave the town," she said. "Take the spell with you. If it's here, he'll never stop, and he may try to hurt you to get what he wants."

"You can't leave the town," Mr. Canis said as he stepped forward and reached into his coat. He took out the Book of Everafter and set it before them.

"You had the Book all along?" Daphne asked.

"Why did you steal it from us?" Sabrina cried.

"I did not mean to make you worry, but I had to have it. I needed to make some changes, and—"

"What changes, Canis?" the Wicked Queen demanded.

"When Relda was taken over by Mirror, I knew his plan would succeed. He would be able escape the barrier inside her body. The Book offered an opportunity, and since it was an emergency—"

"You rewrote a story?" Sabrina gasped.

"No, I tried to rewrite a story. I found Snow White's original story and attempted to make a change—one that would keep Mirror inside the town—but every time I added something, the words I wrote vanished before my eyes. It was as if the story were trying to protect itself from me."

"It was," the Wicked Queen said. "You shouldn't have tampered with it. That book's magic is beyond your understanding, old man."

Canis's face flashed with rage as potent as when the Big Bad Wolf had controlled him. "Who do you think you are? I'm not some burden. Wolf or no Wolf, I have been an important part of everything that has happened to this family for more than twenty years, and you will not talk to me like I'm feeble or senile. This kind of nonsense is exactly why I took the Book without asking. While you people were trying to wrap your heads around what to do with old Mr. Canis, he was working to stop the end of the world!"

Sabrina flipped through the Book, looking for the changes Mr. Canis had made, but she quickly realized there were far too many stories within. She was about to give up when she noticed a short story at the very end, and her own name jumped out at her. She immediately understood what Mr. Canis had done, and her heart sank.

"He wrote us into the Book," she gasped, then began reading aloud. " 'Once upon a time there was a family called Grimm. They were detectives who lived in a town called Ferryport Landing. Their names were Relda, Henry, Veronica, Jacob, Sabrina, Daphne, and Basil, and they had many adventures. The end.' "

"You turned them into Everafters," Ms. Lancaster seethed.

"He did what?" Veronica cried.

"I couldn't risk Mirror escaping the town," Canis explained. "Or jumping into another human body when he discovered Relda's wouldn't get him what he wanted."

"This is why he can't get out of the town," Daphne said, understanding. "Granny Relda isn't human anymore. So we're fairy-tale characters now? Cool!"

"Very clever, old hound," Baba Yaga said with a horrible smile.

"Your body might be shaky, but your mind is sharp. Unfortunately, we are burning precious seconds, and the child grows sicker with each one."

"She's right. We need to get to Mirror," Sabrina said.

Sabrina was too ill to walk, so Puck spun around on his heels to transform into a majestic white stallion. Uncle Jake helped both Sabrina and Daphne up onto his back. Charming's wounded leg kept him from walking, as well, so he rode on Poppa Bear's back. Soon, they were all marching down the hill toward Mirror.

"Are you OK?" Puck asked Sabrina.

"Just doing what you told me," she whispered. "Faking it until I make it."

She tried to sound positive, but it felt like the magic was eating her alive. Twinges of pain escalated into gut-searing agony, but she gritted her teeth. There were a few moments when she was sure she would black out and fall off Puck's back, but Daphne wrapped her up in her little arms to keep her balanced. Henry and Uncle Jake walked on either side of Puck, holding Sabrina's hands. Veronica, Basil, Mr. Canis, and Red followed closely.

"I see him," Pinocchio said, pointing at the terrifying storm clouds that hovered over the town. Sabrina was too tired and too ill to be afraid. The magic was building. All she could focus on was letting it loose.

The group came face-to-face with Mirror on Main Street, close to where the barrier ended. Mirror, still inside Granny Relda's body, stood in a wide stance with his arms outstretched. It was a mocking welcome, and it made Sabrina angry. He wasn't taking her seriously. It was as if this confrontation were nothing more than the last annoying thing on his to-do list.

Sabrina asked the others to help her down, and once she and Daphne were on their feet, Puck transformed back into a boy. He seized his wooden sword and prepared to charge Mirror. But Sabrina held him back.

"You stay here," Sabrina said, and then turned to her sister. "You too."

Daphne shook her head. "We stick together. We're Grimms. This is what we do."

"But—"

"We're going," Goldie said.

"All of us," Red promised.

"Let's go crack this mirror in half," Pinocchio said.

The rest of the crowd agreed and followed Sabrina's every step forward. Only Veronica remained behind, with a squirming Basil in her arms. Mirror had touched the lives of every member of Sabrina's army, and they would stand with her until the end. In no time, they were standing before the Master.

"There's something different about you, Sabrina," Mirror said. "Did you change your hair?" He frowned. "I see you brought along your gang of misfits. I suppose that means

Atticus is dead? Can't say that bothers me too much. That brother of yours was a bit of a lunatic, Billy—always shouting and carrying on. 'I'm going to kill my brother! I'm going to have my revenge!'"

"Now he'll never get the chance," Snow said.

Mirror cocked an eyebrow at her. "So, our little schoolteacher stood up for herself, did she? How inspiring," he mocked. "Is that why you're all here? You're going to kill me, too?"

"We don't want to kill you," Sabrina said. "But we have to stop you somehow. I'm going to give you the same offer we gave your Scarlet Hand thugs. Stop now, and you won't be harmed. Let my grandmother go."

"I may be able to give you a body of your own," the Wicked Queen said.

"Oh, Mother, are you finally going to be kind to your baby?" Mirror sneered. "You abandoned me. You created me, and then you turned your back. I think it's a little late for a mother and child reunion—but enough whining! All I want is the spell that lowers the barrier."

"We've already told you," Sabrina said. "It's not going to happen."

Mirror's fingers crackled with energy. Suddenly, Veronica and Basil were yanked off the ground by an unseen force. It held them dangling high above the crowd.

"Put them down!" Henry bellowed.

With another blast of energy, Henry joined his wife and son.

"Hank, this doesn't have to get ugly," Mirror said. "Just have your girls hand me the paper, and I'll let you down."

"Let them go, Mirror," Sabrina said, her voice croaking from the tremors of pain. She felt like she might explode, or break in half. She turned to Daphne, who offered her a brave smile.

"Sabrina, do not give him the spell!" Uncle Jake shouted, and he, too, was swept off the ground and into the air above the crowd.

"I can let them go with a snap of my fingers," Mirror said. "It's that easy, Sabrina. But, from you, I just need one little piece of paper."

"Daphne, give it to him," Sabrina said.

Daphne shook her head. "Sabrina—"

With a wave of her hand, Sabrina forced the paper from her sister's pocket. Daphne couldn't do anything to stop it from floating into Mirror's hand.

"NO!" Daphne cried.

"I can't let anyone else die!" Sabrina said.

Granny Relda's face twisted into a sick smile as Mirror gazed down upon the paper. With a laugh, he recited the ancient words. Sabrina heard an odd tinkling sound, and then she watched the sky above turn bright red. The dome evaporated, and Ferryport Landing was free.

Mirror smiled at the gathered Everafter army. "Congratulations, my friends. You're free. You are all finally free!"

The crowd shuffled uncomfortably, as if unsure of what to do.

"Don't get too excited, bub," Daphne said. "As long as we're alive, we're going to be all over you. We won't stop chasing you until you're back in your frame and our granny is safe and sound!"

Mirror turned to the girls, his eyes glowing red and his hands crackling with flames.

"Oh, Daphne, you do have a talent for pointing out the obvious," Mirror growled. "As long as someone in your family is alive, you will always manage to find a way to ruin my party."

Mirror pointed one flaming finger at the girls, and a powerful force sent them flying. Just before she slammed into the ground, Sabrina felt her pain bubble over, as if she were a shaken-up soda bottle. A metallic shell appeared, enclosing both girls and protecting them from harm as they skidded across the ground. When they came to a stop, they helped each other up as the shell cracked open and crumbled to the ground.

"Neat trick," Daphne said. "Any idea how you did it?"

"Not a clue." Sabrina shrugged.

The girls walked back through the crowd, stopping once more before Mirror.

Surprise painted Granny Relda's face, and Mirror blasted the girls again. This time, a shield of pink light glowed from Sabrina's right hand and pushed back against his attack.

Sabrina waved her left hand to see what would happen, and the earth cracked open, creating a wide chasm. Mirror fell inside the newly created gorge.

Sabrina reeled from the magic that continued to grow inside her body. On the one hand, it felt good to be so strong, but on the other, she felt a dark desire to stand over Mirror and laugh. She had to burn the magic out of her as quickly as possible. She took Daphne's hand, and together they ran to the crevice and peered into the darkness.

"Mirror!" she shouted.

"You have to go easy on him," Daphne said. "Remember: When you attack him, you attack Granny."

"I know," Sabrina said. "I just . . . this power isn't good for me. There's too much."

Just then, Granny Relda's hand appeared over the edge of the crevice, and Mirror pulled himself out of the hole. He was furious, eyes still aglow. Suddenly, the ground bubbled, and geysers exploded all around the army, sending steam high into the air. Silver ooze gurgled out of the geysers and collected in pools. From these pools, new soldiers rose. Each was the size of a large man but made from the same liquid material as the magic mirrors. Once they solidified, the new creatures attacked Sabrina's army.

"Now, where were we?" Mirror sneered as blinding strands of electricity crackled from his hands. Before he could blast the girls, Daphne reached into her pocket for an amulet. In a flash, she and Sabrina vanished, reappearing directly behind Mirror.

"I didn't know you had something like that," Sabrina whispered.

"Neither did I," Daphne replied, and then kicked Mirror in the backside. "Sorry, Granny."

Mirror roared, and the ground beneath them shot into the air, twisting into a knotted pretzel of earth, trees, and roads. It grew higher and higher, rivaling Mount Taurus, and took everything and everyone with it. The sisters lost their footing and slipped right over the edge, but Sabrina managed to snatch onto the roots of an old tree. Daphne clung to her leg. Together, they hung there, struggling to pull themselves to safety.

Sabrina took a deep breath and focused on her magic. They soared to the top of the new mountain like rockets, landing on its peak. The cold wind whipped violently around them, further aggravating Sabrina's fever.

"Do you see Mom and Dad?" Daphne shouted.

The visions hit Sabrina like a tidal wave. Her mother and Basil were safe below, having taken shelter in the woods. Her father was on a ridge just beneath them, still fighting one of the mirror men. Uncle Jake was pulling himself up to the top of the mountain, and Puck was flying in their direction. The rest of the army was alive but busy fighting off Mirror's horrible warriors.

"Everyone is fine," Sabrina assured her.

"What about you?"

Sabrina shook her head. There was no more faking it.

"Where are you, Sabrina?" a voice bellowed from below.

Sabrina peered over a ridge. Mirror was hovering in midair. "Ah, there you are. I'm done with this, child. I've held back until now."

"We're not going to let you destroy the world!" Sabrina shouted just as Puck landed beside her.

"I'm not going to destroy the world, kiddo. Where would I live? No, no, I'm just going to rule it. I'm stronger and smarter than a human, so it only makes sense. You think I'm arrogant. But shouldn't the most powerful be in charge?"

"This is the part where the villain tries to explain his stupid way of thinking, isn't it?" Daphne replied.

"That's a rookie move," Puck said.

"Then let me explain something that you can relate to," Mirror said as he floated up to the peak and landed before them. He locked eyes with Sabrina. "Anger. Betrayal. Abandonment. You know what it's like to have people you care about turn their backs on you. You know what it's like to be angry."

"I'm not angry anymore," Sabrina said shakily.

"Then, let me remind you," he said. With a wave of his hand, he sent Daphne sailing through the air and over the edge of the cliff.

"Daphne!" Sabrina screamed.

"On it," Puck said, launching himself off the cliff's edge after Daphne.

A silver ooze, much like the one Mirror had used to make his army, seeped over Granny Relda's body until she, too, was a living mirror. In the reflection, Sabrina saw the day she'd arrived at Granny Relda's house. She looked so angry, so hopeless, like she didn't believe she would ever really be loved again. The pain of that time came rushing back, but she turned her head away to block it out. She had felt love: from her sister, from her grandmother, from her uncle, and from Puck. She'd felt it from the dozens of new friends who were now as close as family. Their love saved her. It made her strong. It helped her save herself. It was powerful magic.

Sabrina stepped toward Mirror, and he flinched, but she hugged him. "I'm done fighting you, Mirror. I understand how you feel, and I'm sorry that you didn't get the love that I did. But I'm not like you. Let me show you."

Mirror pulled back, and the silver ooze melted away, revealing Granny Relda. Sabrina placed her hands on her grandmother's face and let all of her magic loose. But it wasn't an attack. It was love—the love others had given her—and it was pure and brilliant and strong.

She sent Mirror every moment of kindness she had ever received. She gave him her memories of friends. She gave him the feelings she had for Mr. Canis and Red and her uncle. She gave him her father reading her a bedtime story and her mother giving her a wink. She gave him Granny Relda's hugs and the softness of baby Basil's cheek nuzzling into her shoulder. She gave him Elvis's happy kisses. She gave him the surprise of Puck's first kiss, and the odd, fluttering feeling inside her whenever he talked about their future together. And then she gave him Daphne—sweet, loving, hilarious Daphne. She gave him the joy she felt when Daphne laughed. She gave him their nights asleep together, their many escapes and daring rescues. She gave him every meal with Daphne stuffing her face. She gave him her sister's sense of right and wrong, and how the little girl could see the good in everyone. She gave him every day that Daphne had made Sabrina feel stronger, braver, and happier. She gave him an hour of Daphne brushing her hair. She gave him their secrets and silly giggles. She gave him every single new word Daphne had ever invented. She gave him what had saved her own life—her sister's love. She even gave Mirror the love that she had once felt for him—all of it opening like an overstuffed box into his heart.

"I . . . I never knew," Mirror whispered.

The mountain sank back down to level earth, twisting itself back into the land. The mirror men leaked back into the soil, and the wind sailed away. With the last of her magic, Sabrina created a cushion of air that caught her friends before they collided with the ground. Everyone was safe.

Mirror looked down into Sabrina's face. She could see her grandmother there, just beneath the surface. He was letting her go.

The Wicked Queen approached, and Mirror's eyes sparkled with happiness. "Hello, Mother," he said, this time without scorn or rage.

Ms. Lancaster flashed Sabrina a confused, uncomfortable look, but Sabrina just nodded.

Sabrina then turned back to Mirror. "You have to give me back my grandmother, please. I love her very much."

Mirror nodded. "Sabrina, would you do me one small favor? I know that you have no reason to, but . . ."

"What would you like?"

Mirror reached out his hand. "Before I go, will you forgive me?"

Sabrina took his hand in her own and held it tightly. "Mirror, of course I forgive you. I am your friend."

He smiled and sighed. Then, Granny Relda's mouth opened, and the black spirit that was Mirror's essence slipped to the ground. Granny Relda collapsed. Ms. Lancaster helped revive the old woman while Sabrina watched the dark mass flop in the dirt like a fish out of water. Sabrina scooped him up and whispered that everything would be OK.

Then, Mirror melted into a puddle of glistening silver. He dribbled between her fingers, into the soil, and was gone.

Fluttering wings announced Puck's return. He landed at Sabrina's feet with Daphne clinging to him. "You know, you two get tossed off tall things a lot. I think you should start wearing parachutes all the time," he said.

Sabrina swept her sister into a hug.

"How are you feeling?" Daphne asked.

"It's gone," Sabrina said, relieved. "The magic is gone."

Granny stirred, and Sabrina helped her sit up just as Uncle Jake, Daphne, Henry, Veronica, Basil, and Elvis rushed to join them. The old woman blinked and looked around.

"Welcome back, *liebling*," Sabrina said.

Granny Relda beamed and gave her a big hug. "Have you girls been up to shenanigans?"

Daphne hugged their grandmother so tightly that Sabrina worried the old woman might break. Elvis pushed his way in to shower her with kisses. Henry and Jake helped their mother to her feet. She wobbled a bit but finally found her footing.

"How do you feel, Relda?" Veronica asked, embracing the woman.

"I suppose I should be exhausted, but I'm actually just very hungry," Relda said with a laugh. "Oh, dear, I've lost my hat."

"We'll get you another hat, Mom." Uncle Jake laughed.

Basil squirmed in Veronica's arms. "Who's this, Mommy?"

Veronica smiled as a happy tear escaped her eyes. "Honey, this is your grandmother. She's part of your family."

"Do you have a boo-boo?" he asked Granny Relda.

Granny Relda wrapped him up in her arms. "I do! But I bet a kiss would help."

Basil gave her a big kiss on the cheek.

"I feel better already," Granny cooed.

Puck stepped toward the old woman. "Just so you know, I pretty much saved the whole world," he gloated.

"Oh, I have no doubt," she said, wrapping him up in a hug and showering him with kisses. Sabrina was sure he'd squirm away, but he didn't.

"Billy, look," Snow said as she stepped to the edge of the river. "I'm outside the barrier."

Charming joined her, and the two looked out on the horizon.

"Oh, dear," Granny said, her face full of worry.

"It's going to be OK, Granny," Daphne promised.

Sabrina turned to her army and smiled. "You're free."

The Cowardly Lion, Baba Yaga, Red, Mr. Canis, Boarman, and Swineheart—so many faces. They all took a step forward and stood on the other side.

"It's too big," Beauty said.

"What is?" Sabrina asked.

"All the possibilities," Goldie answered knowingly.

A week later, many of the Everafters were gone. The Frog Prince and his daughter were the first to go, then the Scarecrow and the Cowardly Lion, all of King Arthur's remaining knights, and Little John. It seemed that everyone else would soon follow.

Veronica had held a seminar on the basics of modern life, including how to use a computer, apply for a job, and get an apartment. She was very surprised to find that nearly everyone in town came to hear her.

But not quite everyone was ready to give up on the town. Sabrina marveled at those who decided to stay. Boarman and Swineheart reopened their construction business. There was so much destruction that they were both convinced they would soon be the richest Everafters in town. They proudly introduced their new partner, Mr. Hamstead. The former sheriff and his wife, Bess, were moving back to the little town. They were over the moon with happiness, as they were expecting their first child.

The town held an emergency election for mayor. Charming ran, but he lost to his girlfriend, Snow, who was surprised to find herself a write-in candidate. Charming graciously conceded. Mayor White's first order of business was to finally rebuild the school. She also hired Goldilocks to be the new city planner. She promised that the new Ferryport Landing would be designed with feng shui in mind and would prove to be the most balanced and serene little town on the Hudson River.

Despite Henry's begging, Granny Relda decided to rebuild in Ferryport Landing. She couldn't bear to leave her home, though she did promise to visit the city frequently. As always, Mr. Canis was by her side, now with Red. He and Granny would raise her, and they offered the same to Pinocchio. Their kindness overwhelmed him, and he sobbed into Granny Relda's dress. Later, he would discover that he had grown half an inch for the first time in a hundred years.

As the founders of the new Ferryport Landing made their plans, Goldie took Veronica aside. Sabrina couldn't help but listen in.

"I know it hasn't been easy having me around," Goldie confessed.

Veronica shook her head, though Sabrina wasn't convinced of her sincerity. "You were a big help."

"I just wanted to say . . . you're good for him. Better than I would have been," Goldie said. "You make Henry happy . . . which is hard for me to watch. I still—"

"I know you do," Veronica said. "He's kind of awesome, but I think that if you open yourself up and take a chance, you might find someone who is awesome for you."

The women hugged and parted as friends.

One night, when there was nothing left for them to do, Sabrina, Daphne, Puck, and Red walked down the road toward the marina. They found a piece of dock that wasn't damaged, and they took off their shoes and dipped their feet into the Hudson River. They sat for a long time silently contemplating all that had happened.

Finally, Puck broke the silence. "Jake is leaving town. He says there's magic all over the world that needs to be wrangled. He asked me to go with him."

Sabrina felt a lump in her throat. "What did you say?"

"I'm probably going to go. This little town is no place for the master of mischief. There's nothing left for me to break."

"You could come with us to New York City," Sabrina said hopefully. "I'm sure your mother would like to see you around the kingdom."

He seemed to understand what Sabrina was thinking. "Don't worry, I'll swing by and harass you all the time."

Sabrina smiled. She knew this boy would always be in her life. Then she laughed. *Whether I like it or not.*

"Wait, what is that?" Puck asked, pointing down the river. Sabrina squinted and made out a boat sailing toward the marina. It looked like a bona fide pirate ship, with huge masts and a grinning skull-and-crossbones flag snapping in the wind. The children watched as it drifted toward them and then dropped anchor. Moments later a boy climbed onto the rail of the ship and leaped into the air, flying with a trail of glittering dust trailing behind him.

"It can't be," Sabrina said.

"It is," Daphne said, then bit the palm of her hand.

"Who is it?" Red asked.

Puck scowled. "I'll handle this."

The flying boy stopped short of the dock and hovered in mid-air. He held a wooden sword much like Puck's and wore a little green hat.

"Hey, you!" the boy cried. "Sorry to spook you with the ship. My lost boys and I sort of borrowed it from a few pirates. Our home is overrun with them, so we've decided to start someplace new. We're looking for a town called Ferryport Landing. We've heard it's a good place for folks like us."

"Never heard of it," Puck said.

The flying boy frowned. "It's got to be around here some-where. I heard it's filled with magic and fun."

"I think someone gave you some bad information, kid," Puck said. "This town is as boring as it gets."

"All right, well, thanks." The flying boy shrugged and flew back to his boat.

"That wasn't very nice," Sabrina said.

Puck stuck his tongue out at her. "I hate that kid."

Sabrina looked up the road at what was left of Ferryport Land-ing. She felt like she was mourning the loss of another dear friend. But she was hopeful that one day soon it would live again.

"Is that it?" Daphne asked. "Is that the end?"

Sabrina took her sister's hand and nodded. "Yes, and it's about time."

The children sat on the dock for a long time, looking out at the water.

"Wait. If we're Everafters now, does that mean we're going to live forever?" Daphne asked excitedly.

Puck eyed Sabrina. She could almost see his mind cooking up the millions of pranks he would play on her now that he had all the time in the world. She felt sick to her stomach when he gig-gled mischievously.

"Shenanigans," he said.

Thirteen Years Later

Daphne zipped up the back of Sabrina's gown while she studied herself in the full-length mirror.

"Well, I guess it's official," Sabrina said. "I'm getting married."

"The wedding dress is a big tip-off," her mother said, adjusting the train. "You look like a princess."

"Which one?"

Daphne laughed. "I don't know. But I could go out into the church and bring a few back here to compare."

Sabrina looked at herself in the mirror one more time. The ivory dress seemed to glow in the light. If she hadn't known better, she would suspect it was enchanted. "I hope everyone is wearing their disguises. Bradley is still not super comfortable with the talking animals, and his folks still don't have a clue about our family business."

"Everyone looks human," Daphne said. "Well, except Hamstead's boys. They brought their rocket packs."

Sabrina sighed. "All I need is a bunch of teenage pigs and cows flying around St. Paul's."

"Nothing is going to ruin this, Sabrina," Red said from the doorway. Looking at Red, now a young woman, no one would ever know there was a monster living inside her. Apparently, her routine of yoga and meditation was working well.

"Red! Get in here and help me," Sabrina said.

"Are all the guests here?" Daphne asked as she took a brush and started combing her sister's hair.

"Baba Yaga is here," Red said as she eyed the bouquet of white roses. "She's wearing a fur coat. At least, I thought it was just a coat. But I could have sworn I heard it hiss at me."

"Uncle Jake made it," Veronica said. "Goldie's here with her fiancé, too. Snow and Billy are up front with their kids. Wendell and his girlfriend just arrived, and Bunny is in her seat—you know, the regular bunch—oh, Pinocchio."

"Pinocchio! He came? We haven't seen him in a million years," Red said.

"I saw him. He's looking very grown-up," Veronica said.

"He's hot," Daphne said offhandedly.

Everyone eyed her in disbelief.

"What? He is!" she cried defensively.

Sabrina nodded. "Anyone else?"

She saw a look pass between her mother and sister.

"There was no way to find him," Daphne said.

"Who?" Sabrina asked.

"You know who I'm talking about. I tried," Daphne said. "He's just hard to track down. I used every spell I know."

Sabrina hadn't seen "him" in almost five years. She did not want to think about "him."

"Well, that's good," Sabrina said. "He'd just ruin it for me.

He'd probably toss eggs at the minister or something. It's for the best."

"You're not having second thoughts, are you?" Red asked.

"NO!"

"'Cause you need to be sure. We can call this off if Bradley isn't the one you love," Daphne said.

"Oh, you're giving me relationship advice? How many boys have you broken up with this year?"

"I have to break up with them if they're not right for me," Daphne said. "Most of them are too—"

"Normal?"

Daphne shrugged.

"There's nothing wrong with normal," Sabrina said. "I love normal. After dealing with an office full of Everafters every day, it's nice to go home to something normal."

Daphne giggled. "That's the price you pay for being a fairy-tale defense attorney."

There was a knock at the door, and then Henry entered, smiling and crying at the same time.

"Dad?" Sabrina asked.

"You look so beautiful," he blubbered.

"He's been like this all day," Veronica said, wrapping her arms around her husband's waist. "I love it."

Sabrina hugged her father, too, but Veronica broke them up.

"No tears on the dress!" she chastised, which made everyone laugh.

From the open door, the sounds of a pipe organ floated into the room.

"It's showtime," Red said, handing Sabrina her bouquet of white roses.

Sabrina checked herself one more time in the mirror. Today was the start of a new adventure. Bradley was exactly the big, beautiful, grounded man she wanted. And together, they would build a big, beautiful, grounded life.

Bradley is a good man. He is kind and loving and sweet and handsome and normal. Oh, so wonderfully normal. He's the kind of man who makes me want to throw off immortality and grow old with him. I need him. He keeps me sane.

"I wish your grandmother were here to see this," her father said as he offered Sabrina his arm. Together, they walked to the back of the church. "I'm sure she's watching, wherever she is. She's probably making a big dinner for your grandfather—all weird blue food made from squid and daffodils."

They walked up the aisle, through a sea of smiles. There were many faces Sabrina hadn't seen in thirteen years, and some new faces she suspected masked more familiar ones. A man sat quietly licking his hand—ah, the Cowardly Lion. Mr. Swineheart, Mr. Boarman, Snow, and Charming sat next to Bunny and her seeing-eye wolf. Even the Scarecrow had made it back from Oz. And there, with his shock of white hair, was Mr. Canis. As she passed, he smiled and said, "Relda would be so proud."

On the other side of the church, there were real, honest-to-goodness humans who had no clue they were at a wedding filled with magic. And, at the altar, was Bradley, his blue eyes gleaming. He had shaved his trademark goatee for the special day. It was odd to see him without it. Sabrina barely recognized him.

The minister smiled down at her. "Who gives this woman to be married?"

"I do," her father said, and placed Sabrina's hand into Bradley's. It felt warm and comforting. Henry kissed her cheek, then joined Veronica and Basil in the front pew. Basil, who wasn't a baby any longer, stood nearly six feet tall. He grinned and winked at her.

"Marriage is a journey," the minister said, "down a long, twisting road. Some days the path is clear and bright, and other days it's murky and mysterious. Today, the two of you take the first step down this road together. Before we start, it is customary to ask the congregation to witness this union. I ask those gathered here: Do you promise to support this marriage, in good times and bad, to help this couple down their road whenever possible?"

Sabrina turned to look at the crowd just as they all said, "We do."

The minister smiled. "Very good. It is also customary to ask those gathered if anyone can give cause or reason that this union should not take place. If anyone objects, speak now or forever hold your peace."

Sabrina cringed and looked out at the crowd once more. But no one spoke. No one stood. No one threw an egg.

He wasn't there. He wasn't going to ruin her wedding. So why was she . . . disappointed?

"Very well," the minister said. "I believe the bride and groom have written some vows they would like to share with each—"

His voice was drowned out by the sound of flapping wings, as loud as thunder. Everyone craned their necks to see what was making that noise, but Sabrina didn't have to look—she knew.

When Bradley's side of the church gasped and screamed and ran from their seats, she sighed. When Henry and Veronica scowled, and when Daphne bit down on the palm of her hand, Sabrina did not even have to look up.

"It's—it's an angel," the minister said, falling back in shock.

"Hardly," Sabrina muttered.

And then the "angel" floated down before her, the light from the stained-glass window silhouetting him. He was no longer a boy. He was a man. And he was beautiful.

"Hello, stinky," he said with a wink that infuriated Sabrina. But not enough to stop her from grinning.

Sixteen Years After That...

August 16

I love my backyard. It's small—just a few flowers, a stone path, a bird-bath, a hammock, and a shed for tools. But it is my heaven. I can spend hours here, reading, relaxing, and practicing the yoga Red and Mr. Canis have recommended for my stress. (Well, I don't actually do that, but someday I could!)

In my backyard, there are no headaches. No lawyers or judges, no negotiations, bail hearings, or hung juries. There are no meetings with the mayor, no reporters digging for a story, no campaign dinners, and no elections. Lying in my hammock, I can forget about how the brownstone needs a new roof, and how the neighbors are making me crazy with their construction, and how our dogs, Bono and Edge, need a bath. And best of all, for a brief moment, I can forget that I am the mother of two lovely but extremely difficult girls.

The younger, Emma, is a lot like Daphne was at her age—funny, kind, precocious. But, unlike Daphne, Emma enjoys antagonizing her sister. Admittedly, Alison is a handful—a total Grimm! Six months ago, she turned fourteen, and along with the presents came a surprising change in attitude. Suddenly, my sweet, loving, happy child has turned into a teenager—head-strong, rude, impatient, and forever embarrassed by her parents. It is as if, sometime in the night, goblins snuck in and replaced her with one of their own.

Daphne says I was exactly the same way, but I don't remember being so self-centered. Well, Daphne will be a lot more sympathetic soon enough with her twins. I guess Basil's the smart one in this family. He says he's going to stay a bachelor for life. I just have to laugh at him. Love does not allow you to make plans. I remember—

Suddenly, Sabrina heard a scream. She threw down her journal and reached under the garden table, where she had taped a dagger. Yanking it free, she dashed into the house. If it was them, she would make them pay. She'd seen their mark in the streets. She would not let them harm her family.

She dashed up the stairs two at a time, then ran as fast as she could down the hallway. Emma was waiting by her sister's bedroom door.

"The spaz won't open up," Emma said.

Sabrina tried the doorknob but found it locked. "Allie, open the door!"

But Alison didn't open the door, and the screaming didn't stop.

"She's probably just got a zit, Mom," Emma said. "You know how dramatic she can be."

"Alison! I'm coming in right now," Sabrina shouted, and then she kicked down the door and charged inside.

"Wow!" Emma gasped. "You have to teach me how to do that!"

Sabrina was fully prepared to face a monster, but all she saw was Alison, looking right at her, tears streaming down her face. Sabrina looked around the room for intruders, then quickly hid the dagger in the pocket of her shorts.

"What is it, honey?"

"It's horrible!"

"Did Parker break up with you again?" Emma asked.

"Emma, stop teasing her," Sabrina snapped. "And, Allie, please tell me what's wrong!"

Alison turned her back on her mother, and Sabrina thought she was shutting her out, but then she saw something poking out of the back of her daughter's shirt. There was a loud pop, and then wings—huge, glorious pink wings—unfurled from Alison's back. They fluttered at a fantastic speed and lifted Alison off the ground. She hovered in midair awkwardly until her head slammed into the ceiling.

"That's no zit!" Emma cried.

"Mom? What is going on?" Alison sobbed.

"Honey, I know you are a little freaked out right now—"

"A LITTLE? I'm turning into a bug!" she shrieked.

"You're not turning into a bug!" Sabrina said. "Now, both of you, calm down. I promise everything is going to be fine. Your father will be home soon from the castle, and—"

"The castle?" the girls cried in unison.

Sabrina sighed. She wanted to run and hide in her backyard.

"When he gets here, we can explain everything," Sabrina said, trying to remain calm.

"What am I?" Alison cried.

Sabrina cringed. "You're a fairy princess."

"What!" Alison burst into tears.

"Girls, I need to tell you some things about our family," Sabrina said. "Have you ever heard of the Brothers Grimm?"

THE END

. . . for now.

Collect all of Sabrina and Daphne's adventures!

Book 1:
The Fairy-Tale Detectives

Book 2:
The Unusual Suspects

Book 3:
The Problem Child

Book 4:
Once Upon a Crime

Book 5:
Magic and Other
Misdemeanors

Book 6:
Tales from the Hood

Book 7:
The Everafter War

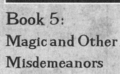

Book 8:
The Inside Story

Book 9:
The Council of Mirrors

ABOUT THE AUTHOR

Michael Buckley is the *New York Times* bestselling author of the Sisters Grimm and NERDS series, *Kel Gilligan's Daredevil Stunt Show*, and the Undertow Trilogy. He has also written and developed television shows for many networks. Michael lives in Brooklyn, New York, with his wife, Alison; their son, Finn; and their dog, Friday.